Set on the eve [illegible] War Two, award-winning noveli[illegible] novel in two decades is built around a fascinating historical figure, Dr. Eduard Bloch, an Austrian doctor who had been physician to Adolf Hitler and his family when Hitler was a boy and young man, and who cared for Hitler's mother during her illness and death from breast cancer. The historical Bloch was the only Jew for whom Hitler ever personally arranged departure from Europe, and he must now, living in the Bronx, face accusations over the special treatment he received from the Nazi dictator.

1940 focuses on Dr. Bloch's relationship with Elisabeth Rofman, a medical illustrator at Johns Hopkins Medical School, who has come to New York from Baltimore to visit her father, only to find that he has, mysteriously, disappeared. The story grows more complex when Elisabeth's son, Daniel, a disturbed adolescent, escapes from the institution in Maryland where his parents have committed him, and makes his way to New York where he is hidden and protected by his mother . . . and by Dr. Bloch.

1940 is a fiercely original novel that travels to dark places where it exposes us to people who, like ourselves, inhabit a troubled world that is very much in transition.

❖ ❖ ❖

"An exquisite novel of mystery and exploration of the human heart, **1940** is also a page-turner, a thrilling read."
BINNIE KIRSHENBAUM

"A strange and intriguing contribution to the body of work that seeks to cast light on the dark phenomenon of Naziism."
ANITA DESAI

A NOVEL

JAY NEUGEBOREN

Published by the Two Dollar Radio Movement, 2008.

ISBN: 978-0-9763895-6-9
Library of Congress Control Number: 2008900720

Cover design and author photograph by Eli Neugeboren.
Interior layout and design by Two Dollar Radio.

Distributed to the trade by Consortium Book Sales & Distribution, Inc.
The Keg House
34 Thirteenth Avenue NE, Suite 101
Minneapolis, Minnesota 55413-1007
www.cbsd.com
phone 612.746.2600 | fax 612.746.2606
orders 800.283.3572

TWO DOLLAR RADIO
Book publishers since 2005
"Because we make more noise than a $2 radio."
www.TwoDollarRadio.com
twodollar@TwoDollarRadio.com

For Kathleen

1940

"For the most part the boy's recreations were limited to those things which were free: walks in the mountains, a swim in the Danube, a free band concert. He read extensively and was particularly fascinated by stories about American Indians. He devoured the books of James Fenimore Cooper, and the German writer Karl May – who never visited America and never saw an Indian."

DOCTOR EDUARD BLOCH
"My Patient, Hitler,"
in *Collier's*, March 15, 1941

"Perhaps everything terrible is in its deepest being something helpless that wants help from us."

RAINER MARIA RILKE
Letters to a Young Poet

ONE

So: Would he be pleased to see her? Elisabeth was bringing good news – when you visit again, bring only good news, her father had said to her when they had parted the last time, at Pennsylvania Station – and the good news was that Professor Max Brödel of The Johns Hopkins Hospital and School of Medicine had offered her a full-time position as a medical illustrator, an appointment that would become official on the first day of the New Year.

Professor Brödel was a German émigré who had introduced the discipline of medical illustration into the United States, and Elisabeth had completed her studies with him the previous spring, after which she had worked with him, part-time, through the summer, fall, and early winter. She had also worked with Doctor Helen Taussig, who was studying abnormalities in children's cardio-vascular systems, especially in so-called "blue babies" – children who suffered from congenital malformations of the heart – and it was her work with Doctor Taussig and these children that she loved most, and that she was eager to tell her father about.

She walked under the elevated subway tracks, along Westchester Avenue. It had been more than four months since she had been in the Bronx, and she hoped that on this visit she would be able to persuade her father to return with her to Baltimore. She had lived in Baltimore for more than five years

– since the time, in April, 1934, when she had placed her son, Daniel, in a private institution on Chesapeake Bay – yet in all this time her father had never visited her. Nor had he seen his grandson in more than two years.

She drew her coat close against a non-existent wind while in her mind she conjured up a child's heart like one she had begun drawing for Doctor Taussig the week before. She rotated the heart slowly in order to consider it in all its dimensions, then sliced it in half so that when she drew it from two discrete perspectives, Doctor Taussig and her medical students would be able to see what was happening simultaneously on both the interior and the exterior of the heart.

A film of snow lay on the streets, from early morning flurries, but the air was warm, almost balmy, and this probably meant that heavier snows were on the way. She stopped and looked back towards the elevated subway station from which she had come. Buildings that were parallel to the tracks blocked the railroad trestles from view now, and when she looked up the hill she had just descended, a train, entering the station, seemed suspended in the sky above the rooftops, as if unmoored.

In Mister Klein's butcher shop, she bought three lamb chops, and in the fruit and vegetable store, string beans, mushrooms, garlic, and parsley. In the grocery store, she bought candles and wine, and in the bakery, a braided *challah*. None of the shopkeepers indicated, by gesture or word, that they recognized her. At the rise of the hill where Waters Place met Iverson Street, she bought tulips from Francine, a girl who lived in a first floor apartment in her father's building. Francine was eleven or twelve years old, a half dozen or so years younger than Daniel, and Elisabeth asked her about her family, but Francine, wrapping the flowers in brown paper, did not reply.

Elisabeth took the flowers, picked up her suitcase, and walked on towards her father's building. To the north and east, dairy farms and single family dwellings stretched out on low-lying, snow-covered land. The peacefulness of the landscape comforted her, and she found herself imagining the look on her father's face when he would open his door. *So, you're here again, are you?* he would say – his usual greeting – before smiling and embracing her.

On the third-floor landing, she knocked on her father's door, but there was no response, and she heard no sound. She was puzzled. Her father had never given her a key to the apartment, and it was not like him to be away when she arrived. She let her hand rest on the doorknob, felt the door move, pushed it open, entered the kitchen. The room contained only an ice box, a stove, a sink, a table, and two wooden chairs. The linoleum, a checkerboard of beige and gray squares, had been freshly waxed and polished.

She set down the groceries and her suitcase, then walked through a slender passageway that led to the bedroom. In the bedroom, the two beds were neatly made, identical cream-colored chenille spreads covering them, and across the iron rail at the foot of the bed that was hers, as in a hotel, a fresh green towel and a white wash cloth.

She took off her hat and coat, laid them on her father's bed, returned to the kitchen, and opened the ice box, where she found bottles of milk and orange juice, a jar of raspberry jam, butter, and eggs. On the counter next to the stove was an unopened box of Schrafft chocolates.

The bathroom had been cleaned – immaculately so – and there was a new white curtain hanging from silver hoops above the tub. She fingered the curtain, which felt very much to her touch like the fabric used in surgery to drape patients. In the bedroom, she pulled down the two window shades, took off her shoes, and, giving in to her exhaustion – she had risen at four-thirty in the morning in order to put in a half-day of work at the hospital – she lay down.

❖ ❖ ❖

When she awoke, she imagined that her father's hand was on her shoulder, waking her so she could get ready to go with him to work. When she and her father lived together in Brooklyn – her mother had died of tuberculosis three months before Elisabeth's fifth birthday – her father had worked as a sandhog, and sometimes as an electrician, in the building of the city's new subway system. In those years she had often gone with him, crossing Brooklyn Bridge in a cable car and spending whole days in places he found for her – alcoves, storage areas, and caves that had been cut into the dirt and rock of the island. Most days she would amuse herself by drawing pictures or playing with her dolls. She would build and furnish houses for the dolls out of scraps of wood, metal, and fabric, and would surround the houses with forests, lakes, gardens, swamps, and bridges she made from sticks, stones, grass, dirt, and flowers.

She had loved to draw machines and engines, especially the large hydraulic presses that drilled through stone, and she had also loved to draw mules, horses, and carts, along with the various shovels, picks, axes, and mauls she often saw leaning against walls and looking as if, like the men who used them, they too were resting from their labors.

The men her father worked with had marveled at her ability to draw their likenesses, and once she had finished a drawing of one of them, she would present it to the man, who would usually give her a penny or two in return.

She reached to the bedside table, turned on the lamp, and looked at her watch. It was nearly midnight, which meant that she had slept for more than five hours. She thought of telephoning Alex, her ex-husband – he was the one person in New York her father might notify if something was wrong – but there was no telephone in her father's apartment. Her father did not believe in telephones in the same way he did not believe in airplanes or radios, X-rays or moving pictures that were accompanied by sound. He did not trust what he could not understand. Nor did he, to her knowledge, have any friends other than the women with whom he occasionally spent nights.

From the cabinet above the kitchen sink she took down a pair of silver candlesticks and a silver goblet, objects her father had managed to bring with him from Poland when he came to the United States at the age of sixteen. Despite the hour, she lit two candles, covered her eyes with both hands, recited the prayer for welcoming the Sabbath, then poured wine into the goblet, recited another prayer, and drank the wine. She placed the *challah* on a plate, covered it with a napkin, made a pass above it in the air with a bread knife, recited a third prayer, tore off a piece of the bread and ate it. Then she sat at the kitchen table and poured herself more wine. Sometimes, on Friday nights, she and her father would finish an entire bottle together.

Feeling a slight draft, she turned and saw that the front door had come open. She closed it, then put the candlesticks in the sink so there would be no risk of fire during what remained of the night. She returned to the bedroom, bringing the goblet of wine with her, undressed, and put on her nightgown.

If her father were not with a woman, it occurred to her, it was possible he was working the night shift at the nearby railroad yard, where, though retired, he sometimes filled in for sick or disabled workers, helping to repair the electrical systems of trains. But if he was at the railroad yard, why hadn't he left her a note telling her so?

If he didn't return by morning, she decided, rather than wait around worrying about him, she would perform the favor one of Professor Brödel's friends, Doctor John Kafka, had asked of her, and pay a visit to John's uncle, Doctor Eduard Bloch, who was living nearby, a block or two from the Botanical Gardens, on East Tremont Avenue. Doctor Bloch, a recent émigré from Austria, had been Adolf Hitler's doctor when Hitler was a boy, had attended to Hitler's family during the boy's growing up, and to Hitler's mother during her illness and death from breast cancer. According to the nephew, Doctor Bloch had been able to get out of Austria due to an unprecedented act – the intervention of Hitler himself, the only Jew for whom the German dictator had ever performed such a service.

She finished her glass of wine, turned out the light, and told herself that her father had not left a message because he was probably preparing a surprise for her, and that if he wasn't there when she awoke, he would surely be there when she returned from visiting Doctor Bloch. *So*, she imagined him asking. *Where have you been? I've been waiting for you all morning.*

TWO

From the Journal of Doctor Eduard Bloch
December 6, 1940

Because once again I have been asked to convey my impressions of the man who granted me passage across the seas and so was responsible for the political and personal liberty which, in the United States, I now enjoy – a liberty compromised only by those conditions that might accompany any experience of exile – I have willingly chosen to set down in words, without concealment, my recollections, and to do so with the hope that they might be of use to others in understanding the difficult passage through which our several nations are now passing.

In this way, I trust, I will be able to return the multiplicity of kindnesses that individuals have bestowed upon me, as happened once again today in the person of a most unusual woman, Elisabeth Rofman, who is an acquaintance of my nephew, Doctor John Kafka – John and I are cousins to the Czechoslovakian writer of the same name, though neither John nor I have ever met him – and a colleague to the esteemed Max Brödel, Professor at The Johns Hopkins Hospital and Medical School.

John had written to inform me that Miss Rofman's father lived nearby, here in what is called the Westchester Heights region of the Bronx, and that he had suggested she pay me the courtesy of a visit when she was next in this city. He told me she was an exceptionally gifted woman – a divorced woman, it seems, and with a son whom she put away in an Institution several years ago – and of rare intelligence, but what I was not prepared for was the extraordinary beauty of her person, and, despite or perhaps because of her extreme shyness, the palpable warmth of her presence.

Miss Rofman has an exceptionally high forehead, wide set pale grey eyes, and unusually broad cheekbones that suggest Slavic ancestry. Her nose is long, slender, and, though it doubtless embarrassed her as a child, is made intriguing – truly enchanting! – by a tiny birthmark near its extremity. Her mouth is wide and full, her smile winning, her jaw and chin strong. Her features, in their sharp angularity, and in a certain overall darkness of mien – her hair, short and straight, is a deep silken black, like that of a raven's wing – put me in mind, upon first impression, of certain portraits of women made by the American painter John Singer Sargent.

I wonder – and wonder I will, you see, since in these pages I intend to hide nothing, no matter the embarrassment, from myself or from others – if John thought there might be a romantic attraction between us.

I speculate in this manner since John, in his description of Miss Rofman, emphasized the fact of her divorce, and since it seemed a most obvious fact while she and I were becoming acquainted, palpably there between us in the room like a table or chair, that here we were, each of us separated from home and from work – she temporarily, and I, I fear, permanently – and both of us previously married (I am a widower, my dear wife, Marta, having left this world some eleven years ago). Moreover, it is my belief – a belief my nephew John shares (I took John in when he was a boy, raising him as if he were my own son) – that first impressions carry force out of all proportion to the actual passage of time, and are often the most reliable indicators of those true feelings upon which confident judgments and wise choices can be made.

I will be sixty-nine years old upon my next birthday, and I

am in excellent health, capable still of working full-time as a physician, should the opportunity present itself. I regularly take long, brisk walks even on the coldest of winter days, and do so without suffering shortness of breath or any other form of fatigue, either of limbs, lungs, or heart. Although Miss Rofman is younger than I by some two decades, and in appearance would be taken for a woman of no more than forty years, my estimate of her true age, and the very age that Marta was when she passed away – this gleaned from answers to questions I put to her in a manner I trust was not rude – is that she is between forty-four and forty-five years old.

Her eyes seemed to drink in every word and gesture of mine, along with each detail of my rather shabby dwelling. In these lovely and, yes, these *hungry* eyes, the grey (with hints of a blue like that of a clear late afternoon winter sky) is nearly transparent, a quality I often saw in women who had emigrated to Austria from regions of Western Poland – an area now part of the Ukraine – and there was an inquisitiveness in them that allowed me to see the less reserved woman she might have been before she married and divorced, and before she bore a child.

Although Miss Rofman would not often return my gaze directly, yet were her answers themselves consistently direct. Nor did she weigh them down with the kinds of equivocations I have found many Americans employ, as if, in people of this nation, there is a lamentable yearning never to be found in disagreement with those whom they wish to please.

Miss Rofman had no such scruples, however, which raised her considerably in my estimation, and allowed for a marvelously free exchange of information between us. What did surprise, though, given her shyness, was the intense and comprehensive manner in which she returned my questions with pointed inquiries of her own: What, she asked, was it like to be among people with whom I could not converse in my native language? Did I mind the isolation? How often did I see my daughter,

Gertrude, and her husband, a young physician, who, she had learned from conversations with John, also lived in New York City? Did I have a close relationship with my daughter? Given the apparent cruelties he is wreaking upon both large portions of Europe and many members of our faith, did I harbor regrets about having served the ruler of Germany and his family? Did I cherish, resent, or regard as good fortune – or ill fortune! – the unique privilege that had allowed me my exodus? Was I a practicing Jew?

I answered her questions with an exactness that seemed to satisfy her. For my part, it was, in sum, a great and distinct pleasure to spend an afternoon with an attractive, intelligent woman of impeccable manners and unique forthrightness, and one who – quiet joy! – spoke German with a minimum of errors, and with the merest trace of an American accent.

Thus it was that we moved, in our conversation, back and forth from her language to mine without seeming to notice when we were doing so. I found this quite remarkable, and when I inquired of her knowledge, she explained that although she had never visited Europe, she had studied German for four years in high school and for an additional four years at University (Barnard College, which is part of Columbia University). More recently, during a three year apprenticeship to Professor Brödel, she had, intensively, taken up the study of German again.

It is her admirable facility with German that has inspired me to set down my own impressions in the English language, for by so doing – by writing in a tongue that is *not* native to me – I will be forced to think more painstakingly about what it is I choose to say, and about the choice of words with which I will say them. By passing my experiences through a language that remains ultimately foreign to me, my experiences will, I sense, become objects that will seem to have an existence apart from me, and so, I trust, will allow me to actually *see* my experiences with greater vividness and clarity. Moreover, I expect, thinking and writing in English will force me to slow down the very processes of writing and thinking and thus *dis*allow me the ease that might, were I writing in German, permit for a certain facility with language that would encourage a disjuncture between experiences and the words used to describe experiences, much as in the famous "screen memories," when individuals replace the memory of actual events with less accurate (and less painful) memories, thereby leading too easily to superficiality.

It was a particular thrill when engaged in conversation with Miss Rofman to tell her that just as she had learned to speak German at a young age, so I had had the good fortune to learn English when I was a young man, not only as a student at University, but previous to this. An uncle of mine, I explained – my mother's eldest brother, Samuel Joshua Kaufman, was a physician, and from the time I was born he had been particularly fond of me. After his marriage to a wealthy English woman he met in Berlin, herself a Jew and the daughter of a physician, he had moved to England, and distant though we were in miles, he had maintained his interest in me, and, especially, in my education. It was he more than any other who was instrumental in encouraging me to make a career as a physician, a choice he made possible both by his example (he was a highly esteemed member of the Royal College of Physicians and Surgeons; I spent several summers with him and his wife – they were childless, a fact that doubtless contributed to his affection for me – in their London townhouse, where he had his medical office), and by his generous financial contributions both to my studies and to the funds that became necessary when I set up my medical practice in Linz.

In addition – what, above all, allowed for the quality of dialogue Miss Rofman and I were able to enjoy, and what is most responsible for whatever facility I possess with regard to the English language – he kept me supplied, by post, with American and English novels. I was particularly enchanted, during my early years – this when I was still in *Gymnasium*, in the years before I entered medical school – by the novels of Robert Louis Stevenson and Jack London.

I remarked (to myself) that it revealed something of Miss Rofman's character that she did not, for her part, credit her linguistic facility to an innate talent or to diligence as a student, but rather to the happenstance that when she was a girl between the ages of four and eight, the woman who cared for her while her father was at work spoke German. Miss Rofman's mother, I surmised, was not present during those years. The woman, by the name of Ulla, was Jewish, a fact that surprised me, for I had not imagined that German Jews would have served as domestic help to East European Jews, but I did not pursue the subject since Miss Rofman indicated her discomfort concerning this period of her life by moving away from it with haste.

It was at this juncture of our dialogue, in fact, that, with a certain abruptness, she changed the matter of our conversation from the personal to the public, and to that subject about which all who meet me in America, knowing of how and why I am here, inquire.

Her questions became, at once, less specific. They became, that is, questions *anyone* might have asked – as many *have* asked! – and they were phrased in ways that left to me the choice of how much or how little I wished to tell, so that what I found myself doing, and I had no premonition this would happen, was saying to her that rather than replying in the perfunctory way to which I have become accustomed, I would prefer to set down my responses, both my considered thoughts and my random musings, in writing.

If I did so, I asked, would she be willing to read what I wrote?

Miss Rofman, I had noticed, has a habit of smiling frequently, a swift almost mechanical though not unpleasant smile she provides before and after she asks or replies to a question – a habit that bears little if any relation to what she may be saying, and no relation at all to anything patently humorous – but at this moment her smile was, of a sudden, anything but mechanical. It was broad, natural, and, to my surprise, rather playful.

Are you, then, she asked, seeking an illustrator?

I had not considered the possibility, I replied.

Well, consider it, she said. I am quite a good illustrator.

I said that I did not doubt the truth of this, but that what I was suggesting was offered without thoughts of a collaboration. In truth, I added, her questions were themselves the inspiration for what I was, to my surprise, proposing.

When I said this, her smile faded, and she apologized, though she did not say for what, specifically, she was apologizing. My suspicion is that her suggestion about serving as illustrator was a polite way of letting me know that my recollections of the German leader were of little importance to her. In this most welcome lack of interest – and in the ironic way she presented it to me (an irony I was slow to perceive) – she again showed evidence of an impressive singularity of mind.

Still, her visit is the proximate cause for my beginning to set down, on this evening near the end of the first week of December in the year 1940, these words. In this task, I was further encouraged by what she said when she took her leave.

I would be honored to read whatever you write, she declared.

I informed her that although members of several Intelligence and Military Agencies of the United States Government, along with editors from a number of newspapers and magazines, had been pressing me to set down my recollections, and to submit to interviews, I preferred at this time to keep my knowledge and impressions private, since doing so, I believed, would allow me a greater freedom both in the retrieval of memories and in the setting down of these memories.

Will the writing you propose be for me, then, or for a wider audience? she asked.

Perhaps for your eyes first, I answered, and later on, and with, should we judge it appropriate – the more personal passages excised – for others.

Thank you, she said then, and she said nothing more. She took her leave so swiftly, in fact, that I did not have the chance to say to her that I also see this as an opportunity to respond to the several accusations being made against my person, accusations so absurd and reprehensible that men and women of ordinary good sense will, I trust, give them no credence, yet accusations – for example, that, by ministering to a young boy's mother several decades ago, I have, if without conscious intent, brought about the German leader's hatred and oppression of the Jews – I cannot, in honor, ignore.

❖ ❖ ❖

Thus I begin the story others have urged me to tell, and I do so by recounting an incident that took place on the high seas, and one that made clear to me the unique history I was bringing with me across these seas.

After I had made my way from Linz, largely by train, across Austria, France, Spain, and Portugal, I was able to obtain passage on a small Spanish liner, the *Marques de Comillas*, out of Lisbon, and bound for New York City. I had accomplished my journey to Lisbon with only moderate difficulties and, to my surprise – and relief! – without the authorities – police (trains, hotels) and military personnel (border crossings) – seeming aware of or remarking upon the unique privilege that had been granted to me, a Jew.

On our third day out of Lisbon, however, our ship was stopped and boarded by British Control Officers. We had just passed through two days of horrific weather – swells that seemed the size of small mountains, along with fierce driving rains and much thunder and lightning – and the storm had left a majority of the passengers, along with a goodly number of crew members, quite ill and dangerously depleted. I was able to tend to them, insisting as I made my rounds that, to avoid dehydration, they begin to take in fluids, and following on this, both fluids and foods rich in potassium, calcium, and phosphates.

On this third day out, however, shortly before eleven o'clock in the evening, we were all, passengers and crew members alike, ordered to assemble in the main lounge, and to bring with us our identification papers, passports, and visas.

I was lodged one level below deck, and from the porthole of my cabin I saw that a large military transport had made anchor nearby, a transport that, irony of ironies, was named for the great Jewish statesman, Benjamin Disraeli. The British officers, along with a dozen or so British soldiers, had made their way to us aboard two small launches that were tied to the starboard side of our ship, and these officers now commenced to examine us one at a time, scrutinizing our passports and other documents, while the soldiers, who struck me as mere secondary school lads, manifestly frightened themselves, stood at attention, guns at the ready.

The tension in the air was as heavy and discomforting as had been the weather less than twenty-four hours before. Many of the passengers, asleep when the order to appear in the lounge was given, were huddled in whatever ill-fitting garments, overcoats, robes, and blankets they had been able to secure. Most of them, I assumed, were, like me, fleeing from Germany, Austria, or other nations, Czechoslovakia and Poland most notably, where the German occupation was in force.

Given the storm, and the events that had determined the place in which we found ourselves – between lives, so to speak – we had had neither opportunity nor desire to exchange much information with one another. I had assumed, rightly, it would turn out, that most of my fellow passengers were Jews, and though Britain was engaged in a war against Germany, yet did we harbor anxieties – due to our common status as Jews in transit, and to pervasive attitudes towards our people held even by those, like the British, who were at war with the enemy who was the cause of our flight – about what might be done to us. Doubtless, we feared, as I did, that some of us might on this night be removed from the ship, to what fate was unclear.

Women and children were among us, and several of them – those who spoke no English, in particular – were weeping. One elderly lady fainted, and when she did, I went to her at once, telling her companions to set her gently on the floor in a supine position. I loosened her garments and elevated her feet. Nobody intervened to stop me, although a soldier moved swiftly to my side. I patted the woman's cheeks, touched her forehead and lips with the cold water another soldier brought, and when I saw the woman's eyes open and her coloration return, I returned to my place in line. A few moments later, the officer in charge, reaching me, took my passport, opened it, glanced through a few pages, and smiled.

You were Hitler's physician, weren't you, he said.

Yes, I answered, but said no more.

He smiled again, in a way I can only characterize as enigmatic, after which he returned my passport with a slight bow of his head, and moved on to the next person.

I wondered, of course, how he knew who I was, and I wondered, too, exactly what it was he knew of me and how he had come by his knowledge. I should add, at once, that although I have characterized his smile as enigmatic, it was also *kind*, and that – this in retrospect, for I was nervous in the moment itself – given the tensions under which he was operating, I find his kindness remarkable. Surely had he so wished, he could have had me removed from the ship, detained me for questioning, and caused me other considerable difficulties.

And so, what I did not say to him – what he did not, in that moment, in his generosity, inquire of, yet what I sensed was passing in the air between us – I will elaborate upon here.

The Jew, I will state first of all, is to the world what Austria is to Germany. I emphasize this, as I will to all who interrogate me, because it is a thought I have been formulating for a considerable time, and one that is pertinent to what I will have to say about the ruler of the German Empire. And because I am both Austrian *and* Jew, I believe I am able to bring to the subject, as to the man, a unique and valuable perspective.

Although there have always been rumors to the effect that Hitler's paternal grandfather was Jewish, and although some of Hitler's childhood friends would tease him by remarking on the fact that he *looked* Jewish, and that there are commentators who speculate that such things may be a source in him both of shame and of a desire for vengeance and vindication, yet, believing as I do, with the philosophers and poets, that the child is father to the man, it will prove most useful, I submit, to consider first of all what his early life in Linz was like. Upon that early life I can comment knowledgeably.

Yet before I do this, there is another matter I must offer for consideration. I refer to the extraordinary similarities between the Jewish people and the German people, and here, as elsewhere, I note, I will, generally, speak of the German and Austrian peoples as being one.

Franz Kafka himself noticed much the same thing, and made the finer point: that the more Jews entered fully into German society – the more we resembled them – the more did they resent us. In specific, what Kafka, who, had he lived, would be more than a decade younger than I, wrote of our commonalities was this – that we were, each of our peoples, ambitious, able, diligent, and thoroughly hated by others – in his words: pariahs to the world.

Kafka wrote this many years before Hitler came to power, when, as Kafka noted, other nations feared, admired, envied, and ridiculed Germans much as they feared, admired, envied, and ridiculed Jews, while it was only we Jews who actually seemed to love the Germans. Consider, for example, our great poet Heinrich Heine – Jewish *and* German, though living much of his life in exile – declaring that the ancient Hebrews had been the Germans of the Orient! Or Goethe, expressing the wish that Germans be dispersed throughout the world as Jews had been, and that Germans should, following our example, be a light unto the nations and should strive for the improvement of mankind.

We may add to such sentiments both the well-known affinities Germans and Jews have when it comes to industry, frugality, and thrift, and our mutual love for and near-worship of family life. Moreover, both peoples share a marked and common respect for the printed word – we are The People of the Book, they The People of Poetry and Thought – as well as a proclivity for abstract speculation, and, less happily, have often been characterized by others for alleged qualities of arrogance, ill manners, stubbornness, overweening pride, self-loathing, and excessive sensitivity.

Therefore, in returning to the statement with which I began this passage of abstract speculation, I call attention to the fact that just as Jews have been relegated to inferior positions within the German Empire, so has Austria been relegated to a secondary place within the Third Reich.

❖ ❖ ❖

Imagine, then, the city of Linz in which Hitler came of age more than a quarter of a century ago. Linz, then as now the capital of Upper Austria, was a major port on the Danube, a thriving industrial and commercial center noted for its iron and steel works as well as for its manufacture of machinery and textiles. Yet it was also, with a population at the time of slightly more than eighty thousand, a beautiful city architecturally and one with a rich, lustrous history.

Before becoming capital of Upper Austria, it had been, in the late fifteenth century, a provincial capital of the Holy Roman Empire, and it retains many marvelous buildings that attest to its history, including a glorious eighth century Romanesque church, a Provincial Museum (which, in addition to many fine paintings, contains Roman artifacts and – what especially fascinated Hitler on his youthful visits there – a considerable store of folk art), and a splendid, newly completed Gothic cathedral.

Spread out majestically on both sides of the Danube, Linz is also a city that draws nourishment from its bucolic setting – in particular, from the many farms, predominantly dairy, that give the city and its outlying areas those picturesque qualities that, I believe, first inspired young Adolf in his passion to become an artist.

In this connection – the presence, in Linz, of these two distinct and contrasting elements: noble architecture and pastoral beauty – we may sense the origins in Adolf not only of his desire to become an artist, but of the means he chose to earn a living when he too was far from home and fell upon hard times. For what he did in order to survive during this passage in his life was to paint and sell postal cards of pastoral settings that he recalled from his childhood in Linz, along with Viennese street scenes, several of which cards I received from him and managed to save, and one of which, inscribed with renewed expressions of his gratitude, I showed to Miss Rofman today.

I will also state this: that in all the years during which I ministered to him and to his family, never once did the question of race – of our differing races – arise. This was especially noteworthy during that most crucial episode in our relationship: our interactions at the time of his mother's fatal illness, a time when he might have had occasion to show evidence of negative feelings. About young Adolf's feelings during his mother's sad, slow dying, however, I will comment later, but not on this night, for the hour is late and, tiring, I begin to lose that mental acuity necessary to the authenticity of this project.

My own life, I will add, is not central to this story; nevertheless, since I am to be guide to those who read this, I will conclude these introductory remarks by noting several basic facts about myself.

I was born in Frauenburg, a small village in Southern Bohemia, one which, in the course of my lifetime, has existed under three flags: Austrian, Czechoslovakian, and German. My family was Jewish, and although we observed our people's religious practices with minimal rigor (we attended the local synagogue only on the New Year and the Day of Atonement, which we did as if attending the most regal of occasions; my father, grandfather, and uncles wore top hats and formal attire), I was always aware that I was a Jew, and that this was a fact in which I was to take pride. We spoke German in our home (I was touched by Miss Rofman's understanding that this – the loss of language – is ever the most painful loss of all), and to indicate how deep was the feeling in our community for the essential beauty and nobility of the German language, I note here that those of our fellow Jews who were peasants – which we were not: my father was a successful merchant, in dry goods – and who spoke Czech all week long, both at home and in the street, would, on the Sabbath, speak to one another only in German.

When I had completed *Gymnasium*, I journeyed to Prague, where I studied medicine, after which I joined the Austrian Army as a Military Doctor. In 1899 I was ordered to Linz, at that time the third largest city in Austria, and when I had completed my military service, in 1901, I chose to remain in Linz. Until a short while ago, I have practiced medicine there, where, with my wife and daughter, I have enjoyed a good, enviable, and unremarkable life.

The Hitler family moved to Linz in 1903, two years after I had begun my medical practice there, and they did so largely because of the mother's determination to provide her children, young Adolf especially, with a good education. In those years, as now, Linz was rightly known for the excellent quality of its schools.

In those years, too, Linz, and my life in it, was as quiet and reserved as Vienna was gay and noisy. My consultation rooms were lodged on the first floor of the house in which I lived – one entered directly into my waiting room from the street – an ancient baroque structure for which I had, and have, much affection, and one situated on Landstrasse, the city's main thoroughfare.

Let me also, albeit in a summary way, here list some basic facts about the Hitler family while these facts, from the stimulus of Miss Rofman's visit, are fresh in my mind.

The family background was well known. Alois Schicklgruber Hitler, the father, was the son of a poor peasant girl. When he came of age, he became a cobbler's apprentice, after which he worked his way into the government service, eventually becoming an inspector at Braunau, a tiny frontier town located between Bavaria and Austria, some fifty miles distant from Linz.

As soon as he became eligible for pension, at fifty-six years of age, he retired. Proud of his own success at rising in the world, Alois was eager for his son to enter government service as he had done, but young Adolf, determined to become an artist, opposed his father in this. Father and son fought, often violently, over this issue, while the mother, Klara, endeavored to maintain peace within the family.

When, in fact, Hitler decided to go to Vienna to study at the Academy, Klara, who struggled valiantly to make ends meet, suggested ways to pinch the family budget in order to send him a small allowance. Credit goes to the young man, however, for he refused, and went even further, signing away his minute inheritance to his sisters. He was eighteen years old at the time.

As long as he lived, Alois Hitler persevered in his attempt to shape his son's destiny to his own desires, wanting Adolf to have the education that had been denied him, an education that would provide him – his major concern – a job that was *secure*. Thus, in concert with Klara, he moved his family from the hamlet of Braunau to the city of Linz. There, he purchased a small farm for his family on the outskirts of the city, in Leonding; given his previous government service, Alois knew that he would not be required to pay full tuition for his son at the *Realschule*.

The family was rather large, and forever in difficult straits financially. Alois had had two previous wives, both of whom had died, and Klara – who was Alois's niece on his paternal side (Alois's father was her granduncle) – had served as housemaid to the family during his first two marriages.

Young Adolf had a half-brother, Alois, named after the father and older by several years. This brother left home at an early age and became a waiter in London, after which he returned to the European mainland and opened his own restaurant in Berlin. The brothers were not close.

Hitler's closest relationships, other than the relationship with his mother, were with his sisters. Hitler's older sister, Paula, married a Herr Raubal, an official in the tax bureau, and after Herr Raubal's untimely death, and following on Hitler's rise to power in 1933, she relocated to Berchtesgaden, where she became housekeeper at Hitler's villa. His sister Klara, the mother's namesake, remained in Linz, though for a while she lived in Vienna, where she managed a restaurant for Jewish students at the University. Angela, the youngest sister – and Hitler's favorite – married a Professor Hamitsch of Dresden, in which city she still resides.

There was also – a fact less well-known – a half-sister, from Alois Schicklgruber's second wife, who had been his kitchen maid during his first marriage. This sister was, for the most part, hidden away by the family due to the fact that she was diagnosed as a mental case. Of this sister's existence I am certain, for I had occasion once, when she was at home on a rare visit – she lived out her adult life in an Institution for the Mentally Insane

– to examine her, about which meeting (Hitler accompanied his mother when they brought the sister to my office), I will write later.

The sister's sad existence, and the shame the family felt about her, came to mind this afternoon when Miss Rofman, responding to a question of mine about *her* family, talked with admirable frankness of her son, providing a diagnosis and prognosis that was lucid, thoughtful, and without prejudice. Clearly her love for her son is in no way diminished by the fact of his unfortunate condition. I sensed not only her deep affection for the child, but her genuine hopes – which seemed to me not unreasonable or unrealistic – for the life he may yet have. His name is Daniel, and he will soon be eighteen years old.

The Hitler family, except the half-sister, had barely settled into their new home outside Linz, however, when, following on an apoplectic stroke, Alois passed away. This was a cruel blow, especially to Klara, the wife and mother, who was then in her early forties.

Klara was a simple, modest, kindly woman. She was tall, with neatly-plaited brown hair, a long, oval face and, most memorably, expressive gray-blue eyes. Alois, who was more than twenty years her senior, had always managed the family. Now the task was hers, and in conversations with me, she acknowledged that she was worried, and desperately so, about the responsibilities suddenly thrust upon her by her husband's death.

Of the life the family lived in the wake of their loss, and of how this may have shaped young Adolf's life, I will write on another occasion. Remembering Klara's despair, however, calls to mind a look I saw this afternoon in Miss Rofman's eyes – they are paler than Klara's and, while no less expressive, are considerably more penetrating, revealing, as they do, an acute intelligence of a kind Klara lacked – when she spoke of her father. Miss Rofman's father was not in his apartment yesterday when Miss Rofman arrived from Baltimore, and by the time she had left for her visit with me, nearly a full day later, he had not returned. Although Miss Rofman contended that there was doubtless some perfectly ordinary explanation for his absence, her eyes told of her fears. She has promised to pay me a visit again tomorrow so that we may continue our conversation. I will, of course, at that time ask of her father, and, should he continue to be absent, will place myself at her service.

THREE

Elisabeth's train was scheduled to depart from Pennsylvania Station at 6:22, and it was now 4:48. Outside, it had begun to snow again, and she found herself wishing there were someone – *anyone* – who would simply tell her what to do. She sat in the station's main waiting room, without her suitcase – without even a book – and chastised herself for the weakness she had succumbed to in having telephoned Alex.

Beyond the waiting room, she knew, an enormous glass-roofed concourse provided access to the platform where her train would be waiting, and behind her, a long, barrel-vaulted arcade, lined with shops, led to the marble stairway and escalator that had brought her to the main hall a few minutes before. When she had first stood in this hall with Alex years before, he had explained the architectural plan to her, and she recalled the fact that had amused him most: that this vast space – all steel, light, and air – acre upon acre of glass domes, steel-ribbed vaults, and plasterwork arches – was a copy of the Tepidarium of a Roman bath.

How sad, she thought, to have loved a man so utterly once upon a time and to feel now that he was unknown to her. And wherein was responsibility lodged, she wondered: in the shallows of her mind, where judgment had, seemingly, been non-existent? In Alex's extraordinary gift for dissembling and deceit? Or – the more likely possibility – in the confused workings of her own heart, where her inordinate desire and his exceptional charm had all too willingly conspired?

It was only after she had left Doctor Bloch's apartment that she remembered that without a key – she had let the door lock behind her when she left – she would be unable to get back into her father's apartment. Mildly panicked – in addition to clothing and personal items, she had left her work there: sketches she had promised to complete and deliver to Professor Brödel by Monday – she had entered a luncheonette and, from a phone booth, telephoned.

Alex's wife, Sonya, had answered, and when Elisabeth said the matter was important, Sonya had said she would get Alex, but had returned a short while later to say that Alex was occupied. If Elisabeth left a message, however, he would return her call at his first opportunity.

"Tell Alex that I'm in the Bronx," Elisabeth had said, "and that I'm concerned about my father. I'll be back in Baltimore late this evening."

"Your father," Sonya had said. "But of course. When you said it was important, I thought it might be about Daniel."

"Daniel is well," Elisabeth said.

"Daniel well?" Sonya had said. "Surely you're joking."

❖ ❖ ❖

Elisabeth arrived at Alex's house by taxicab shortly before 6 P. M. The house, at the corner of Fifth Avenue and 69th Street, designed by Alex and modeled after the August Belmont mansion that had been located at Fifth Avenue and 19th Street, occupied, with its inner courtyard and gardens, an entire city block. Elisabeth had not telephoned again because she knew that if she had, Alex would have found a reason to refuse to see her. She knew him well enough, though, to know that once she was there he would be unable to resist the chance to invite her in and show her the life she had given up.

"Tell Doctor Landau that Elisabeth Rofman is here," Elisabeth said to the housemaid who opened the door.

In the small vestibule, a vase of chalk-white lilies sat on a marble-topped table in front of a gilt-edged mirror. Elisabeth looked at her image in the mirror, and noted that her skin, next to the lilies, appeared almost preternaturally healthy: rose-colored, with hints, in the shadows, of dull gold and moss green. Mirrored from behind, the lilies' pollen-laden pistils and stamens were hidden from view, yet the flowers' fragrance was so thick in the small space as to seem almost liquid.

On the wall to her left, beside the inner door, four small antique oil lamps used for the celebration of Chanukah were suspended from wrought iron hooks. To her right were framed etchings of synagogues and of bearded Jewish men at prayer. Alex took great pride in his collection of Jewish art and ritual objects, and Elisabeth, letting an index finger rest within the curved well of one of the menorahs, was able, despite Alex, to feel an affection for the objects themselves. She recalled how happy Daniel was the first time he'd been allowed to touch a match to the oil, to watch the oil flare up, and to touch a match to an additional well on each successive night of the eight nights of Chanukah.

"Doctor Landau says to please come in, Miss Elisabeth, and he requests the pleasure of your company at dinner," the housemaid said when she returned.

As soon as Elisabeth moved from the vestibule to the foyer, large oak-paneled doors that led from the foyer to the hallway opened, and Alex came towards her, smiling broadly, hands extended. He was dressed in a dark purple-and-red paisley smoking jacket. As always, he wore a black skullcap of the kind rabbis and cantors wore in synagogue, one whose shape was not unlike that of a woman's pillbox hat.

"I am honored – " Alex began.

"No you're not," Elisabeth said.

" – and pleased," Alex continued. He took Elisabeth's hands in his own, and because, with Alex, she had learned that it was best not to protest since this only encouraged him, she did not object. "You'll join us for dinner then?" he said. "It will please the children."

"I need your help," Elisabeth said.

"Of course," Alex said. "Sonya told me. But of course, of course." He moved quickly, his hands on her shoulders, and again she neither protested nor resisted when he took her coat. Then he stepped back and spoke with what seemed genuine warmth. "You look wonderful, Elisabeth – " he declared " – the winter air has always had a salutary effect on you. And you're feeling well yourself? You're not working – well – overly? But please come and let us talk. I'm delighted that you felt free to stop by this way. We are, after all, still family to one another, yes?"

Elisabeth let Alex lead the way into his study, which, suffused in soft orange lighting – from the stained glass shade of a large lamp, and a small fire in the fireplace – made her feel, briefly, faint – assaulted by memories, by Alex's physical proximity, and by the room's lush furnishings: the dark leather armchairs, the heavy wine-red drapes, the books, the manuscripts, the silver ritual objects set upon shelves – spice boxes, menorahs, wine goblets, and smaller objects whose purposes were mostly unknown to her.

Still, she realized, the room was not that different from what it had been like when she had last been here with Daniel three years before, or from what it had been like when she had lived here. Despite Alex's pride in saying or doing the unpredictable thing, he remained a man addicted to his habits, and to his daily, domestic routines.

"The rabbis say that the unexpected visitor, like the prophet Elijah, is always the most welcome visitor," Alex said.

"Do they really say that?"

Alex closed the door behind them. "Actually, *I* say that." He paused. "Ah, Elisabeth – I sometimes forget how difficult it is to fool you. You are a splendid literalist – the only person who regularly expresses skepticism at the rabbinic aphorisms I send forth into the world." He laughed. "It is amazing, though, how people will nod in agreement when I lower my voice and preface some homily I've invented with the words, 'The rabbis say . . . .'"

"I arrived in the city yesterday afternoon for a visit with my father," Elisabeth said. "I wrote to him in advance, but when I arrived, his door was unlocked and he wasn't there. He hasn't returned since, and I have to leave for Baltimore tonight."

"And therefore you think – ?"

"I don't *think* anything in particular."

"I would doubt that – you always think things in particular."

"I *am* worried, though, or I wouldn't be here," Elisabeth said. "It's not like him to simply disappear. Where would he go? And it's not like him to make me worry about him."

"I agree."

"Will you help me then?"

"Of course." Alex bowed his head slightly. "You may depend on me."

"Will you have to call the police?"

"Perhaps. But let me reflect on this during dinner. After dinner, we can talk. I sense your urgency – the urgency of the situation – but I don't want to act hastily. I want to consider the best course, naturally, and then . . . ."

Alex went to a window, pulled a cord and opened the drapes. Outside, on Fifth Avenue, snow was falling so heavily that Elisabeth could not see to the far side of the street, or to the stone wall that bordered Central Park. She imagined snow falling silently on the fields near her father's house, fields in which she had walked with her father the previous summer, picking wild blueberries. Then she was imagining Doctor Bloch gazing out of his window at the snow, and wondering if the scene would conjure up memories for him of the winter landscape in Linz, and, thinking of him, she reminded herself to telephone him before she left for Baltimore, as she had promised she would.

"Would you consider staying the night?" Alex asked. "I can have the maid prepare one of the guest rooms."

"No."

"Be practical, Elisabeth. If your train is delayed this evening, as is probable, where would you stay? Surely it will be unnerving to return to your father's apartment and to sleep there alone. You could take the first train tomorrow morning. My coachman would bring you to the station." He paused. "And there's also *my* well-being to consider, for I would worry about you."

Elisabeth remained silent.

"Had you not come here," Alex continued, "I would have had no cause for concern. But since you have . . . ."

"I appreciate your offer, but I'll take my chances with the train. They'll need me at the hospital early on Monday morning, and I have work to prepare before then."

"And too, if I am to be of genuine assistance," Alex said, "I'll need more information about your father, whom I have not seen for several years. Do you have a recent photograph?"

"No."

"If you stay here, you can have a decent night's rest. It will be no trouble – rather the opposite. My children are, after all, brother and sister to Daniel. It would be a gift were they to spend time with you – it would diffuse some of the mystery and fear in which, alas, our son's life has been shrouded."

"That fear could easily be dissipated if you'd visit him more often – or, better yet, have him visit you here on a regular basis."

Alex smiled in a way that irritated Elisabeth, and when he talked about their mutual need to accept the reality of Daniel's situation and, receiving no response from Elisabeth, began quoting from the Bible, as he often did in their conversations – about the life of the flesh being in the blood, and about rabbinic interpretations of this notion – Elisabeth felt her irritation turn to rage. The rage, wonderfully uncomplicated, carried with it distinct sensations of pleasure, and she pictured it as it moved through her – a thin, steaming river of fire – so that, observing its movement even while she listened to Alex's words, she was able to trace its course – to watch it enter and leave her heart, push through valves, pulse from chamber to chamber and then from organ to organ as it flowed to distant cells, depositing its nutrients while receiving bodily wastes.

"With all respect," Alex was saying. "We disagree."

"Oh yes," Elisabeth said.

How strange, she mused, to be capable of listening to Alex while at the same time being able to watch the flames within – to see them lick the walls of the pericardium, and singe the membranous sac that contained the heart and its great ascending and descending blood vessels. Still, she knew, her anger and the sustenance she derived from it were accompanied by a profound exhaustion. But I could draw a picture of my father, she thought. I could go to a hotel – to the Barbizon – and register for the night, order room service, and luxuriate in a warm bath. Afterwards, I could relax in an easy chair, drink good wine, make the drawing, call the concierge, and have the hotel deliver the drawing to Alex. I could go to sleep on soft, freshly laundered sheets, and in the morning I could return to my father's house, find the building's super, and get a key from him.

Elisabeth put on her gloves. "For a sincere man, Alex," she said, "you remain the most insincere person I've ever known."

At this remark, Alex's eyes brightened with pleasure. He smiled and then, looking past Elisabeth, his smile broadened. Elisabeth turned and saw that Alex's three children were standing in the doorway – Hannah, who was born a few months after Elisabeth moved to Baltimore and would now be six years old, and the boys, Jacob and Noah, who were three and two.

Sonya, dressed in a lilac-colored full-length gown, stood beside her children. Alex had been past forty and Sonya nineteen when they married, and childbearing had done little to diminish her beauty. If anything, she appeared more beautiful now – the lines in her face less soft and childlike – than when Elisabeth had last seen her.

"I've been trying to convince Elisabeth to spend the night with us," Alex said, and then: "Come, Hannah. Come, boys – Jacob. Noah. Come forward, please, and say hello to your Aunt Elisabeth – to Daniel's mother."

Without hesitating, the children approached Elisabeth. The boys were dressed in matching Navy-blue sailor suits, while Hannah wore a pink flowered dress, her golden curls tied with a pink ribbon.

Hannah stood in front of Elisabeth, curtsied and, holding out her hand, spoke: "I'm most happy to see you again, Aunt Elisabeth."

Elisabeth removed her gloves, and took Hannah's hand in her own. "I'm very pleased to see you again, too, Hannah."

Jacob and Noah, waiting their turns, now greeted Elisabeth with extended hands. Their manners were impeccable, their smiles bright.

"You may be excused, children," Alex said. "We'll have supper in a few minutes."

The housemaid took one boy by each hand and, Hannah following, led them from the room. Elisabeth looked at Sonya, and Sonya returned Elisabeth's gaze in a way that was not without kindness. Sonya smiled, her cheeks flushing slightly, and Elisabeth felt an urge to take Sonya's hands in her own. Perhaps what Elisabeth had previously taken for condescension in Sonya was merely modesty. It was no small thing, after all, she thought, to have married a much older man – a divorced man with a disabled child – and to have become the second Mrs. Landau (within a week of Alex and Sonya's wedding, Elisabeth had filed legal papers in order to become Elisabeth Rofman again), when, given Sonya's beauty and her family's standing in the uptown Jewish community, Elisabeth assumed that she could have had virtually any man she or her family chose.

"If you'll excuse me," Sonya said. "I'll begin feeding the children." She offered her hand to Elisabeth. "It's truly good to see you again, Elisabeth, and I hope you'll be able to stay."

"You're very kind," Elisabeth said, "but I'm afraid I won't."

Sonya left, and a few moments later Elisabeth found herself sitting in a plush easy chair by the window, across from Alex, who, after asking questions about her father's schedule and habits, began telling her about a research project on which colleagues of his at Columbia-Presbyterian Hospital, where he was Chief of Surgery, were working. The project was one he believed would eventually enable parents to determine whether or not their children might be born with or without particular – and tragic – defects. It was their hypothesis, to cite one intriguing example, that certain rare conditions that afflicted East European Jews had, in fact, come into being centuries before, at times when Jewish communities – forced into isolation by persecution, and in times of increasing mortality that coincided, as it had during the time of the Black Plague, with decreasing genetic variation – had intermarried at significantly higher rates than they did now. Thus it might yet turn out, he said, that blood was, literally *and* scientifically, thicker than water.

Then he was talking about *Arrowsmith*, and asking if Elisabeth recalled conversations they had had about this book, and about the debate – ongoing, ever ongoing, he said – between those who believed in investing resources in pure research, and those who demanded research that promised more practical and immediate dividends in clinical settings. This conflict had pervaded much of the history of Johns Hopkins earlier in the century, as Elisabeth surely knew. Did she remember the character of Doctor Max Gottlieb, Martin Arrowsmith's hero, who believed in not granting patents for seriological processes, and in not allowing premature, and therefore dangerous release of vaccines?

And was it possible, he asked, that fifteen years had passed since the publication of that book, and since the time the two of them had sat where they were sitting now, talking and arguing about it?

Alex showed Elisabeth a signed copy of the book, from Sinclair Lewis, which book he had also had Paul de Kruif inscribe a month before at the Rockefeller Institute of Medical Research. Elisabeth would probably recall that de Kruif, the great bacteriologist and medical adventurer, had collaborated on the book with Lewis. And had Elisabeth heard, perhaps from colleagues at Hopkins, that the Rockefeller Institute was considering offering Alex a position there?

Elisabeth stood even while, in her mind, she was revising her earlier estimate: what troubled her was not that Alex had become unknown to her, but what was a distinctly less pleasant thought – that she dearly wished he might *become* unknown to her.

Aunt Elisabeth?! she wanted to say. Have we, then, in your vain reckonings, become brother and sister?

"We are really talking about our son, aren't we?" she said instead, and saying this, she felt her anger return, and found that this enabled her, calmly, to ask for her coat, and to leave.

FOUR

Elisabeth had sent telegrams to Doctor Brödel and Doctor Taussig, informing them her father was still missing, and that she was going to stay in New York until he returned, or until she found out what had happened to him. In the meantime, she wrote, she had mailed off the set of sketches she had promised to deliver Monday morning. She had also been able to obtain art supplies, and would continue to work on their ongoing projects. She trusted her absence would not cause them any great inconvenience.

Both Doctor Brödel and Doctor Taussig had replied by telegram, urging Elisabeth to attend to family matters and not to concern herself about the work. They each gave her their home telephone numbers and told her to call them collect if there was anything they could do to help.

Four days earlier, after spending the night at the Barbizon on Sunday evening, and after finding Charles, the super for her father's building – he lived in a basement apartment with his elderly mother and a lame Collie – Elisabeth had moved the kitchen table into the bedroom, where it had been serving as her drafting table. The drawing paper she was using – stipple board surfaced with heavy white layers of clay and covered with microscopic pits that could hold carbon dust – was extremely sensitive to moisture and grease. A drop of water, a speck of saliva or dandruff, or the mere touch of a moist finger, could fix the drawing on the spot and take up the dust more easily than the rest of the drawing. It could also cause the surface to become shiny and slippery, which made the carbon dust brush off without adhering. If this happened, the surface of the paper, though dead, could be rejuvenated, but to do this required applying several layers of fixative, and the fixatives available commercially were less than adequate.

Therefore – her great triumph on Tuesday, her first full day of work in the apartment – using Professor Brödel's recipe, she had made up two jars of her own fixative from powdered, bleached shellac and absolute alcohol.

She had been at work for more than an hour – it was seven-twenty – and for the first time she was feeling a faint longing for food. The cold morning light, from the bedroom's north window, where she had set the table, was especially wonderful at this hour. Spending most of her waking hours at her drawing, she was happy, and a good measure of her happiness, she knew, derived not only from the act of drawing, but from the absence of human voices. Alone in her father's apartment, she felt the way she remembered feeling when, as a child, she had been by herself in one of the underground alcoves he had found for her.

It was not so much that she had stopped worrying about his disappearance, but that, in the pleasure of long days filled with work she loved, she found, simply, that it was occurring to her less and less to speculate on what had or had not happened to him. What she had come to believe – wanted to believe? – was that by his disappearance he had given her a gift and that he had intended to do so. The alternative – that something truly bad had happened to him – was not a possibility she was willing to entertain yet.

The previous evening she had received a telegram from Alex informing her that he had information concerning her father, and that he could give her the information if she came by on

Friday afternoon. She should do so before five o'clock – he would be at home from two o'clock on – since the Sabbath began at 5:18, and she was, of course, invited to celebrate the Sabbath with him and his family. If Alex had had bad news, she reasoned, he would not have sent a message, but would have delivered the news himself.

She looked at her drawing – held it up to a mirror – and imagined that Professor Brödel would be pleased with it. The previous week he had asked Doctor Taussig if he could "borrow her" in order to have her illustrate what he had named 'The Operative Story of Goitre.' The procedure was one wherein the right lobe of the thyroid gland had been removed, with a slice being left posteriorly to preserve the parathyroid glands and the recurrent laryngeal nerve. Due to the dense overlapping of nerves, arteries, veins, muscles, and cartilage in the neck – so similar in their way to the jumbled mass of cables, wires, coils, and tubes inside subway panel boxes her father had worked on – the drawing was as complicated as any she had previously attempted, and she was flattered that Professor Brödel had entrusted the assignment to her. When, before leaving Baltimore, she had shown him a set of preliminary sketches, he had complimented her on her approach: a saggital view of the operative field that showed only the right side of the neck, with an insert in the lower left portion of the paper that would present the position and arterial blood supply of the para-thyroid glands in a frontal view.

She touched her own neck, and was amazed at the difference: at how smooth and uncomplicated it was to her touch, and then, looking at her neck in the mirror next to her bed, to imagine the extraordinarily intricate world that lay below her skin. To divine the unseen from the seen, Professor Brödel taught, was the essence of their craft. And in the exercise of their craft, he maintained, it was equally important to understand that each and every line tell a story.

She heard a dull, insistent pounding sound, and stood, looked out the window, but saw nothing unusual. She sat, and imagined that her father was standing next to her and that she was explaining to him, as Professor Brödel had explained to her, that an illustration like the one he was looking at – unlike a photograph, which was merely imitative – had to comprehend its subject from all perspectives: topographical, histological, pathological, medical, surgical. From this knowledge a mental picture would come into being, and from this picture the plan of the drawing could take shape.

That was why, Professor Brödel taught, a clear and vivid mental picture – what was left in and, more important, what was left out, always had to precede the drawing itself. It was the *planning* of the illustration, more than the actual drawing, that was paramount.

The pounding, Elisabeth realized, was coming from the kitchen – someone at the door with a telegram? – and she quickly covered the drawing with tissue.

When she opened the door, however, it was not a Western Union messenger who stood there, but Doctor Bloch, in a heavy Persian lamb coat.

"I am greatly relieved to see that you are here," Doctor Bloch said. "You are all right, yes?"

"But why wouldn't I be here? And yes, I'm all right – but how did you know where I lived?"

Doctor Bloch's silver-gray mustache was rimmed with a scrim of ice, his cheeks bright red, his eyes watery. He removed his hat.

"Let me explain," he said. "I was concerned that I had not heard from you since Sunday, nor had I seen any notice in the newspapers about your father – whether lost or found, as you say here – and so I looked, first, in the telephone directory, and finding no Rofmans listed for this region of the Bronx, I next visited the local police station, where I told them I was in search of a distant cousin named Rofman who, I was certain, resided nearby. The police were quite friendly, treating me with such kindness that there were moments when I had to wonder if they were truly officers of the law! They consulted several lists, following which one of them accompanied me here, which is how, my child, I came to find you."

"I see," Elisabeth said. "But I was at work, and I wasn't expecting you, and so I'm somewhat preoccupied. And –"

"Yes?"

"We haven't located my father."

"You speak of *we*?"

"Doctor Landau, my ex-husband, is helping in the search."

"But he is merely a physician, yes?"

"I *am* all right, but forgive me, please – my apologies, Doctor Bloch – please come in. May I offer you some tea?"

"Most happily," Doctor Bloch said. "It is alarmingly cold outside. Bitter, bitter."

"*Bitte?*" Elisabeth asked.

Doctor Bloch laughed, and laughing with him, Elisabeth stepped aside so that he could enter the apartment.

❖ ❖ ❖

This newer part of Saint Raymond's cemetery, Doctor Bloch explained, was built on swamp land. Consecrated in 1877, it covered nearly fifty acres of salt meadowland and was within walking distance of the Throg's Neck region of the Bronx. There, several German taverns and beer gardens dating from the turn of the century were still in existence, he had discovered, and he hoped Elisabeth would join him in one of them as his guest for dinner that evening.

"I'm afraid not," Elisabeth said. "But I thank you."

"But here – " he said, leading her to a section of more elaborately sculpted tombstones " – here is where, this in April, 1932, Mister Condon paid a ransom of fifty thousand dollars to

Bruno Hauptmann – a German, but not, fortunately, a Jew – for the return of Doctor Lindbergh's child. My researches – I like to know the history of places in which I reside, you see – convince me that where we are now standing is the very place in which the transaction took place."

The temperature had fallen well below freezing, and the wind, blowing moist air in from Long Island Sound, carried with it what felt to Elisabeth like tiny blades of frozen salt. She held lightly to Doctor Bloch's arm.

"And who can I pay for the return of my father, do you think?" she asked.

"But the Lindbergh boy was *not* returned," Doctor Bloch replied. "The infant was found dead some six weeks after the ransom was paid."

"Would it make sense, then, do you think, for me *not* to pay money to somebody who will *not* return my father?"

"I do not understand," Doctor Bloch said.

"And yet you claim to be a relative of Franz Kafka."

"Aha!" Doctor Bloch said, tossing away the stub of a cigarette. "You are being ironic! Yes. I understand now. But it *is* true, you know – my daughter, Gertrude, can verify it, as can John – that Kafka was a cousin. And contrary to what people believe, you may be interested in learning, he was actually quite proud of the writing he did for the state. He worked in disability insurance, you see, and he would send handsomely bound copies of his reports to us and to other members of our family in Austria."

"And are you storing them with young Adolf's post cards?" Elisabeth asked.

"Oh no," Doctor Bloch replied. "Nobody took the reports away from us. They simply disappeared."

"Like your neighbors in Linz?"

"Bitte," Doctor Bloch said, and covered Elisabeth's gloved hand with his own. "Given my circumstance, I can understand the saving grace of your ironic humor in a time like this." He patted

her hand. "I do take pleasure from your wit, you know – from the sharp edges of your acute intelligence – and I do not mean to discourage your expression of it. Rather the opposite. But –" he gestured with his free hand " – but when I see how beautiful this cemetery is, I also think of what has been transpiring in my homeland. I think, that is, of how our own cemeteries have been vandalized and desecrated. I am grateful, of course, to be living in safety on these kind American shores, but I assure you that I am acutely aware that we do live in dreadful times."

"I didn't mean to offend," Elisabeth said. She shivered, and withdrew her arm from Doctor Bloch's. "I'm very cold."

Doctor Bloch nodded decisively and turned towards the gates through which they had passed a short while before.

"Doctor Lindbergh, with the eminent Doctor Carrel, you may be aware, has been trying for some years, in their work on perfusion pumps, to invent a mechanical heart," he said as they walked, "and I, for one, wish him well. He is a supremely brave and intelligent man, resourceful in what I think of as a particularly American way, yet a man who has suffered inordinately for the fame attending upon his heroism."

"I may receive information about my father later in the day," Elisabeth said. "I'm hopeful."

Elisabeth looked back and saw what appeared to be a stone lamb on top of a small tombstone. Such lambs, she knew, signified the graves of infants. She thought for a moment of the children whose hearts Doctor Taussig attended to, and reminded herself that when some of them died, their hearts would be given to Doctor Taussig for her research, and that she – Elisabeth – would be given the task of dissecting them and of drawing them in a way that would allow them to appear, still, to be organs composed of moist, living tissue.

The animal moved – it was a cat, not a lamb, Elisabeth realized – leaping from the tombstone to the ground. Elisabeth walked alongside Doctor Bloch, telling herself that there was no reason to tell him that she'd already been to the beer gardens in the Throg's Neck area several times with her father, or that she'd also been to the islands in Long Island Sound that one looked out at from the beer gardens.

City Island, a fishing village with a large Italian population, was closest to land, and she and her father had often gone there to feast on meals of clams, oysters, and fried fish. Elisabeth also knew that Bellevue Hospital, acting as a depot for several city hospitals, shipped some two hundred corpses a week, along with wooden boxes filled with amputated arms and legs, to Hart's Island, which lay a few miles north of City Island. There, the plain pine coffins were laid three deep in the ground.

And nearer to shore, a half-mile east of City Island, was Rat Island, which had become a resort for vacationers. It was curious, she thought, to think of how misnamed these places were: City Island was not physically part of the city; Rat Island was too rocky to house rats; and Hart Island, where the dead had no one to mourn for them, was a place without heart.

They left the cemetery, walking past Old Saint Raymond's Church and back in the direction of her father's apartment, and she took Doctor Bloch's arm again.

"I was thinking – " she said " – not tonight, but perhaps another time – that if your offer's still good, we might go to one of the taverns together one evening."

❖ ❖ ❖

What Elisabeth imagined was that the next time she entered her father's apartment she would find a manila envelope on the table beside her drawings, and that inside the envelope there would be a letter from her father along with a thin stack of hand-written pages.

She was moving in and out of sleep as she often did when she rode the subways. The train was about forty feet above ground, traveling towards Manhattan, and she looked out the window at the East River, below, at barges, tugs, and fishing boats, and at a large ship that was cutting a path north towards Long Island Sound, its decks laden with enormous spools of silver wire.

The train descended below ground, and in the curve of the tunnel wall – on the other side of the train's window – she imagined words appearing which she recognized as being in her father's handwriting.

His handwriting had always been surprisingly graceful and legible, the loops and circles sweetly curved, the backs of letters rigid, parallel, and at a slight slant, the words evenly spaced. She remembered how proud she was to bring notes from him to school, and to have her teachers remark on the excellence of his penmanship.

My Dearest Daughter Elisabeth, the letter began. *I am leaving these rooms in order to end my days in a place that was for me the source of highest joy in life . . . .*

She let her eyes close so that she could watch herself slip through an open window of the subway car, into the tunnel, and into warm, dark water.

I want to tell you the story of how I came to America, and of how I fell in love with and married your mother, and of how I lost her, and of why it is that in the years since, when you and I . . . .

Elisabeth saw herself lying prone, her hands pressed to her sides, while she floated feet first through the dark, as if drifting downstream. Warm fumes, like morning mists, rose from her skin. She slept.

❖ ❖ ❖

The room was warm, and Elisabeth felt sweat slide along her right side and down towards her waist. Despite Alex's entreaties, she had not taken off her coat. As she had expected, he had no specific information about her father's whereabouts, though he had received a report from the Transit Authority stating that, according to witnesses on two separate occasions, a man answering to her father's description had been seen walking along the subway tracks at night near the Rector Street station.

"I trust you'll let me know at once if you hear anything further," Elisabeth said. "But what about the police – will they want to talk with me?"

"I've tried to spare you that," Alex said.

"Spare me?"

"Oh Elisabeth," Alex said. "I *am* doing my best to help you locate your father, though I must say you do not seem pleased by the news that he is probably alive." Alex paused, to allow Elisabeth to reply, and when she said nothing, he continued: "What I can tell you is that I am making all proper and – well – some *im*proper inquiries. I have friends in the department who can do a good deal of work before an investigation becomes official. The problem, though, as you might imagine, is that once an investigation becomes official, there are effective ways of doing things that the police cannot put into practice. Thus, the less you or I know about this, the better."

"I'll be going then," Elisabeth said. "I don't want to keep you from your preparations for the Sabbath."

"You're adamant about not joining us?"

"I'm not adamant, but no – I can't stay."

"Then I will talk with you now about Daniel," Alex said. He moved away from Elisabeth, and sat behind his desk. "Doctor Ogilvie was here last week – a day or two before your visit, and – "

"And – ?" Elisabeth sat across from Alex, and did not try to hide her irritation.

"As you know," Alex said, "Daniel will be eighteen years old in two months, which means that technically, though not legally, given his condition, he will be entering his majority."

"Therefore?"

"As you also know, the Home has become concerned about the ways in which he's become increasingly difficult, especially when it comes to his advances upon several of the female residents. His control of his impulses is negligible, and if – "

Elisabeth stood. "This is nonsense, Alex, and you know it," she declared. "The boys and girls live in separate facilities, and – "

"Please," Alex said. "There's no need to excite yourself."

"I know where this is leading, and I won't listen to it," Elisabeth said. "If the Home has anything to say – any recommendations – they can make them directly to me. When it comes to Daniel I won't have you acting as go-between."

"Of course, of course," Alex said. "We both want what is best for him. That's precisely why – "

"No," Elisabeth said. "You want what will make life easier for you."

"It's only that we know how sensitive you are on the subject," Alex said, "and we only wanted – "

"You only wanted to *spare* me, yes?" Elisabeth said. Then: "What Doctor Ogilvie probably suggested is what he's suggested before, am I right?"

"Possibly."

"And you'd love to have me name things now, wouldn't you?" Elisabeth said. "Would *that* give you pleasure, Alex? To hear me repeat the good doctor's suggestion that we submit Daniel to a procedure that will assure his inability to father children for the rest of his life?"

"Oh my dear Elisabeth," Alex said. "How wrong you are! Do you think I love Daniel less than you do – am less protective of him? He is my first-born son, after all, and according to Jewish tradition – "

Elisabeth turned towards the door. "Our conversation is over," she said.

"I see how upset you are," Alex said, "but I trust, when you've calmed down, and have had time to reflect on this, that you and I can have a rational conversation about what's in the best interests of our son."

"I will not argue with you."

Alex moved in front of Elisabeth. "But we *will* talk, yes?" he said. "You're too emotional now, for us to – "

"No," Elisabeth said. "I'm not emotional enough. I can be fully rational if I have to, and if I have to I can refute each of your arguments – and theirs – for this is little but . . . ." Elisabeth thought of saying that this was little but Social Darwinism with a vengeance, but she knew the wiser course was to do what she had said she would do, and not to argue. "I have to go," she said. "Please move away from the door."

"But you *are* upset," Alex said. "I can see it. And there is, also, the continuing mystery of your father's disappearance. I will do what I can to accelerate the search, though it would not surprise me, given his history, that the man others claim to have seen wandering in the subway tunnels is, in fact, your father."

Elisabeth said nothing.

"As to Daniel," Alex said, "what I suggest is that when you return to Baltimore, we arrange to meet at the Home with Doctor Ogilvie and with the Home's medical staff and their legal counsel. How does that sound?"

"Despicable."

Alex put his hand on her arm. "But Elisabeth, please realize this: even if I came to agree with you about Daniel – if I could be persuaded of your point of view – I'm not sure that, legally, we would prevail."

"Daniel is my son."

"And mine," Alex said. "Such facts, however, do not constitute arguments."

Alex opened the door and, wishing Elisabeth a peaceful Sabbath, let her pass in front of him.

FIVE

From the Journal of Doctor Eduard Bloch
December 15, 1940

I have seen Miss Rofman twice within the last two days, once in her father's apartment, and again this afternoon in mine. Her father, alas, has not been found, nor is there any word of his fate. In addition, Miss Rofman has confided in me – this only a few hours ago, when she visited before leaving for Baltimore – the possibility that the Institution in which her son resides may try, despite her protestations, and, apparently, with the collusion of the boy's father, to perform a medical procedure that will deprive the son, forever, of his reproductive capacity.

I am honored to be the vessel of her confidence, but alarmed not only by the effect of this news upon her, but of what I suspect she is planning to do about it. In brief, I fear for her in ways that are troubling in the extreme.

There is this too: that while I listened to her rehearse the essence of the conversation she had with her son's father – about the ways this man and the Director of the Institution in which the boy resides hope to circumvent her objections – I found myself possessed of a curious notion: that her father does not actually exist.

It occurred to me, that is – a fleeting thought that has become insistent in the hours since her departure – that her father may have disappeared, but not within the past few weeks. There are several things that lend credibility to such a possibility – the fact that Miss Rofman has chosen not to alert the police concerning her father's disappearance; the fact that since Miss Rofman's move to Baltimore six years ago her father has never visited her there; and the fact that the apartment in which I found Miss Rofman, austere in the extreme, seemed hardly to have been lived in by man *or* woman, though there were, on a bedroom dresser top, along with items belonging to Miss Rofman, some personal objects of a kind only a man would use.

Once one begins thinking in such a manner, however – once one posits a hypothesis, no matter how contrary to reason or reality – consider the fancies we physicians often engage in when making our differential diagnoses! – disparate and ordinary occurrences can always be marshaled by the imagination to give validity to that hypothesis. There is certainly nothing about Miss Rofman, in behavior or reasoning, that suggests she would be a person in whom illusions could, in any sustained or substantive way, displace reality.

It occurs to me, therefore, that it may well be my own feeling of displacement – the ways in which, in my new American life, I frequently feel I am living in a dream invented by someone else – that has given birth to such frivolous speculations.

In addition, despite being in the midst of vexing problems, Miss Rofman's ability to retain her sense of humor – ever a sure sign to me of an individual's state of mental stability – has not forsaken her. For example, when I remarked, in English, that I was somewhat embarrassed to be receiving her in my present setting, but that I choose to think of this one room which must serve as dining room, living room, study, and kitchen, as my "drawing" room (and a curiously constructed room it is, into which, for no apparent reason, one steps past an iron railing down into what is termed a *sunken* room), she responded by saying that I should not feel embarrassed, given that she had received me just yesterday in *her* drawing room.

I thought, as one way of calming Miss Rofman's fears about her son, of saying that Hitler has, by his policies concerning disabled individuals, been giving eugenics a bad name, and that this is especially so, according to my nephew, John, within the medical profession here in the United States. Given the high state of anxiety Miss Rofman presented this afternoon, however, it seemed to me the better part of kindness not to engage her in extended dialogue on the subject, but simply to listen to her.

Despite preoccupations concerning father and son, Miss Rofman showed a generous interest in my life, reminding me that she and I had agreed to go to dinner one evening, which dinner we will arrange upon her return from Baltimore, asking also about my daughter and son-in-law, and about when she might read those portions of my journal I would be willing to show, for I had told her during our visit yesterday that I had, in fact, acted upon my proposal of a week ago.

Her visit once again providing the stimulus to have me take pen in hand, I will now attempt to render, to the best of my recollection – but with, of course, the knowledge that memory, like the imagination, is rarely our most trustworthy guide – what happened in the Hitler family following upon Alois's death.

At the time – 1903, by my calculations – Adolf, a lad of fourteen years old, was both too young and too frail to become a farmer, and so the best choice for the mother, Klara, was to sell the farm and rent an apartment in Linz, a decision I encouraged. With the proceeds of the sale, and the pension that came to her because of Alois's government service, a sum I estimate as being the equivalent of approximately twenty-five American dollars per month, Klara moved the family into three small rooms at No. 9 Blütenstrasse, a two-storey house in Urfahr, a suburb that lay across the Danube from the main portion of Linz, and that gave, from the upstairs windows, an excellent view of the surrounding mountains.

I visited this home often, and my predominant impression was of its cleanliness. Klara was a superb housekeeper. There was never a speck of dust on the chairs or tables, a stray fleck of mud on the floor, nor a smudge on any window. I would sometimes jest with Frau Hitler, who had a somewhat depressive disposition, that the very word *sauber* had been added to the German language by someone who had visited her home, and at this jest she would give me one of her rare smiles.

In general, however, Frau Hitler's life, reduced by her limited income to essentials, was as spare as her home – devoid, that is, of extravagance. Still, the lives of her children, in large part due to her efforts, though not extravagant, were, as with most young people in Linz, in essentials as well as in cultural amenities, more than adequate. As an example, let me note that we had the usual provincial opera in Linz, and seats in the gallery of our theater, the *Schauspielhaus*, which was always filled with students, could be had for the equivalent of as little as 10 to 15 cents in American money. Occupying one of these seats to hear what was doubtless an indifferent troupe sing *Lohengrin* proved such a memorable occasion, in fact, that, in later years, Hitler saw fit to mention it in *Mein Kampf*.

The young boy's life, thus, was not without those pleasures available to all of us in Linz – walks in the mountains, swims in the Danube, and especially, given his artistic spirit – the presence in his environment of music (the opera, free band concerts in the town square), art and architecture (he frequented our museums religiously, and when he settled in his beloved Munich on the eve of The Great War, declared his ambition to be that of an *Architekturmaler* – an architectural painter), and literature (he was particularly fascinated by stories about American Indians, devouring the books of James Fenimore Cooper and the German writer Karl May, who himself never visited America and never saw an Indian!).

As a boy, and later as a man, I myself tried to read some of May's novels, which were hugely popular, and confess that though others far wiser than I – Thomas Mann and Albert Einstein among them – were his devotees, I was not. The endless accounts of death, torture, and decapitation were not only too violent for my tastes, due perhaps to the actual violence I witnessed in wartime, but in their repetitions, of a sameness that made them predictable. In a single one of his novels, for example – this I have on the authority of a critique I happened upon while in the military – more than two thousand separate individuals are killed or physically assaulted.

Adolf was, I have already noted, a somewhat frail young man, but this was not due to diet, for though the family was not well-to-do, food was cheap and plentiful in Linz, and the Hitler family ate much the same rugged, simple diet as did other people in their circumstances: meat perhaps twice a week, and meals consisting, typically, of cabbage or potato soup, bread, dumplings, and pear or apple cider.

For clothing, the family employed the rough woolen cloth we call *Loden*, and young Adolf invariably dressed in the uniform all boys his age wore: leather shorts, embroidered suspenders, and a small green hat with a feather in its band.

These, then, with regard to food, clothing, shelter, and recreation, were the basic elements of his daily living.

But what kind of boy was Adolf Hitler, and how does the boy I remember relate to the man he has become?

To answer this question, we must turn, I believe, to the time of his mother's illness and dying, for this was when he most tellingly revealed himself. I have never, I state at once, in all my years as a physician, seen any individual so prostrate with grief as Adolf Hitler. Nor have I ever witnessed a closer attachment than that of young Adolf for his mother.

He was no "mother's boy," in the usual sense of those words, but surely his love for his mother was his most striking characteristic, and this love was, by the mother, reciprocated in kind. To those who choose to see something aberrant in this relationship, I reply, as an intimate of the family, by asserting unequivocally that this was not the case.

The mother, quite simply, adored her son, and, as many mothers will for a favored child, allowed him his way whenever possible. Thus, for example, when Adolf tired of school, she allowed him to take leave of his studies. And when he declared his ambition to become an artist, she allowed him to reject a position offered him in the post office, in order, as I have previously written, to continue with his painting.

Let us note at this point, too, the particular events that had made her children's lives precious to Klara. Before Adolf and his sisters were born, Klara had suffered the deaths of her first three children, all of whom, in the years immediately preceding Adolf's birth, died when very young. Adolf was, in fact, her first child to survive infancy. Moreover, a fifth child, Edmund, died in the year 1900 before he had attained his sixth birthday (Adolf was eleven at the time). Thus was Klara, after her husband's death, not only the solitary means of sustenance for her surviving children (she also cared for one of her younger sisters, Johanna, a rather ill-tempered hunchbacked woman who lived with the family, and who was fond of Adolf), but remained grateful for their existence, and intensely protective of them in ways only a mother who has suffered such losses can be.

Should we be surprised, then, or find it unnatural that her children returned this love in kind? Why would a young man whose mother worked and sacrificed for him in the way Klara did, not love her with a devotion matching her own? Thus, in a remarkable instance of understatement, did Hitler write in *Mein Kampf*, a tract otherwise lacking in matters personal, that he "honored" his father but "loved" his mother.

Others have declared that the young Adolf Hitler was a harsh-voiced, untidy, defiant ruffian, but in my experience he was none of these things. Largely to the credit of the mother, he was quiet, well-mannered, neatly dressed – in his adolescent years he came to affect the dress of a dandy, and would stroll about Linz with an ivory-handled walking stick – and obedient.

These, then, are the essential impressions I retain of him from his early years, impressions that do not set him apart from many other young men of that time and place. There was, however, also about him (in this one must, as ever, be quick to wonder, given the weight of intervening history, whether or not memory, as is its wont, is here transforming reality) a certain inwardness – a strangeness, in truth – that did distinguish him from others, for to a very large extent, he was a lad who seemed to live within himself.

This impression was due, at least in part, to his appearance: to his sallow complexion as well as to the large, melancholy eyes – so like Klara's! – that made him appear unusually old for his age. He appeared, that is, to be both very much a boy and not a boy at all.

Whenever he came to my consultation room, he would sit patiently among others, waiting his turn. Although exceptionally quiet and shy – qualities I associate with his physical frailness – he was not a sickly boy. He had the usual maladies young people had – colds, fevers, inflamed tonsils – yet his recuperative powers were more than adequate, and when an examination was over, he would, like any well-bred boy, bow and thank me in the most courteous way.

I am, of course, aware of the stomach troubles that beset him later in life, and these, I submit, were probably due to the inferior diet he ingested during his years in Vienna.

But even as I begin to move forward in time to the moment of his mother's illness, another scene interjects itself, and I will digress to record a strange recollection, one I had not known I would recall when I began writing today. I have previously mentioned the half-sister, Maria Anna, who, I believe, lived her life out in an Institution, and she was the daughter either of Alois's first wife, or, perhaps, an illegitimate child born before the first of his three marriages (in all, Alois seems to have fathered nine children). What I had initially recalled was that the child, who had the shapeless body and manner of a tired middle-aged woman but the wide plain face, much, in my memory, like a cabbage, and blue innocent eyes of a young child – said hardly a word, and recoiled from me when I attempted to examine her. I had recalled, also, and intended to report, the way in which young Adolf spoke to her, in a whisper, so as to calm her and make her amenable to cooperating with me.

This woman had, by Klara's word, been having distressing difficulties with her bowels and, in the night-time, often howled inconsolably, as though in severe pain. This howling, upon Adolf's prompt, she repeated for me – and then pointed to the spots on her abdomen where the pain was located.

What I remembered as being remarkable was his ability to charm the savage beast within this miserable and troubled woman. Since he had always been, in my presence, a boy of few words, I was astonished to hear the long and quite gentle stream of words he lavished upon her even while he was caressing her cheek, and – I recall this vividly – doing so with the *back* of his hand.

What I had forgotten was that after she had allowed me to examine her (I could find no specific cause for her maladies, and suspect either ulcers or duodenitis, the result perhaps of bile backing up into the stomach through a distended or misshapen pylorus), as if in a hysteria of gratitude, she threw herself upon the floor of my consultation room and, on all fours, began to chew noisily on the edges of my carpet. Neither Frau Hitler nor young Adolf moved to stop her, and I was so astonished – and appalled (my paralysis reinforced by the rather charming way she would intermittently stop her chewing in order to smile up at me) – that I too simply stood there, unmoving.

When Frau Hitler did, firmly, ask her to stop, Maria Anna commenced her howling again and it was at this point – what I had not remembered until a few moments ago – that young Adolf set himself on the floor beside his sister, on hands and knees, as if it was something he had done many times before, and he too began to chew at the edges of my carpet. He did so for what was perhaps a minute – no more – at which point her howling ceased. He then stood and reached for his sister's hand, which she willingly took, after which she stood and rested her head upon her brother's shoulder.

I prescribed a bromide, warm compresses, and a diet free of acidic foods, along with several glasses of milk each day. Adolf and his mother thanked me, and left.

This moment in time, I am certain, might have remained locked away in my unconscious forever had Miss Rofman not visited me this afternoon, and, more specifically, had she not spoken of her fears concerning her son, and it is to her credit – to the fact of her visit – that I owe this sudden release of memory and association. (Whether or not this occurrence is the origin of the habit of chewing on carpets that the leader of the German people is rumored to practice when enraged, I would not venture to guess.)

Hitler's alleged stomach troubles, along with the references I have seen to lung troubles that supposedly plagued him as a youth are a mystery to me. I was the only doctor treating him during the years when he is said to have suffered from these ailments, and my records, now the property of the German authorities, would show nothing of the sort.

As to his achievements as a student, Adolf himself, in *Mein Kampf*, reports with honesty that he was an indifferent student, and this is in accord with my recollection, confirmed by conversations I remember having with Doctor Karl Huemer, who was an acquaintance (his wife Frau Huemer was my patient), and Adolf's history teacher at the *Realschule*, which Adolf chose to go to instead of to the more academically demanding *Gymnasium*. In point of fact, so weak was Adolf's record at the *Realschule* that, in the year of his father's death, he had to pass a re-examination in order to advance to a higher class. This happened again the following year, when he was allowed to re-take the examination only on condition that he leave the *Realschule* in Linz for the *Realschule* in Steyr, some fifty miles away, a school he came to detest. And it was while he was in Steyr that, with his mother's permission, he left his schooling behind forever. It was at this point in time – and after she had bought him a grand piano and paid for lessons, an indication that the family's economic circumstances were not nearly as meager as Hitler and others have since led us to believe – that he journeyed to Vienna for the first time.

Encouraged by his mother, and by his *Hanitante*, his Aunt Johanna, who, for this and/or a subsequent trip, gave him a large loan (the equivalent of a year's salary for a young lawyer or teacher), he sojourned in Vienna for perhaps a fortnight, and it was during this visit (in 1906, if I have calculated correctly) that his ambitions to become an artist, and his desire to enter the Academy of Fine Arts in Vienna, were fully born.

By the time he made a second visit to Vienna, in 1907, Klara was already gravely ill with breast cancer.

She had come to me one day earlier that year during my morning office hours, complaining of a pain in her chest. I recall that she spoke in a quiet, hushed voice, and told me that the pain was so great that it often kept her awake through the night. She had not come to my office earlier because of her many household and familial duties, and because she thought the pain would pass. Alas, it did not.

More unfortunate, upon examination I found an extensive tumor of the breast, although I did not tell her so. I feared the worst, and summoned the children to my office the next day, whereupon I explained the situation to them in the frankest terms. Without surgery, I told them, there was absolutely no hope of recovery, but even with surgery there was, in my estimation, only the slightest chance she would survive. It was to them, in family council, to decide what was to be done.

Young Adolf's reaction to this news was intense and touching. His face contorted in pain and helplessness, and tears flowed from his eyes. It was at this moment that I had a glimpse into the depth of his feelings for his mother. Did his mother, he asked, have *any* chance?

A malignant tumor is serious enough today, but it was even more serious three decades ago when surgical techniques were not so advanced and knowledge of cancer was much less extensive. I explained that she did have a chance – we always do, for each disease makes its home in each of us in a different way – but that the chance was meager indeed. Still, even this shred of hope seemed to give young Adolf comfort.

He and his sisters brought my message to their mother, and, as I expected, she accepted the verdict with fortitude. Klara was a deeply religious woman, and therefore assumed that her fate was in God's hands. It would never have occurred to her to complain.

I brought the case to Doctor Karl Urban, the chief of the surgical staff at the Hospital of the Sisters of Mercy in Linz, and one of the finest surgeons in Upper Austria. He examined Frau Hitler, and concurred: she had little chance of survival; surgery offered the only hope.

The operation was performed in the early fall of 1907, and at Frau Hitler's request I remained beside the operating table while Doctor Urban and his assistant performed the surgery. Some two hours later I drove in my carriage across the Danube to the Hitler residence, where the children awaited me.

The girls received the report I brought with calm and reserve, but the boy's face was streaked with tears, his eyes tired, puffed, and red. When I had finished giving them the news, he had only one question: "Does my mother suffer?"

In the weeks and months that followed, Frau Hitler's strength failed visibly, and during this period Adolf spent virtually all his time at home, where he could be found at her bedside during the day, and where, during the night, he took to sleeping in the tiny bedroom that adjoined hers so that he could be summoned at any time. Throughout this period I ministered to Frau Hitler as best I could so as to relieve her pain and suffering, which I did with iodine-impregnated gauze, and with injections of morphine, treatments that could, alas, provide only temporary relief. Still, Adolf was enormously grateful to me even for the short periods of respite I was able to provide.

Yet there is something else that must be noted: it was during the period of his mother's dying that young Adolf journeyed to Vienna and took the entrance examination for the Academy of Fine Arts, and it was during this period that his application was rejected. It seemed never to have occurred to him that he would fail the examination, so that when he received the rejection, it struck him, as he famously wrote in *Mein Kampf*, "as a bolt from the blue." He never revealed this unhappy news to his mother – or, until years later, to the rest of his family – but remained in Linz, and remained also, to the end, a faithful son to the gentle soul that was his mother.

During the time of her dying, Frau Hitler spoke never of herself or her impending death but only of her worries for her family – about what their lives would become when she was gone – and, especially, of Adolf. "Adolf is still so young," she would say repeatedly. "Adolf is still so young."

Then, one morning several days before Christmas, Angela came to my office with the news that her mother had passed away during the night. Might I come to the home and sign the death certificate? I put on my coat and drove with her to the cottage, where the postmaster's widow, Klara's closest friend, was with the children. Adolf, his face showing evidence of sleeplessness and grief, sat beside his mother. In order to preserve a lasting impression, he had sketched her as she lay on her deathbed.

I sat with the family for a while, as I often did in similar situations, and said that in this case death had been a savior.

They did not disagree. And at the Catholic cemetery in Leonding, where Klara was laid to rest beside her husband, Alois, for a long time after everyone else had departed, Adolf remained behind.

Several days after the funeral the family came to my office to thank me. The girls spoke of what was in their hearts, yet Adolf remained silent, so profound was his grief. I recall the scene vividly, for as I have said earlier, in all my years as a physician – and given all such sad experiences to which I have been witness – I have never seen anyone so prostrate with grief as this young man.

He wore a dark suit and a loosely knotted cravat. Then, as now, a shock of hair tumbled over his forehead. While his sisters spoke, his eyes stayed fixed upon the floor. When his turn came, however, he stepped forward, took my hand, and looked directly into my eyes. "I shall be grateful to you forever," he said. That was all. Then he bowed and left.

Is it any wonder, given the feelings he had for his mother, that, virtually alone among men of his station in political life, he has often referred to the German nation not as Fatherland but as Motherland? And is it any wonder that I, revisiting this time of his life – and my own! – find it as fresh as if it happened yesterday? I ask a question: Had Adolf Hitler not abandoned his career in art and architecture for the life that has led him to be the leader of the German and Austrian nations, would I have remembered it less? My answer: I think not.

Yet even while I record such a scene, what I find myself wondering also is this: What will Miss Rofman think of what I have written? Given the cruelties exacted upon many by Adolf Hitler in recent years – especially upon those of our faith – will she find my depiction of him too generous? Perhaps. To which my only response, necessarily, will be that I must write down what happened in the way that I remember it happening.

Given the privilege I have experienced, of knowing the man who is now perhaps the most popular national leader in the world, and perhaps, too, the most powerful, and given that I knew him in what was perhaps his deepest if not his only experience of true human feeling – of experiencing affection, warmth, and love for another human being – it is, at the least, my responsibility to record as truly as I can what it is I remember and know.

But why, I also wonder, the strange melancholy I am now, by writing and remembering, experiencing? It seems almost as if, by setting down what I have never before recorded, I am somehow erasing the experience itself. It is as if, I fear, once I have recorded my memories in writing, the memories and experiences themselves will no longer be mine.

Still I am, at one and the same time, comforted in my melancholy and – yes – my sorrow. For though I feel sorrow for the memory of a good woman who died in pain and before her time, as well as for the sense of mortality that was mine then and that, more palpable in such times, shadows all our lives, still am I consoled by the very act of writing, and – more – by knowing that whatever else may issue from these words, they will have at least one caring reader. I remain comforted, that is, by the memory of Miss Rofman's leave-taking, when, to my surprise – she refused, almost belligerently, to allow me to accompany her to the subway – after I had wished her a successful journey home, and told her I would be eager for a report of her journey's issue, she suddenly, at the door, moved forward and embraced me, kissing me lightly on each of my cheeks.

SIX

When Antoinette Lanana, a four-year-old whose health had been failing rapidly, spoke more than a sentence or two, the effort caused her to snort slightly with each intake of air and to turn a remarkable, and chillingly beautiful, shade of cerulean blue. Elisabeth sat on the floor beside Antoinette, sketching the girl's portrait – softening the shadings below the eyes and laying in light, curved cross-hatchings with pencil in order to suggest the roundness of the child's cheeks, and while she worked, she considered her plan.

She would telephone Alex and tell him she was going to meet with Doctor Ogilvie in order to inform him of what she was now informing Alex: that she had retained legal counsel. She would not provide Alex with the name of the attorney she had hired, but she would tell him that her attorney had assured her that the Home could not legally perform any surgical procedure upon Daniel without her consent, and that anyone complicitous in performing a procedure would face severe consequences. After this, and without announcing her visit ahead of time, she would arrive at the Home. And after that . . . .

Antoinette's mother sat on the floor beside her child while the father sat upright in a chair beside them, his checkered cloth cap, of the kind newsboys wore, on his lap. Antoinette was the couple's only child, and the mother, who had nearly died from toxemia during pregnancy, would never again be able to bear children. The couple spoke in Italian to Antoinette, encouraging her to sit quietly so that the doctor – despite Elisabeth's attempts to correct them, they persisted in calling her 'doctor' – could draw her portrait.

Elisabeth had made her first drawing of one of the children on an evening more than a year before, when, done with her work, she was passing through the ward and was so moved by a sleeping child's beauty that she found herself taking out a sketch pad. Professor Brödel, finding Elisabeth there, had praised her warmly and, the next day, encouraged her to take time from her regular duties to make more such drawings. He found the drawings especially touching, he said, because they brought to mind those early Renaissance still-lifes where, when you looked beyond the gorgeous puffs of blossoms – the brilliant colors and lush groupings – you noticed the insects that were already at work, eating away at the plants and hastening their decay and death.

Over the previous four years, Elisabeth had spent hundreds of hours on the Pediatric Cardiology Unit, a unit where Doctor Taussig and her staff treated children so hungry for air that many of them would, from the least exertion, lapse into unconsciousness. Their noses, ears, toes, fingers, and entire bodies, due to the reduced hemoglobin in their blood, would at times turn ink-blue with cyanosis, and they would spend large portions of their waking hours squatting on the floor or lying completely still in order not to aggravate what Doctor Taussig had named – translating Professor Brödel's German phrase, *hungrig nach frischer Luft* – their *air-hunger*.

Elisabeth took out her soap eraser, shaved it quickly to a fine point, then brushed at Antoinette's curls, lifting shading so as to create highlights that made the golden curls appear even more golden. *There!* she thought, and gazed at the finished drawing as if at a drawing that had been made by someone else. When she had completed a drawing she could rarely recall when and how she had made it, and it still amazed her that mere pencil and eraser could create such vivid impressions of life. It amazed her, too, that her mind was capable of containing so many disparate images simultaneously, for while she was working at Antoinette's curls, and while she was considering her plan, she was also conjuring up an image of Antoinette's heart and watching it materialize slowly on a blank piece of drawing paper.

She reached into her bag of supplies, took out a jar of fixative, and sprayed the fixative lightly across the drawing. She looked up and saw that Professor Brödel was at her side, and realized that he might have been standing there for several minutes.

"It is quite good," he said. And then: "I am most happy to see you here this morning, Elisabeth. Most happy."

He touched her shoulder with his hand, and moved away. He would, he said, be waiting for her in his studio.

A few minutes later, when the fixative had dried, Elisabeth gave the drawing to Antoinette, and before her parents could stop her, the girl was racing across the ward to show the drawing to other children. She showed it first to Paolo, a six-year-old boy who was less severely debilitated than Antoinette, and when Paolo saw the picture, he laughed and pointed to Elisabeth, calling out something she could not understand. Then both he and Antoinette began to cough uncontrollably.

Within a week or, at most, a month, Elisabeth knew, Antoinette would be gone, and having already received the necessary permission from Antoinette's parents, Doctor Taussig would be asking Elisabeth to dissect and to draw Antoinette's heart, a heart that would not be much larger than a plum. What Doctor Taussig believed was that if she could determine with greater accuracy the cause or causes of the conditions that afflicted children like Antoinette, she would be able to find a solution, and that when she did, the solution would turn out to be a rather straightforward matter of plumbing: finding a way to put a length of tubing – a shunt of some kind – in the right place, thereby diverting the de-oxygenated blood around the narrowed pulmonary artery and into the lungs where it could be adequately oxygenated.

Elisabeth's major responsibility was to dissect and draw the hearts of deceased children so that Doctor Taussig, along with her colleague, Doctor Blalock, and their assistants, could learn more about the conditions that afflicted these children. From what the dissections revealed, from the histories of the children, and from observations of symptoms that could be correlated with physical evidence gleaned *from* the dissections and drawings, Doctor Taussig and her staff hoped to be better able to diagnose and to propose remedies, and to do so *before* opening the children's chests for surgery.

And while she was imagining various ways of drawing Antoinette's heart, Elisabeth was also thinking of times, forty years before, when she would sit on the ground of an open subway trench drawing pictures. It occurred to her, as it had earlier in the week, that when she returned to the Bronx she might start on a series of drawings that drew on her childhood experiences, and, maybe, on something else – on images that had been grazing at the edges of her consciousness from the time she had, a week before, imagined seeing her father's handwriting in the subway tunnel: of the life her father had lived before he came to America, and before Elisabeth was born, and before her mother had died.

If she did, she thought – and she smiled at the notion – she might propose an exchange with Doctor Bloch: if he let her read what he was writing, she would let him see the story she was drawing.

The images – of the subways, of her father and mother, of Daniel and the Home, of Antoinette's heart – fell upon one another in her mind like a series of vellum transparencies, and she realized that she was playing the kind of game she'd often played as a child: closing her eyes and trying to see how many different pictures her mind could hold before it lost sight of the picture with which the series of pictures had begun.

She stood, gathered her supplies, shook hands with Antoinette's mother and father, and wished them luck. Antoinette's mother spoke to Elisabeth in broken English, thanking her and inviting her to visit them in their home. They could not possibly afford to pay for such a picture – Elisabeth had earlier tried, unsuccessfully, to convince them that the drawings were a service the hospital provided – but they did want to show her their appreciation. Did she like fruit?

❖ ❖ ❖

A framed drawing of the escutcheon of the Saturday Night Club, which, Elisabeth knew from conversations with Professor Brödel, would be meeting this Saturday as it did every Saturday, hung on the wall above Professor Brödel's desk. Professor Brödel had become a member of the Saturday Night Club nearly thirty years before, upon the invitation of his friend, Henry L. Mencken. Although Mencken, the club's leader, had been born in Baltimore and had written for several of its papers, he thought of Professor Brödel as of a German compatriot, Elisabeth knew, and boasted often of his own German ancestry, and of the fact that he was related to Otto von Bismarck.

Mencken was unabashed in his enthusiasm for Professor Brödel's work, and had written several times in *The Baltimore Sun* that he considered him the greatest anatomical artist since Da Vinci. Elisabeth agreed about the quality of Professor Brödel's drawings, though she thought of his work, because of his ability to replicate the wet, living quality of human flesh and tissue – due largely to the technique he had invented of laying in carbon dust with sable brushes – as being closer to that of Dürer.

And despite what she perceived as his distinctly Germanic devotion to the *correct* way of doing things – to what was *richtig* – what had endeared him to her from the start was his playful, boyish imagination. Thus, in a cartoon of Doctor William Osler that hung next to the Saturday Night Club's escutcheon, Professor Brödel had depicted Osler, the hospital's most revered physician, walking barefoot through a tornado – striding through its cloud like a saint, a halo around above his head and angel's wings sprouting from his back. Below him was a silhouette of the hospital, its domes and towers rising at the horizon, while in the foreground various lifelike pathogens – amoebas, malarial parasites, staphylococci, and streptococci – were in frantic retreat. Only the typhoid bacilli, standing upright and unmoving, seemed to fear neither the storm nor Doctor Osler.

The Club's escutcheon was divided into quadrants, a crudely drawn figure in each (a violin, a beer mug and sausages, a lobster, a pretzel and two cloves of garlic), each figure symbolic of the ways the men spent their time together. Two hours for music, and two hours for eating and drinking – this was his recipe for the group, Mencken had explained to her, and it never failed. In addition to doctors and writers, Mencken had also awarded membership to several professional musicians, some who taught at the local Peabody School of Music, and he and Professor Brödel, both of whom played the piano well – and *loudly*, Mister Mencken would emphasize – would often play at one piano together, as they had after dinners in Professor Brödel's home. It was, in fact, their passion for German music – for Bach, Brahms, Beethoven, Schumann, and Wagner – that had initially brought them together.

As soon as Elisabeth entered his studio, Professor Brödel asked if she had had word of her father. Elisabeth said that she had not, but that the police were investigating his disappearance. Professor Brödel again assured Elisabeth that she should not be concerned about her obligations to him or to the hospital and medical school. Her drawings had arrived safely within a day, and she could, when she had time, continue to do as she had been doing: working in New York City, and sending the sketches and drawings by mail.

For his part, he said, he had already spoken to people at Bellevue Hospital, and had arranged to have specimens – hearts preserved in formalin – sent there. Professor Brödel handed Elisabeth an envelope within which was a letter that would identify her to the staff at Bellevue, along with instructions as to where she should go to collect the specimens, and what she should do with them after she had completed her drawings.

Then he reached across the short distance that separated them, and took one of her hands in his own.

"But how are *you*, Elisabeth?"

"I'm all right," she said. "I'm fine."

"No," he said. "I do not think you are answering my question. Given what you are going through – your anxieties about your father – how are *you*, my child?"

"Oh *that*," Elisabeth said. "Well, better to lose a father than a child, yes?"

Professor Brödel tapped on the back of her hand, then let go. "Well, I see that your humor has not abandoned you, so it must be as you say – that you are all right. Still, you should not be like we German men, strong on the outside but afraid to reveal what lives within."

"Are German men *really* like that?" Elisabeth asked.

"How would I know?" Professor Brödel replied.

"But speaking of German men, I meant to tell you before that I've met your friend, Doctor Bloch."

"Ah yes, the good doctor Bloch," Professor Brödel said. "But he is Austrian, not German."

"Still, he was most gracious," Elisabeth said. "I saw him several times."

"I have only met him once," Professor Brödel said, "yet during our visit, we discovered an interesting convergence. I wonder – did he mention it? – that we were born less than a year apart, and in that most historic moment when Bismarck brought together the various German lands in order to establish what we now know as the German nation."

"No – he didn't say anything about this."

"Well, perhaps he was paying deference to an older man." Professor Brödel laughed. "I was born in 1870, you see, the very year in which Germany was born, but he – a mere child! – was born in 1871. Nevertheless, he impressed me as an honorable man, though one with a burden I would not willingly share. He is hounded by many, his nephew informs me, to tell what he knows about this Hitler person."

Professor Brödel stood, seemingly irritated at having spoken the name of the German leader aloud. He moved towards the window, past his drafting table, beside which a headless skeleton hung from a wooden post.

"It disturbs me that an eminently good man like Doctor Bloch must be harried because once upon a time, as a responsible physician, he tended to this person," Professor Brödel said. "In my opinion, there is much too much attention paid to Hitler in the press. As Mister Mencken says, and I agree, he is nothing but a *Trommler und Sammler* – a drummer and rallier – an upstart, a vulgar, uneducated rabble rouser."

"He is more than that, I think," Elisabeth said.

"More than that? Well, he certainly knows how to stir up the passions of ignorant mobs!" Professor Brödel was silent for a few seconds, then spoke again: "Well, yes – of course – from your perspective I can see that you would think the way you do."

"From *my* perspective?"

"Like Doctor Bloch and his nephew, you too are a Jew, so I can understand how you might feel, given the particular wrongs he has set in motion against your people."

Elisabeth stood. "I'm afraid I must be going."

"My dear child, you will forgive me if I have become distracted," Professor Brödel said, "but talking about this man, and thinking of what he has done to Germany – well, it outrages me that a person such as this – a mediocre street-artist who has never accomplished anything on his own in life – has been able to attain such power."

"Thank you for the letter. I should be back in New York City by tomorrow evening."

"You *will* forgive me, yes?" Professor Brödel said. "I am in the clouds today, it seems – very much so – but I was put in mind a moment ago, given our conversation, of a remark Goethe once made." Professor Brödel recited words in German, then translated: "'I have often felt a bitter sorrow at the thought of our German people, so estimable in the individual, and so wretched in the generality.'"

"You don't have to apologize to me on behalf of the German nation," Elisabeth said. "And you didn't have to translate. I understand German quite well."

"Well, it would appear, then, that I am also a *forgetful* old man."

Professor Brödel wished her a safe and successful journey, talked of his hope that she would soon locate her father, and then began praising her work, remarking on the portrait of Antoinette and of how Elisabeth had captured the child's fierce spirit, and when he did, Elisabeth realized that she had been so preoccupied with thoughts of Daniel, Alex, and her father that she had violated one of Professor Brödel's primary rules, though arriving when she was nearly done, he would not have known this.

Elisabeth had asked Antoinette to sit as still as she could when this had been unnecessary. Professor Brödel always urged his students not to waste valuable time trying to draw exactly what was going on in front of them – this was especially true when they were in surgery, observing an operation in progress – but rather to stare as hard as they could, and to keep staring, so as to cultivate the internal eye that belonged to memory. You can never stare enough, he would say. When you attempted to capture on paper what was, in the fleeting moment, taking place in front of you, your attention was distracted from life itself – from the living human being who was there, and whose essence lay in things beyond what was literal. It was the accumulation of impressions firmly planted in the mind, he taught – in memory, in imagination, and in the desire to *re*-create what you had seen – that allowed one to *truly* see and, thereby, to reconstruct what one saw in the most effective way, and, more important, what one hoped others would see.

❖ ❖ ❖

The Salisbury Home for Children was located eleven miles northeast of Baltimore, on the outskirts of Bantra, a small fishing village on Chesapeake Bay. By the time Elisabeth arrived – she had hired a private car and driver for the day – it was a few minutes past noon.

The Home was situated in buildings that had once served to house elderly and impoverished sailors, and its main structure, where, in four buildings surrounding a courtyard, Daniel lived with some two dozen other boys, had Romanesque-style turrets at each of its corners.

A dozen or so children were playing in the snow in front of the building, and dressed as they were in bulky coats and leggings, wool hats pulled down over their heads and scarves wrapped around their faces, it occurred to Elisabeth that it would have been difficult for an uninformed visitor to guess that these children were the castaways and – the word that came to mind – the freaks of their families.

But at least, she thought, they were the castaways and freaks of well-to-do families and were not living like animals in state-run facilities as, when poor, such children invariably did. For such good fortune – the wherewithal to allow Daniel to live and to be schooled here – she was grateful to Alex. But she was less than grateful to him for the conversation they'd had before she left Baltimore, when he had responded to her news about obtaining legal counsel by delivering a lengthy monologue on the virtues of eunuchs – erudite nonsense about how, in ancient civilizations such as Babylonia and Syria, eunuchs were, after kings, the most honored and powerful of men – the guardians, statesmen, and diplomats of empires. This had been so, he explained, because their altered sexual condition gave to these men, whose beardless likenesses were frequently immortalized on friezes, the freedom in the exercise of their duties and the enjoyment of their lives, of being undistracted by sexual urges. Nor – a decisive consideration – were they capable of fathering dynasties.

Then perhaps, Elisabeth had said, to set a good example for our son, you might have the procedure performed upon yourself first, so that, freed from distractions, you too could become honored and powerful among men, and an inspiration to your son.

Her remark had silenced him, and though she had enjoyed her small victory, now that she was at the Home, and was watching the children through the car's window, the victory brought little pleasure.

She knew the familiar taxonomy: children who did not develop full speech and had mental ages below three were idiots; children who could not master written language and had mental ages from three to seven were imbeciles; children who could be trained to function in society and had mental ages of eight to twelve – those previously called feeble-minded, a term generally used for *all* children deemed mentally defective – were morons.

A substantial number of the Home's children, however, despite their deficits of mind and malformations of body, and despite the cruel designations that would in most cases accompany them throughout their lives, were able, with training and in time, to leave the Home and to return to the world from which they had come. Doctor Ogilvie, the Home's Director, was a disciple of the philosopher John Dewey – had studied under him at Columbia University, had accompanied him to China when he lectured at the University of Peking earlier in the decade, and was a fervent and often eloquent advocate for Dewey's theory of instrumentalism and for its pragmatic and utilitarian ethic. The various modes and forms of human activity, Doctor Ogilvie believed – had written in the Home's prospectus – were instruments developed by man to solve multiple individual and social problems. Because problems were constantly changing, so too did the instruments for dealing with them, of necessity, have to change. Truth was, according to this way of thinking – a way of thinking that had first attracted Elisabeth to the Home as a residence for Daniel – evolutionary in nature, and the Home's ways of dealing with the children on individualized, flexible, and humanistic bases were predicated upon this belief.

Doctor Ogilvie took rightful pride in the Home's successes: in the many children who, housed and schooled here for a time, were again living with their families; in those children who, after leaving, were able to live on their own and to be gainfully employed; and in those – Elisabeth's hope for Daniel – who had returned to the world and were actually living with families of their own making.

Daniel was neither idiot, imbecile, nor moron. Rather, like many children living at the Home, he suffered from a complex of problems, emotional and cognitive, foremost among them a severe dissociation between thoughts and affects that had led doctors to assign to him – this beginning at about nine years old – a diagnosis of childhood schizophrenia. Yet this designation, Elisabeth knew, was one that even the psychiatrists who consulted on Daniel's case admitted was quite general. It could refer to a broad spectrum of behaviors, most of which, in Daniel's instance, were amenable to melioration, whereas in true schizophrenia this was not considered possible.

Daniel was not schizophrenic, Elisabeth believed – *had* to believe? – and the proof was that he didn't suffer from symptoms usually associated with childhood schizophrenia: an impaired capacity for differentiating self and object, an extreme withdrawal from others as well as from reality, poor motor coordination and/or a failure to develop normal speech and communication patterns. Still, he was plagued by other problems, especially a constant restlessness, which, along with bursts of impulsive and frenetic behavior, made ordinary learning – in school or with tutors – nearly impossible. He was also subject to tantrums that sometimes turned violent; on several occasions he had assaulted and bitten staff members and other children. Nor did he, generally, have any understanding of the source of his behaviors, or – what seemed more significant to Elisabeth – of why his words and actions troubled others.

Still, during his periods of calm, he was – the staff at the Home concurred with Elisabeth's judgment – an essentially bright young man capable of one day living and working outside an institution.

Elisabeth told the driver where he could get lunch, and where he should wait for her. Then she stepped from the car, and the instant she did, children crowded around her, shouting and pushing, snatching at her clothes, knocking her backwards.

They're pawing me, she thought, aware at once of what the words that came to mind implied.

"Children!"

Mister Tompkins, a large round-faced black man of about forty years old, spoke, and his voice, high-pitched yet commanding, made the children stop. Elisabeth watched some of them run away, while others dropped to all fours and crawled off through the snow. Mister Tompkins, standing between Elisabeth and the children, apologized for their behavior.

"They are quite rambunctious today," he explained. "It is

the snow. They do not often experience snow in such abundant quantities."

"I think they're hungry," Elisabeth said.

"Well, yes – it is nearly lunch time," Mister Tompkins replied. "We eat at half-past noon."

Hungry for affection was what Elisabeth meant, but she didn't say so.

In front of Daniel's building, beside a large stone statue of Neptune rising from the sea, two children lay on their backs in the snow, waving their arms and making angels. For a moment Elisabeth imagined that Doctor Bloch was standing in the snow beside her as he had in Saint Raymond's cemetery, and she wondered what, meeting such children, he would think.

"We want money!" one of the children shouted, and others took up the chant: *"Money! Money! Money!"*

"I will escort you into the building," Mister Tompkins said, and he began pushing children aside.

"Thank you," Elisabeth said. "But let them be, please. They mean no harm."

"Daniel is not among the others today," Mister Tompkins said. "I trust, when you informed the office of your visit, that they explained the situation to you."

"Unfortunately, I've had to come unannounced since – because of the blizzard – it was impossible to get a long distance telephone line. But what situation are you talking about? Daniel's all right, isn't he?"

"Oh yes," Mister Tompkins replied. "He is resting in the infirmary, and I can assure you there is no concern about his physical well being. He is a most robust young man."

A heavy-set boy, his face misshapen so that Elisabeth could judge neither his age nor his condition, stood in front of her. He smiled broadly, and when he did, Elisabeth recognized him.

"Is this Arthur?" she asked.

The boy nodded, and Elisabeth extended her hand.

"I'm most happy to see you again, Arthur," Elisabeth said.

The young man, wearing bright orange earmuffs, thrust his hand forward, but instead of taking the hand Elisabeth offered, he suddenly shoved snow into her face.

"Surprise!" he shouted.

Mister Tompkins was upon Arthur at once, pushing him against a tree and wrenching his arm behind him so that the boy howled. Hearing Arthur, other children moved closer and began howling with him.

Elisabeth spat out snow, wiped her face with gloved hands and coat sleeve. "Please leave him be," she said. When Mister Tompkins increased the pressure on Arthur's arm, she spoke again. "I asked you to leave the boy alone, Mister Tompkins."

"As you wish," Mister Tompkins said, and he released Arthur.

Arthur limped off, and Elisabeth watched him join a group of children who were at work building a wall of snow, perhaps three feet high, that seemed to serve no visible purpose.

"If I may say so," Mister Tompkins said when they were inside the building, "I believe it was Daniel's father's visit that probably caused his upset. That is our current thinking."

"His father's visit – ?"

"Why yes," Mister Tompkins said. "Doctor Landau was here this past week. Daniel was, as always, happy to see him. Following the visit, however, he became agitated and tried to follow after Doctor Landau by escaping from the grounds – we are alarmed that this proved possible – and succeeding somehow in climbing over the fence. When we had located him and brought him back, he decompensated rapidly, becoming quite wild and incoherent."

Elisabeth showed nothing.

"I thought it best to inform you of this before you meet with Doctor Ogilvie," Mister Tompkins said. "I am sorry if I have unnerved you."

"No, no – it's quite all right," Elisabeth said. "I thank you for being so frank with me, Mister Tompkins."

"Well, I believe it best to keep families well-informed of what is going on, for if we protect you from the reality of what is happening, it seems to me that we do a disservice to your children."

"I agree," Elisabeth said.

"But there is more," Mister Tompkins said, "and I feel I cannot in good conscience *not* tell you what happened after Daniel was once again in our care. May I?"

"Please," Elisabeth said.

"The cause for our thinking it best that he be kept in private quarters, you see – we are all in agreement on this – is that while one of our young nurses, Miss Mackiewicz, was tending to him in the infirmary, he became aggressive towards her person in a decidedly unwelcome way."

❖ ❖ ❖

I am outraged that you did not inform me of Doctor Landau's visit," Elisabeth said, "and I'll expect to visit with Daniel as soon as our talk is over."

"Of course," Doctor Ogilvie said. Doctor Ogilvie was a tall, thin man with a full head of somewhat unkempt white hair – he was in his late fifties, but looked, despite his white hair, much younger – and he wore a three piece suit, a Phi Beta Kappa key on a gold chain hanging across his vest. "I will take you to him as soon as our talk is over. I know how concerned you must be."

"Perhaps," Elisabeth said. "But I've come here today not because of the incident Mister Tompkins told me about, but to inform you that in this other matter I'm going to do everything in my power to keep you from doing what you may not, by law, do without my consent."

"Please believe me, Elisabeth, when I say that we have Daniel's best interests at heart," Doctor Ogilvie said. "We meant no disrespect to you."

"What you meant and what you did are not the same thing," Elisabeth said.

Elisabeth sat across from Doctor Ogilvie. She had refused the tea he offered, and had no intention of letting go of the rage she felt, for it fueled her determination. All the while Alex had been setting forth his arguments, she now knew, he had been keeping his visit with Daniel and his meeting with Doctor Ogilvie a secret. And yet – what he could not know – his visit, by bringing about Daniel's attempt to escape, had aided Elisabeth's plan.

"Please believe me when I say that we in no way intended to keep you uninformed," Doctor Ogilvie said. "We had assumed, erroneously, it is apparent, that Alex – Doctor Landau – would, in the natural course of things, have apprised you of his visit."

"Doctor Landau has a habit of keeping information about Daniel from me, and you know it," Elisabeth said. "In any event, your failure to inform me of his visit only provides additional evidence of what I'm here to prevent. If I hadn't come here to put you on notice, an action that is venal in intent would probably become criminal in execution."

"Oh Elisabeth – I assure you that we meant no harm – and that we mean no harm."

"But you do and you did, Doctor Ogilvie," Elisabeth said. "You and my ex-husband *do* intend harm to my son." She took a deep breath, then spoke again. "Within a few days you'll get a letter from my attorney. Since Daniel isn't in a hospital yet, may I assume you won't try to circumvent my rights between today and your receipt of my attorney's letter?"

"Of course not," Doctor Ogilvie said. "But if I might persuade you to calm yourself, so that – "

"I have no intention of calming myself," Elisabeth said. "For if I do, it will only encourage you to act in ways that violate my rights and the rights of my son."

"Not at all," Doctor Ogilvie said. "Oh not at all. What I fear you do not understand – what I trust I can clarify for you, as I have for Doctor Landau – is that although you and he have the *right* to be informed, in cases of children suffering from certain regrettable conditions, the courts have not agreed that we are required to obtain parental consent."

"You may clarify matters," Elisabeth said, "but I will correct them. My reading of the law, which my attorney confirms, is that when a child is not a ward of the state – and God help those who are, apparently – you *are* required to obtain the consent of the living parents for any significant medical treatment not deemed a life-saving or emergency measure." Elisabeth rose from her chair. "And since we've concluded our discussion of this matter, I'll be going."

"But – " Doctor Ogilvie said, rising and coming around his desk.

"But nothing," Elisabeth said. "There's nothing else for us to discuss until you've reviewed my attorney's letter, at which point you or your legal counsel can communicate with him. And now I want to see my son, and I want to know why he has been deprived of his freedom to be with other children."

"But my dear Elisabeth," Doctor Ogilvie said, "in all fairness, I think you fail to understand what Daniel is like at times. A mother's love will do that, of course."

"Kindly do not talk to me of a mother's love," Elisabeth said.

From a rack on his desk, Doctor Ogilvie reached for a pipe, and while he filled and lit it, Elisabeth remained silent.

"Well, I see that you are more upset and emotional than usual today," Doctor Ogilvie said, "and of course I understand why that might be. But I ask you to consider this: We have cared for Daniel for five years now, am I correct?"

"Yes."

"And we believe we have not disappointed you through these

years, is that not so?"

"You've been generally kind and competent," Elisabeth said. "That's not in question. But neither is it my reason for being here today."

Doctor Ogilvie gestured to the chair where Elisabeth had been sitting, and she sat again.

"May I suggest that you think of it this way," he said. "If you or Doctor Landau could raise Daniel as you might raise a *different* child, let us say, then surely you would not have given him over to our care."

"I don't know why you're telling me these things."

"Because, I suppose, it seems preferable to giving you a detailed description of the behavior that brought about our decision to place Daniel on supervised seclusion. If you wish, I can provide you with the report that Miss Mackiewicz and Mister Tompkins have filed concerning the incident, and to Doctor Hertzenbach's medical report as well, but I give you my word that, once the situation became dangerous, we had no choice but to act as we did."

"We always have choices," Elisabeth said. She leaned forward. "But if you think for a minute that you and Doctor Landau can make use of this alleged incident as ammunition for your determination to de-sex my son, then you err greatly. And you greatly underestimate *my* determination."

"Oh dear," Doctor Ogilvie said, disturbed, Elisabeth sensed, by the explicitness of her language. He set his pipe down on his desk. "Perhaps I can ask Doctor Hertzenbach to join us so that he can explain our thinking to you in medical terms. Would you mind if I did that?"

"What will he explain to me – that we must not allow feeble-minded children to clog the wheels of progress?" Elisabeth asked. "I know just how difficult Daniel can be at times, but he is *not* feeble-minded, Doctor Ogilvie. Will Doctor Hertzenbach explain to me that anatomy is destiny and that therefore we need to restrict breeding in individuals who endanger the destiny and purity of the race?"

"Oh dear no," Doctor Ogilvie said, and reached to the corner of his mouth for the pipe that, he quickly realized, was no longer there. "Oh my dear woman, we believe no such things. What do you take us for? We are devoted to our children and only wish to prevent harm."

Doctor Ogilvie sat beside Elisabeth. "Truly," he continued, "we only wish to aid Daniel in controlling those urges that trouble him and that can cause you and Doctor Landau, as well as Daniel himself, potentially iniquitous consequences."

Elisabeth knew all the arguments concerning the alleged association of deficient or deranged intelligence with immorality and criminality. But hearing echoes of these arguments, and having made her intentions – and her outrage – clear, she decided, as she had with Alex, that it was time to disengage.

What would be served by trying to persuade these men of things they had no least inclination to believe? The best strategy, she knew, was to give the impression that she would continue to contest their actions and that in so doing she would remain the person they wanted to believe she was: an irrational and emotional woman – a desperate and loving mother trying to protect her son from an event that, in their minds, she was powerless to prevent.

"I don't doubt your devotion to Daniel and the other children," Elisabeth said. "And I won't argue with you any more, but I will note that it's my belief that Daniel *does* know the difference between right and wrong, and that if you and your doctors – and his father – try to treat my son like a degenerate animal, I will fight you to the death."

Shy and intimidated as she was in many situations, Elisabeth was aware that this time her will to prevail was pure and cunning in the way that – the words that came to mind seemed happily apt – an untamed animal's might be.

How like a man you are sometimes, she recalled Alex saying to her years before, and though his remark had embarrassed her at the time, now, remembering the words, she heard them as praise.

She stood again, thanked Doctor Ogilvie for meeting with her on short notice, told him it was imperative he do something about Mister Tompkins's tendency to be physically harsh with the children, and asked to be taken to Daniel.

SEVEN

From the Journal of Doctor Eduard Bloch
December 18, 1940

The boy – Miss Rofman's son, Daniel – has now been residing with me for four days and three nights, and I have come to agree with Miss Rofman's estimate: although he is clearly troubled in ways that doubtless make much of ordinary living difficult for him, especially, I imagine, in his relations with children of his own age, he is an essentially sane, intelligent, and likable young man.

He does present several curious ways of thinking and of expressing himself, yet they are for the most part rather charming (the odd German word for this way of being – *Weltfremdheit* – might be translated into English as 'a certain ignorance of the ways of the world'), and in this he is very much his mother's son, although his style is altogether different. Whereas she is the most steady and steadfast of people, yet with an engaging if unpredictable alternation between modesty and forthrightness, he is anything but steady, steadfast, or modest, although he can certainly be quite forthright! Instead, his behavior is generally naïve and childlike in the extreme, and in ways that, initially, I confess, I found disquieting.

He is a tall, pleasant-looking, somewhat heavy-set lad – an inch or two above six feet, and weighing nearly two hundred pounds – and he walks about with a very serious look, his brow constantly furrowed and his lips forever pursed, although his eyes, so like his mother's, are the delicate gray-blue of a boy half his age. He seems not yet comfortable in the body given to him (I suspect he will, by the age of twenty-one, become even taller and heavier than he is now), and his arms and legs are frequently at odds with one another, as if the left side of his body lacks communication with the right side – his gestures, thus, are noticeably awkward, what Americans call 'gawky.' He is continually in motion – forever touching things (each object on the surfaces of the furniture in my apartment, and on virtually every counter of any store we enter), and when he does sit still, he will rub his fingertips against his palms nervously, or pick at his thumbs with the nails of his index fingers, thereby producing, on top of calluses, open scabs which, to ward off infection, I have been treating with hydrogen peroxide and petroleum jelly, or – more curious – he will chew at his wrists but not at his nails, which are like those of a surgeon, for he files and buffs them regularly.

Still, his childlike perturbations, I have concluded, are integral elements in what is otherwise an intriguing young person, one with idiosyncratic ways – in especial, a refreshing and unself-conscious exuberance – and one for whom it is difficult not to feel an immediate affection.

This morning, for example – it is evening now, and he is asleep, so that I am free to set down these thoughts – when I entered the living room, he addressed me, without prefatory comment, as follows: "Doctor Bloch, may I ask you this question today: Do you think I am old enough to go out into the world to seek my fortune?"

Without showing in any way that I found his question strange (or delightful) I replied that yes, I thought he was.

"That certainly is good news," he said then, after which he gestured to the table, already set for a breakfast he had, as on the previous two mornings, prepared for us: orange juice, assorted cold cereals (one called Kix is his favorite because in the mouth, he has told me, it makes the best crunching noise of any cereal), yogurt with honey, buttered toast with strawberry jam, and tea.

He enjoys cooking, and talks frequently about the elaborate meals he would like to prepare, and of the skills he gained in such matters in the kitchen at the Home in which he has been living. At the Home, he explained, all children were required to perform useful tasks: in its kitchen, on its farm, in its stables, and in its dormitories and classroom buildings. He says that one of his dreams is to someday live in Paris where he would apprentice himself to a master chef so as to become one himself.

"That," he says, as he does of many experiences, "would be a true adventure!"

This sense he has of life as an adventure, admirable in itself, is also a quality that enables him to make the best of many situations that might cause other young people frustration and sorrow. On his first night in my apartment, for example (he and his mother arrived late Sunday evening, telephoning beforehand from the Baltimore train station to advise me of their arrival), when I offered him my bed and said that I would sleep on the living room couch – this was only proper, since he was my guest – he not only refused my offer, but refused to sleep on my couch.

"It is not a bed," he stated. "It is your couch, Doctor Bloch, and should not be used for purposes other than those for which it was made."

His sojourn in my apartment, he declared, would be an adventure akin to a military bivouac. He had already taken this probability into account, he informed me, and so would be sleeping on a cot he and his mother had brought with them from her father's apartment. The cot, which they carried here in a laundry bag, is a rather loosely fitted-together apparatus of wood and canvas of the kind, Miss Rofman says, that people have been using at the New York World's Fair these past two years when, sometimes overnight, they have waited on long lines in order to secure entry to exhibitions.

With the boy present, I did not inquire as to why Miss Rofman chose not to have him stay with her in her father's apartment, though I have my suspicions, and will voice them to her as soon as this proves expedient.

On the two mornings previous to this one, when I have risen from bed and entered the living room, the boy, already awake, has greeted me in a similar manner, with a smile, and, as he did this morning, with questions.

Here are two of his questions – First: Was I personally acquainted with Doctor Albert Einstein, and did I agree that he was the smartest man in the world? Second: Was it true that I had been Hitler's doctor, and if so, when was the last time I examined him?

I answered his questions directly – I did not know Doctor Einstein, but admired him greatly and imagined there was no one more brilliant than he; and yes, I had been Hitler's doctor when he was a boy and young man, but had seen him only once in the past several decades, in March of 1938, when, having become ruler of Austria, he returned to the city of Linz in triumph (and when, of course, I did not examine him). Daniel did not ask me to elaborate upon my answers.

Each morning while we eat, he retells the story of how he escaped from the Salisbury Home for Children, which he introduces by stating that it is the story of his *truly* great adventure. And each time he recounts the story for me – he repeats it at other times – he changes fewer elements in it. It is as if he believes that the more times he retells the story, and the more similar each new version is to the previous one, the more likely it is he will remember it, and – more significant – the more likely it is that *he* will believe it is true.

I have come to this conclusion since he has several times asked if I *believe* the story he has told me.

Yes, I have said to him each time.

This morning, however, after a recounting that was virtually identical to the recounting he put forth yesterday evening, he again asked if I believed his tale, and when I said yes, he leaned towards me and asked "But why?"

"Because," I said, "nobody could simply have made all that up."

Upon my saying these words, he broke into a smile more relaxed and natural than any I have seen since his arrival.

"Thank you, Doctor Bloch," he said.

This is the story he told me.

He had been living in seclusion for two days when his mother, accompanied by Doctor Ogilvie, appeared in the doorway of his room and asked Doctor Ogilvie and the attendant in charge, a Polish man named Kucharski, to leave her alone with him. Doctor Ogilive complied with her wishes. Mister Kucharski, and a Mister Polivito – not, according to Daniel, quite as massive or mean-spirited a man as Mister Kucharski – were with Daniel during his waking hours, to prevent another escape attempt, while at night Daniel's door was locked from the outside and he was given a small cowbell which, for his needs, he was to ring if he wanted to summon a staff member.

Once they were alone, his mother asked him to tell her exactly what had happened, whereupon Daniel told her what he told me: that the nurse, Miss Mackiewicz, who is perhaps five years older than he, had, in his words, "led him on." Under the guise of calming him down from the trauma of his escape and capture, she had caressed his brow, had removed his shoes and socks, and placed his feet in a warm Epsom salt bath. She had also suggested he remove his shirt so that she might, to bring about needed relaxation, massage his neck and shoulders.

When he had complied with her suggestion, he said, she made admiring remarks about his body, and tended to him in ways that he understood to be an advance upon his person, and an invitation to hers. He could, he said, come to no other conclusion than that Miss Mackiewicz wished him to reciprocate, and he described the ensuing encounter between them with a clinical detachment that might have come from the mouth of a medical student, except that while Daniel's words were impersonal and precise, his affect was not. He spoke with great feeling of the arousal and pleasure he had felt, of parallel feelings expressed to him by Miss Mackiewicz, and, before anything but preliminary intimacies had been exchanged, of the pain her betrayal had caused him.

Had he become angry with Miss Mackiewicz when she began to reject the advances she had seemingly encouraged? I asked.

"I must confess that I did," he said to me, as he had to his mother, who, he said, had asked the same question. "But I did not strike her as she claims I did."

This is what happened, as he described it: In the midst of their encounter, Miss Mackiewicz suddenly pushed him away and, screaming, rushed from the room, returning a moment later with others, including Mister Kucharski, who, finding Daniel dressed in only his pants, and with his sexual arousal still visible – here his frankness astonished, given how discreet he is about many matters – handled him in a harsh manner, remanding him physically, though not without a struggle, Daniel asserted proudly, to the room in which his mother found him, and where he had been kept for two days and nights.

On previous occasions, when other women made similar accusations, they had done the same to him, he said. Perhaps it was his size, or his physical condition that attracted these overtures and led to such accusations. Each morning and evening, in his dormitory, he explained – this surprised also, given his apparent lack of coordination – he performed several hundred squats, sit-ups, push-ups, and, on a steel bar near the ceiling of the bathroom, at the entryway to the showers, pull-ups and chin-ups. (He does the same in my apartment, employing the iron rungs of the fire-escape outside my bedroom window, despite the cold weather, for his pull-ups and chin-ups). Nor was Miss Mackiewicz, he confided, alone in making advances. Several other staff members – two housekeepers, and one assistant cook – had given him unmistakable invitations, these accompanied by lurid physical gestures. And five or six girls at the Home had sent him what he called "mash notes," telling him they loved him, offering to have secret rendezvous with him, and becoming angry when he ignored or rejected them.

Was he telling the truth? I knew that I could confirm his reports when Miss Rofman and I would have time to ourselves – that is, I could ascertain if he had told her the same stories he told me. Since I do not doubt his sincerity, my expectation is that he has been consistent in these matters. Clearly, he believes in the stories he tells, although – a phenomenon I encountered with some frequency during my years as a physician – once he has invented a tale, or elaborated fancifully upon an actual incident, it may well be that he comes to believe in the story he has told, and that this story, taking on an independent life of its own, becomes detached and separate from what may actually have occurred.

For the moment, I am inclined to concentrate on listening attentively, and to do so without questioning the veracity of his tale, so that, trust gradually established, Daniel will, with time, have no need to distort or hide the truth of any event, memory, or feeling. This, of course, given my years as confidant and counselor to hundreds of individuals, is a way of being that has become instinctive and natural. For if I have learned one thing from these years, it is that the most important element in any physician's armamentarium is the willingness to listen to the patient. When one does this, as others wiser than I have noted, the patient will ultimately provide one with the diagnosis, from which a prognosis and course of treatment will follow. That is to say, it is by engendering trust that a patient may come to provide a story into which one can usefully place presenting symptoms, thereby offering genuine hope of ameliorating those conditions, whether imaginary or endogenous, that are causing pain and suffering.

But how different is this, one might ask, from what any human being requires of another human being from whom he wishes to elicit consolation and aid? How different is this from what we do in our ordinary waking lives when we give to one another that trust which bestows validation and comfort, and is the basis of any true or enduring interrelation?

It is, therefore, my intention, events having conspired to place me at this particular juncture in the lives of these two people, to provide a trust and friendship that will prove of utility in their current crisis. I will believe what the boy tells me, that is, until there is no longer good reason not to believe. And surely, though in his childlike way Daniel is unaware of it, he is living through a most crucial moment of his life – one that is at least as dangerous to him, in its immediate as well as in its enduring issue, as it is to his mother.

In the telling of the tale, there seems also a stark absence of perspective – of realism – for it is as if he sees himself as a character in a novel by Dumas or Stevenson – or Karl May! – or as an actor in a moving picture set in dungeons of ruined castles or on ships that sail the high seas. He has even, for instance, in the midst of his narrative, asked if, as a younger man, I knew of or participated in those aristocratic traditions – in Germany, Austria, and Hungary – wherein young men fought with swords, slashing their adversaries' faces, and wearing their scars with honor. He was clearly hoping for an answer in the affirmative, which, happily, I could not offer.

But why, his mother asked, had he tried to run away? His answer, to her as to me, was that his father's unexpected visit caused him to become fearful of plans the Home had concerning his future.

"Your future?" his mother asked.

"That my future was going to be taken from me," was his reply.

Until his mother's visit – and his flight – he had not, apparently, understood what was implied by the word *future.* He knew he was scheduled for what the Home termed a routine procedure, one sometimes indicated for young men like him, and one presented to him as if it were a privilege.

His father explained that he had taken time away from his medical practice for a visit to the Home because he had been informed that Daniel was being admitted to a local hospital for a few days, and he wanted to wish him well. Having spoken with Doctor Ogilvie and the doctors involved, his father was confident that what Daniel was going to the hospital for was, as Doctor Ogilvie said, indeed routine, but, spurred on perhaps by the way Daniel, notably silent, indicated he was *not* reassured by his father's visit, his father went further, saying he was certain Daniel would emerge from this minor procedure with his life transformed for the good.

Daniel said that he chose not to argue with his father, for not only was his father much more clever with words and arguments, especially about medical matters, than ever he could be, but because he did not want his father to suspect that he had decided, from the first, that he was *not* going to be compliant with whatever it was his father and the Home were planning.

What he knew – "sensed in his bones" was the phrase he employed – was that it was imperative he get away from the Home before the plan was put into action. What he knew was that he was thinking only of escape and of how he would survive until he could arrive in New York City, and also of how he might do so without putting his mother in danger, and without those who would pursue him being able to trace his whereabouts. He did not have great knowledge of the world beyond the Home, and had not *lived* in New York City for more than nearly a half dozen years.

What aroused his suspicions most of all was the fact that his mother said nothing to him about the plan the Home had for his future. If what he was going to the hospital for was minor, he reasoned, surely they would have informed his mother, since she lived nearby and, like his father, was knowledgeable about medical matters. Why would they not want to have the procedure take place in *her* hospital, which was the best hospital in the world, and why would they hide things from her?

These were questions he asked himself, he said, and they were the cause of his doing nothing to arouse his father's suspicion concerning his own suspicions.

Having said this, he added, as though revealing a confidence, that his father was a very religious man and knew a lot about being a Jew, after which he asked this question: When you were Hitler's doctor, did Hitler know that you were a Jew?

Yes, I said, and added that in those years Hitler's anti-Semitic attitudes were, to my knowledge, non-existent.

"I'm not surprised at all," he said, and next he asked if I would, as I had promised, tell him what Hitler was like when he was a boy.

By this time it was mid-morning, and I made more tea for us – Daniel prefers it the way his grandfather taught him to drink it: with a large spoonful of strawberry jam – and I began telling him about my life in Linz, and about Hitler and his family. I also told him that I was writing down the story – since many people had been asking me what Hitler was like, this seemed the most efficient way to deal with their curiosity – and I asked if, when my task was completed, he would like to read what I had written.

"I would consider it an honor!" he exclaimed.

Well, I said to him, I hoped he could be what I knew was quite difficult for him – patient – since it might be some time before I was ready to show what I was writing. What I did not explain, of course, was that while I was recording my memories of years past, I was also recording matters pertaining to the present, and, especially, to the appearance in my life of his mother. Nor could

I say aloud what occurs to me only when I am writing – that is, how reluctant I am to separate out these two stories, for were I to do so – this is the thought that had *not* occurred until I began to write this very sentence – I fear I would be in danger of somehow losing one or the other.

But lose a story how? is the question that immediately presents itself, and to that question, I answer that, if I am to be true to the past – to my initial purpose in setting down these notes – it is apparent that I must also be true to that impulse which has inspired me to record what is happening in my life in the present – in those matters that relate to the entry into my life of Miss Rofman and of Daniel.

And so, without misgivings, I acceded to Daniel's request, recounting for him some basic information about young Hitler, and when I had done this, albeit in an abbreviated manner, he asked if I would also tell him about the time Hitler returned to Linz. His voice was uncharacteristically calm, and this called my attention to the fact that during the telling of my story he had sat in my large armchair in a nearly immobile state, without picking at his palms and thumbs or chewing at his wrist. And by the time I had told much of what I recalled concerning Hitler's return to Linz, he was fast asleep.

This was how his mother found him when she arrived in the early afternoon. Her pleasure in seeing him asleep, and peacefully so, was evident, and when I told her of our morning together – of our exchange of stories – she thanked me and, laughing – a laugh that in its light, gurgling quality put me in mind of the way my dear Marta would laugh when aware that I had been boyishly mischievous with her – said that she never thought her guardian angel would turn out to be an elderly Jewish-Austrian physician!

I laughed with her, and it was our combined laughter that woke Daniel, who, without knowing why we were laughing, joined in the laughter, slapping at his forearms with joy and, when he could catch his breath, asking his mother what she had brought him.

From her shopping bag she took out items, one at a time: several books, including one about Doctor Einstein, a set of colored pencils that were already sharpened, a large sketch pad, a smaller pad of lined paper, a box of chocolate-covered cherries, and clothing (socks, underwear, shirts, and a pair of dark brown corduroy pants), some with price tags still attached. Daniel thanked her for each item, but he did not embrace or kiss her (since his arrival, not even for *hellos* or *goodbys* have I seen him touch her). Instead, after setting books and clothing on his cot, opening the box of chocolate-covered cherries, and putting two in his mouth at the same time, he asked her to tell him how it was that she was able to evade those who might, searching for him, be following her, which, while I prepared lunch for us, she did.

And now, while sleep has not yet dimmed my senses, and memories remain fresh, I will write of the events of March, 1938, when Adolf Hitler, having become Führer of Germany and Austria, returned to Linz.

In order to better understand this event, I will provide some background, and note, first of all, that, following upon the death of his mother and his departure for Vienna, young Adolf disappeared from Linz, and from our lives, for a great many years. He had no friends I know of to whom he might have returned to visit; I may, in fact, be one of the only people in our city with whom he corresponded, and this correspondence, which moved in one direction only, for he sent no return address, consisted of several of his hand-painted postal cards, all of which save one – an excellent watercolor depicting the Danube, houses of the Urfahr section on its far side – were confiscated by the Gestapo following the *Anschluss* and Germany's annexation of Austria. On most of the cards he wrote simply that he sent his greetings, and he invariably signed the cards, as he did the one

I have retained, with a conventional "Yours, always faithfully, Adolf Hitler." In a card I gave over to the Gestapo, however, he was slightly more expansive. After extending best wishes to me "from the Hitler family" for a Happy New Year, and before signing his name, he wrote, "In everlasting thankfulness." On the reverse side, strangely enough, given his lack of religiosity and his abstemiousness when it came to alcohol – as a young man, when even small amounts of wine were served to him, he would add large amounts of sugar to his glass – was a picture of a hooded Capuchin monk hoisting a glass of bubbling champagne, and the caption, *"Prosit Neujahr* – A Toast to the New Year."

Not until he became active politically in the years following The Great War did any word of him reach us, and the news, which we gathered from items in our local papers, had to do with his activities for organizations in Munich, which activities consisted primarily of speech-making. That he had become a successful and influential public speaker, I note, given how laconic he was as a youth, was unexpected. Not until the ill-fated Beer-Hall Putsch of 1923, in which several dozen people died, and Hitler was, for his part in this brutal and futile undertaking, imprisoned for a short while, did he achieve anything resembling national or local notoriety.

When this happened, I believe that most citizens of Linz who had known him reacted as I did: How could it be that the man behind those vulgar and violent events was the shy, quiet boy we had known in Linz – the son of the gentle Klara Hitler?

Eventually, though, given his political views, even the mention of his name was, in our native land, prohibited. What news we received of him, especially after 1933, when he became Chancellor of Germany, was alarming in the extreme: stories of persecutions he launched and of those he countenanced, and, most of all, of German rearmament and of the war we feared had become inevitable.

By this time there was a local Nazi party in Linz, and although it was officially outlawed by the government, in practice the authorities gave it their blessing. Denied the right to wear their uniforms publicly, for example, our local Nazis identified themselves to others by wearing white stockings, or small wild flowers (much like the American daisy) on their coats, or by giving the Nazi salute when passing one another in the street; they would also place Nazi flags on the graves of loved ones – frequently on Klara's grave – and at Christmastime they burned blue candles in the windows of their homes.

On the evening of Friday, March 11, 1938, shortly before eight o'clock, Austrian Chancellor Kurt von Schuschnigg, who became Chancellor after the assassination by Nazis of Engelbert Dollfuss in 1934, interrupted a radio program of light music to announce that, in order to prevent bloodshed, he was capitulating to the wishes of Reich Chancellor Adolf Hitler, and that the frontiers of our two nations would henceforth be open. He ended his address with words that caused tears to well in my eyes: *"Gott schuetze Oesterreich"* – may God protect Austria.

It was not long after this, preceded by extensive German troop movements onto our soil, that we received news that Hitler himself would be returning. Our city, truth be told, went mad with joy, a sad reminder of how popular the *Anschluss* was, this popularity evidenced by the way my fellow townspeople greeted German soldiers who soon paraded through our city: with flowers, cheers, songs, and the constant ringing of church bells.

For me, of course, the news brought with it wariness. I had read portions of *Mein Kampf*, Hitler's rather poorly written and somewhat incomprehensible book (one given, in Germany, and now in Austria, to all newly married couples on their wedding day), and so I knew of how his views towards Jews had changed – of how he believed a million German lives could have been saved during the war if a few thousand Jews had been gassed, and of how – the image was, for me, painfully evocative – Jews had become "a cancer on the breast of Germany," and, therefore, along with Communists, Socialists, Freemasons, and others, to be, chill word, *ansgerottet* – eradicated.

Then, on a Saturday morning, news arrived that he was on the outskirts of our city. Planes flew overhead, advance units of the German Army marched through our city, and the *"Horst Wessel"* song and *"Deutschland ueber Alles"* filled the air. All windows along the procession route – Landstrasse, where my home was – were ordered closed, but I watched through my bedroom window, and I soon saw below me, flanked by a motorcycle brigade, a great black six-wheeled Mercedes and the frail boy I had treated some thirty years before standing erect and triumphant in the automobile, returning the joyous greetings of the citizens of Linz.

For many years he had been denied the right to visit Linz, or Austria, yet now, having the day before passed through the city of his birth, Braunau, he was returning as ruler of the nation that had ostracized him. And when he smiled, and waved the Nazi salute to one and all, and, passing my home, glanced upwards, I thought for a moment that he remembered where I lived, that he was searching for me, and – my nose pressed to the window – that he saw and recognized me.

Then he was gone, moving towards our town square, Franz Josef Platz – soon to be renamed Adolf Hitler Platz – where, from the balcony of our town hall, he gave a long speech that was broadcast on radio. Germany and Austria, he declared, now and forever, were one nation! One blood – one Reich!

From the town hall he went to the Weinzinger Hotel, where he was given, at his request, a room with a view of his beloved Poestling Mountain, the mountain he had looked out upon all through his childhood. On the following day he invited several old acquaintances to his quarters: Kubitschek, the musician; Liedel, the watchmaker; Doctor Huemer, his history teacher.

Despite all that I had meant to him and to his family, I did not, since I was a Jew, expect that he would invite me. Yet he did, I was told afterwards by Doctor Heumer, inquire of me. Was I still alive? he asked. Was I still practicing medicine? And then, Doctor Huemer reported, he made a singular statement, one that was doubtless offensive to our local Nazis. "Doctor Bloch," he declared, "is an *Edeljude* – a noble Jew. If all Jews were like him, there would be no Jewish question."

That same day, a Sunday, he visited his mother's grave, after which he reviewed local Nazis as they marched proudly past him – not yet equipped with uniforms, they wore knickerbockers, ski pants or leather shorts, swastikas hand-painted onto white armbands and onto varicolored headgear. The next day he departed for Vienna.

What followed after his visit – what I have spoken about with neither Daniel nor his mother, and will reserve for these pages – was disastrous, though more for the other Jews of Linz than for myself. At the time there were some seven hundred Jews living in our city. Immediately upon Hitler's departure from Linz, by decree, all of our shops, homes, and offices were marked with yellow banners – made of paper, they were of the kind that had been used in Germany – the word *JUDE* stamped on them, which banners, we knew, were merely the outward announcement of more dire humiliations to come.

I, however, was treated differently. A few days after this decree, an officer of the Gestapo telephoned and told me I was, immediately, to *remove* the yellow banners from my home and office. Next, my landlord, who was not Jewish, went to the Gestapo's headquarters and, since many Jews were already being displaced, and without compensation or benefit of court hearings, asked if I were to be allowed to remain in my apartment. "We wouldn't dare touch that man," the Gestapo officer in charge told him, as my landlord, with more respect than ever I had known from him, reported to me. "His case is to be handled by Berlin."

Soon after this, and for no apparent reason, my son-in-law – Gertrude's husband, Paul – was arrested and put in jail, the right to have visitors taken from him. Nor were we able to receive any news of him. My daughter, however, a brave and headstrong woman, went directly to the Gestapo and this is what she said: "Would your Führer like to know that the son-in-law of his old physician has been sent to prison?"

Initially, the Gestapo treated her rudely. Had she not seen that the *Jude*-banners had been removed from her father's house? Was that not enough? Were Jews *never* satisfied?

Shortly after her visit to the Gestapo, however, Paul was released.

My medical practice, which had been one of the largest in Linz, had begun to dwindle at least a year before Hitler's arrival, and in this surely I should have seen a portent of things to come. But when the heart chooses to deceive, it is ever more powerful than the mind. Thus, though many of my older patients informed me, with admirable frankness, given what was happening since the ascendancy of the Nazis to power, that they could no longer patronize a Jew, I continued to think that things would change, and that all would be as it had been before.

I was wrong. After the *Anschluss*, my practice, by law, was limited to Jewish patients, and though at first I rejected the idea of retirement, retirement was decided for me, since it soon happened that to be a doctor to Jews was to be a doctor to no one.

On November 10, 1938, the ruling we had heard rumors of was made public: all Jews were to leave Linz within forty-eight hours. All Jews, many of whom who had lived in Linz for their entire lives, were to sell their property, pack, and depart – our destination: Vienna.

I telephoned the Gestapo to verify the news, and I was informed that in my case an exception had been made. I would, and on highest authority, the officer told me, be permitted to remain. What of my daughter and her husband? I asked. Since they had already signified their intention of emigrating to the United States, they too would be permitted, on a temporary basis, to remain. Like all other Jews, they would of course be required to vacate their home; until their emigration, however, they would be permitted to live with me.

Within two days, where there had been seven hundred Jews, there were now seven – Gertrude, Paul, myself, and four others, all of whom were past eighty years of age and in failing health. (Although they were my patients, I do not know what became of them.)

Let me now list the favors I received. I was allowed to keep my passport, a privilege, I believe, not given to another Jew in all of Austria. When food became scarce, there was no *J* stamped on my ration card, a privilege that proved helpful in many ways, given that Jews were allowed to shop only during inconvenient and restricted hours. I was given a ration card for clothes, something generally denied to Jews, though it may be that my war record, wherein I had charge of a one thousand bed hospital, and for which I was twice decorated, was partially responsible for such a consideration. When, four months after the departure of Gertrude and Paul, I was given permission to leave Austria, I was permitted to take with me sixteen marks instead of the customary ten, and also – an especially remarkable consideration – a small satchel of medical instruments (stethoscope, blood pressure manometer, thermometer, head lamp, two small scalpels, three retractors, and several suturing needles along with a small quantity of fine China silk thread).

Two days before my departure, I received from the Nazi organization of physicians a letter of recommendation that stated I was "worthy of recommendation" because of my "character, medical knowledge and readiness to help the sick." I had, the letter concluded, "won the appreciation and esteem of my fellow men."

To show my gratitude for these favors, a Nazi party official strongly suggested I write a letter to the man who was responsible for my good fortune: the Führer. And so, on a cold, foggy November morning – a mere month ago! – I wrote the following:

Your Excellency:

Before passing the border I want to express my thanks for the protection which I have received. In material poverty I am now leaving the town where I have lived for forty-one years; but I leave conscious of having lived in the most exact fulfillment of my duty. At sixty-nine I will start my life anew in a strange country where my daughter is working hard to support her family.

Yours faithfully,

Eduard Bloch.

What I wonder, though, is this: did Adolf Hitler ever receive my letter, and if so, how did he react? I wonder too: were I to write to him now, and appeal to our common experience and humanity – to the memory of his mother, and to the life we shared when he was a young boy in Linz – would he listen to me, and might I have some influence upon him, and upon the policies, especially racial policies, he has been pursuing? Surely I am not the only *Edeljude* in Germany or Austria. Surely the love and kindness he received from his mother and others, along with the gratitude he expressed to me, might be rekindled so as to allow him, at the least, to be generous to others in the way he has been to his boyhood physician.

But what I wonder about more than such matters, which, even as I write about them, seem the stuff of melodrama, is this: What will Miss Rofman make of what she learns from these writings?

Doubtless, on a personal level, she will be pleased that good fortune has enabled me to survive, to emigrate, and to be here – in part, I hope, because it has allowed us to begin a unique friendship, and in part because it has given her a home in which her son, Daniel, can be protected from those who would inflict harm upon him. Still, the question cannot be gainsayed: What will she think of a man whose good fortune is balanced – and vitiated – by shame? To ask this, however, is only, in effect, to ask of her the question I have been asking of myself:

In accepting favors granted to me by Adolf Hitler that were, to my knowledge, granted to no other Jew, have I been dishonorable?

There is also this question: How in *her* mind and heart does she regard the fact that the source of her good fortune may have less than honorable roots?

What I have concluded is this: unlike characters in classic tragedies, I am *not* a man more sinned against than sinning. Rather the opposite. I am a man whose good fortune seems out of all proportion to his good works. Good works I have doubtless performed in my lifetime, and yet, given the news that reaches me from the land from which I have departed – in especial, the treatment of my fellow Jews – my *Stammesgenossen* – why is the reward given me so singular, and what, if anything, am I to make of it, or, if this is not what a psychiatrist might call an ordinary expression of a "guilt complex," what am I now to do with the life given back to me, and to the life that, in the months and years to come, will be mine?

I am, by all accounts, it would seem, a survivor. But of what? My fellow Austrian Jews have been displaced to the East, we are told, and certainly their losses and discomforts, given the haste of their exodus, are far greater than mine. Nor have I suffered the indignities many of them, in Linz and elsewhere, have suffered since the Nazis rose to power. True, I have been exiled from my native land and my beloved community; yet I live, if modestly, in a nation that welcomes me, my basic needs are provided for, my daughter and her husband are nearby, I have a kind and lovely woman who has chosen to befriend me, and I have, as a companion, a fascinating young man I can care for and to whom I can impart some of what I know (he is, like his mother, gifted artistically, and I have begun helping him with anatomical drawings). My losses, thus, are more than equaled, in actuality and in prospect, by gains.

It has not been my habit of life, or mind, to speculate on matters as I am doing here. For the most part I have always strived to do what was right and what was required of me – as a son, husband, father, brother, uncle, citizen, and physician. I have tended to my patients diligently, and while I listened to their reports of symptoms and illness, and paid attention to the context in which these conditions occurred, it has been my practice, and habit, to attend, by and large, to what can be seen, heard, touched, and smelled – that is, to matters physical: to those biological organisms or those events which might have given rise to specific, observable, measurable, or reported conditions, whether lesions, growths, mental deficits, physical disabilities, or loci of pain.

Yet now, without a clinical practice to carry me through my waking hours, and without the occupation – and pre-occupation – of caring for and considering the well-being of patients, questions and feelings previously relegated to the ante-rooms of my mind are demanding more light. Thus my self-indulgence in setting these ruminations down on paper, and thus, too, my somewhat dim intimation of worlds of feeling and of sensation that, perhaps, have ever been mine but which – like the proverbial stepchildren of fairy tales? – if unintentionally, I have ignored or slighted.

What I know with certainty at this moment in time – in my bones, as Daniel might put it – is that nothing will ever be the same. For even while much of the life I have lived and known is forever lost to me, so is a new life, and of a most unforeseen kind, being born. And, curious to tell, I am acutely aware that this is so not when I am alone with my thoughts and feelings, as now, and not when I am with Miss Rofman (and an affection for her stirs inside me in mild yet pleasantly confusing ways), but when I am with Daniel.

For it is this young man's oft-times inability to know what it is he is feeling, along with his inability to express his feelings in ordinary ways, that seems to have stimulated in me an equal and opposite reaction. Let me, if in a somewhat inchoate fashion, explain, and I do so not primarily to understand Daniel – though I wish to do that also – but to understand myself, and the strange new stirrings that flow through me.

In Daniel's mind, I suspect, and I posit this as a clinician, there is some neurological anomaly that inhibits him from relating to other human beings in what we would consider normal and appropriate ways. I agree with Miss Rofman that he should not be diagnosed with childhood schizophrenia. Yet he is afflicted with a most real condition, and one for which we as yet have no name. Surely he is not lacking in intelligence, nor in feeling itself. Nor is he, for want of a better term, 'repressed' in his expression of thoughts and feelings in the way, say, that most Austrian men are.

What I think of when I think of Daniel's mind and of how it works – or, rather, what I *see* – is this: that his mind is like a map of an unexplored country, or, more exactly, that it is made up of a series of maps, one on top of the other, with trails and routes on one map intersecting with others, both vertically and horizontally; when he talks, or when he is silent, or when, as now, he sleeps, I find a great desire swell within me – a yearning to *see* these maps so that I might understand the boy better, and might, by tracing and retracing the routes along which his thoughts and feelings travel (in *their* infinite movements and interactions), be of use to him. It is so difficult to imagine, or know, the worlds of feeling, thought, and sensation that lie within *any* other human, and more so, given his unusual modes of perception and expression, within this young man.

On the first afternoon we were together Miss Rofman said something that has served, perhaps, as stimulus for this way of thinking. Miss Rofman was talking about her father, who worked on the construction of the New York City subway system in the early years of the century, and she told me that she has, ever since she was a young girl, thought of subway lines as being like paths of memory. She apologized for what she termed the somewhat vague fashion in which *she* explained herself, but, continuing, said that she would sometimes imagine that her own memories were passengers in subway cars – or were the subway cars themselves! – and that these memories would, jogged by specific images, events, scenes, or feelings, often transfer from one train to another – from one subway line to another (there was only one major line when she was a girl; now there are three, and they are somewhat independent of one another) – and thereby, on a different set of tracks, and in different trains, become transformed into different if related sets of memories.

Recalling this conversation with Miss Rofman, and imagining the maps that might lie inside young Daniel's mind, and contemplating their unpredictable and random ways, this thought also occurs: Should something happen to Miss Rofman, what would become of Daniel?

He is profoundly bound to her, yet were some accident of life, or biology, to take her from us, I suspect that he would not grieve in any conventional way (it is hard to imagine him crying under *any* circumstances, except perhaps from extreme physical pain) – in any way, that is, that would seem congruous with the expectations others would have of a young man in his situation.

It is the recognition of this deficit in him that has, then, made me value the newly discovered worlds of feeling within me, and to believe that to do so, and to explore them, is not a mere indulgence.

For example, when he told of his flight from the Home

– through the woods (which he described graphically: downed trees, iced-over clearings, boulders and rocks slick with frozen moss), over the iron fence, and onto snow-laden roads – and then, again, when he did what his mother instructed, and re-enacted his flight, and once more ran through woods thick with unknown perils, what he said, somewhat exultantly, was that the more he ran, the stronger he felt.

So it is with me. Although I was quite tired when I began to transcribe my thoughts this evening, I find that the more I write, the more I want to write – and the less tired I feel.

I am reminded, too, writing these words, that Daniel has decided to write a letter to Doctor Einstein. Since Doctor Einstein is the smartest man in the world, Daniel says, Doctor Einstein will surely know what to do to stop the world from pursuing a war that, Daniel is certain, will eventually cross the ocean and, perhaps, destroy the United States and all Jews who live here. (Was it his decision to write a letter to Doctor Einstein that suggested to me the possibility of writing to Reich Chancellor Hitler?) When I recounted for Daniel – but more for his mother, who returned my anecdote with a lovely laugh – Doctor Einstein's remark that though he is a stinking rose to the Germans, yet do they continue, despite his anti-Nazi views, to wear him in their lapels, Daniel wrote this down, and said he would use this remark in his letter. (I wanted to quote for Miss Rofman Doctor Einstein's remark that the only thing in the world truly worth aspiring to is the friendship of excellent and free persons, but to do so at this point in our friendship, I judged, would be premature.)

Nevertheless, though I feel capable of writing more – in particular, of recounting Daniel's description of his journey from the Home to New York City – I am aware that if I do not get a reasonable night of sleep, I will experience a fatigue tomorrow that may inhibit my ability to be of service to Daniel and Miss Rofman (who has not yet had any definitive news concerning her father, and – this I could not help but notice – does not talk about his disappearance unless I question her about it), and so, with regret, I cease here.

EIGHT

When Elisabeth entered her father's apartment, Alex and a tall thin man in a brown tweed suit were waiting for her.

"Oh!" she exclaimed. "But how did you get in here, and by what right have you – ?"

"This is Detective Kelly," Alex said. "He has been working on your father's case."

Detective Kelly inclined his head towards Elisabeth but said nothing. He lifted his hat from the counter, next to the sink and, with the back of his hand, brushed away invisible crumbs from where the hat had been.

"Yes," Elisabeth said. "Of course. Do you have news?"

"We have news," Alex said, "but I'm afraid it's not about your father. I think you had best sit down."

Detective Kelly brought Elisabeth a glass of water, and gestured to one of the two kitchen chairs.

Elisabeth refused the glass of water. "Tell me," she demanded. "Tell me at once, Alex, whatever it is, and then leave, please. You *confuse* me by being here, and you know it."

"You should sit," Alex said.

"You should leave," Elisabeth said. "How *dare* you enter my father's home without permission! By what right do you and Mister – "

"Kelly," the detective said. "Galen Kelly."

"And we do, of course, have a warrant to search the premises," Alex said.

"We?" Elisabeth responded. "*We* have a warrant – ?"

"A figure of speech," Alex said. "But the news *is* alarming, I'm afraid."

Elisabeth saw a man walking towards her along the hallway that led to the bedroom. Stepping backwards, she reached behind and held fast to the glass knob of the front door.

Mister Tompkins, entering the kitchen, bowed slightly. "Good afternoon, Miss Rofman," he said. "I did not mean to alarm you. I regret the cause of my presence in your father's home."

Pretending confusion, Elisabeth turned to Alex. "Please, Alex," she said. "*Please?* Perhaps I – I do feel dizzy – yes – so please just tell me what you came to tell me."

"I'm afraid we now have two missing persons in our family," Alex said. "Daniel has run away from the Home."

"I'll ask you not to speak of *our* family," Elisabeth said.

"I'm not certain you heard what I said," Alex said. "Daniel has run away from the Home. This happened sometime on Sunday, following your visit, and he has not yet been found."

"Yes," Elisabeth said calmly. "Yes – thank you, gentlemen. I appreciate the information – and the esteemed delegation that has come to give it to me – but now that you've performed your duties, I'll ask you again to please leave."

Alex turned to Detective Kelly. "I was afraid she might react this way – that the news would induce a state of shock."

Alex reached towards Elisabeth, to take her by the arm and guide her to a chair.

Elisabeth backed away. "You say he left the Home on Sunday," she said. "This is Thursday. Why did you wait four days to give me the news?"

"We had hoped to find him quickly, as we did the first time he ran away," Mister Tompkins said. "We preferred, of course, not to alarm you unduly. Doctor Ogilvie and Doctor Landau had – and have – every confidence that we will soon locate your son."

"I am outraged," Elisabeth said, and then, more softly, tears welling in her eyes. "I am his mother after all."

Elisabeth sat in the chair that Detective Kelly held out for her.

"I know this news must come as a shock," Detective Kelly said, sitting down across from her. "Still, to help us in our search for your son, I'd like to talk with you about your visit with him this past Sunday."

"Of course," Elisabeth said. "In truth, when I saw you both here, I feared something like this – I had a premonition – but tell me what you know – what you want to know . . . ."

Elisabeth covered her eyes with her hands, and when Alex put a hand on her shoulder, feigning helplessness, she did not push it away. She looked up at Alex. "What are we to do?" she asked.

Alex gestured to Detective Kelly, who spoke in a low, even voice: "We're trained to give bad news gently," he said. "But in my view, ma'am, no matter what we do, there's not much help for these things."

"The weather was fierce on Sunday," Elisabeth said. "I remember that. If Daniel were to become marooned . . . ."

"We're in close touch with the authorities in Maryland," Detective Kelly said, a light Irish brogue in his voice. "What we know is that Daniel made his way through the woods that surround the Home, and – no small feat – climbed the iron fence. Apparently he's a strong and agile young man. So far we've been able to trace his movements to the point at which he left the grounds, and we've had the grounds searched thoroughly, of course. But after that we're pretty much in the dark. We believe he may try – may already have tried – to follow you, which is why we're here, and why your assistance – anything you can tell us about your visit – will be helpful."

"He ran away last week also," Elisabeth said. "After his father's visit."

"We know that," Detective Kelly said.

He nodded to Mister Tompkins, who handed him a large black leather satchel, from which he took out a small paper bag. He opened it and held it in front of Elisabeth so that she could see the stained underpants inside the bag.

"Those are Daniel's," Elisabeth said. "During our visit, he was very embarrassed – he didn't want the other children to make fun of him, so he asked me to take them home and wash them."

"Mister Tompkins informs me that Daniel continues to soil himself regularly," Alex said.

"True," Mister Tompkins said. "Daniel will sometimes, while engaged in a solitary activity, sit in a soiled condition without apparent awareness of what he has done until one of the staff, often summoned by one of our children, calls attention to the problem."

"And what about this – ?" Detective Kelly asked, taking a foot-long tube of papers from the satchel. He removed a rubber band, flattened the papers and showed Elisabeth five drawings, one at a time. "Doctor Landau believes your son made these. We found them here in the bedroom."

Elisabeth looked at the drawings Daniel had made while in Doctor Bloch's apartment: battle scenes of soldiers and sailors, airplanes and tanks, PT boats and submarines, and – her favorite – a cutaway drawing of a soldier's stomach, a bayonet protruding, the soldier's intestines uncoiling from the wound.

Elisabeth smiled. "They certainly are not *my* drawings," she said. "Or have you – ?"

She felt her heart lurch.

"My drawings!" she exclaimed, and moved towards the bedroom. Detective Kelly stepped in front of her and held her by the arm.

"Let me go," she said.

"Where are you going?"

"Where am I *going*?" Elisabeth replied. "To see if – " She stopped. "This is my home, and I don't see why – "

"*Your* home?" Alex said. "I thought it was your father's."

"A figure of speech," Elisabeth said.

"I found these drawings and the underpants in this apartment, and I understand you've been staying here," Detective Kelly said. "So it seemed logical to ask if your son's been here with you."

"Don't be ridiculous," Elisabeth said. She glanced at Alex, who, an elbow on the kitchen counter and his chin propped on his hand, was smiling at her. She turned away quickly, and noticed, despite the snow and slush outside, that the kitchen floor was spotless. She looked at Alex's feet, and then at Detective Kelly's. Both men were wearing boots.

"I had thought," she said to Detective Kelly, "that when I left Daniel's father, I would no longer be required to have to undergo these kinds of veiled accusations."

"I make no accusations, ma'am," Detective Kelly said. "But I found these pictures here, and so I have to ask the obvious questions. It's my job."

"Of course they're Daniel's," Elisabeth said. "He gave them to me for safekeeping when I visited him on Sunday. Now if you'll let go of me, I want to see about *my* drawings."

"I'll go with you," Detective Kelly said. "There are several pictures I'd like you to explain."

"Questioning people this way may be your job," Elisabeth said, moving towards the bedroom. "It was my husband's hobby."

"Oh please, Elisabeth," Alex said. "There's no need for this kind of nonsense now. Our son is *missing*, can't you understand? He may be in danger."

"Or maybe – " she began, knowing she was taking a chance to talk this way, but believing her very hostility would make her innocence concerning Daniel's whereabouts more credible " – maybe, once he discovered what was being planned for him, he decided to remove himself *from* danger."

"This isn't the time to argue about that," Alex said. "What's important is that Daniel has run away, and it is mid-winter, and we both know that he is the least fit of young men to survive on his own. Unless – "

"Unless what – ?"

" – unless you're not worried because you know he's safe," Detective Kelly said.

Elisabeth looked around the bedroom. Her portfolio, on the table, had been opened, its strings untied.

"You two work well together," she said. "Having lived with Alex for a time, your line of questioning, Detective, is familiar."

Alex approached and, one hand on his head, to hold his *yarmulke* in place, he began shouting: "Daniel has run away from the Home! Can you *hear* what I'm saying? Can you *understand* the gravity of the situation?"

"'Heredity, like gravity, has its own laws,'" Elisabeth said calmly. She turned to Detective Kelly. "That's one of Doctor Landau's favorite aphorisms – it's from Zola."

Elisabeth felt Detective Kelly relax his grip, and she chose this moment to dig her nails into the back of his hand.

He cried out, and let go.

"Since I've already seen Daniel's drawings, I'll now see about my own," Elisabeth said. "Then I want to ask *you* some questions, Detective, about Daniel *and* my father – questions I hope will prove more useful than accusatory. It doesn't serve any of us – " she nodded towards Alex " – to become hysterical at a time like this."

"You've drawn blood," Detective Kelly said, his brogue suddenly more pronounced.

"So I have," Elisabeth said. "You would do well to see to your hand. As Doctor Landau can confirm – and as you can see

– have already seen in your search – I work with cadavers."

Elisabeth gestured to the jar of formaldehyde on the floor beneath the drawing table, a jar in which two children's hearts lay.

She opened her portfolio, and began examining the drawings one at a time to see if any were missing, or if there were marks – dirt, oil from fingertips – that needed attention.

"The drawings are remarkable," Alex said. "You've become quite accomplished."

Elisabeth said nothing.

"But this one – the man going through a forest – this is the one I believe Detective Kelly was most interested in," Alex said.

"Yes," Detective Kelly said, returning from the bathroom, a handkerchief wrapped around his hand. "Is this a picture of your son?"

"It's a picture of my father," Elisabeth replied, and for the first time since she had entered the apartment, she felt her body relax, her heart ease. "It pleases me that you see the resemblance. But it's my father, the way I imagined him walking through a forest in Poland in the year 1893."

❖ ❖ ❖

I've never seen you like this," Alex said to Elisabeth when they were alone.

"That's true."

His coat draped over his left arm, Alex stood by the kitchen door.

"And what a wonderful project – recreating your father's life in drawings – imagining what his journey, from the Old Country to the New, was like. I am impressed."

"Good," Elisabeth said.

"The drawing of the infected hand – septicemia, yes? – is the finest thing I've ever seen of yours. It's your father's hand, I assume."

"Yes," Elisabeth said, "and I trust that Mister Kelly won't think I was engaging in some kind of artistic prophecy."

"I trust not," Alex said, without smiling. Then: "I do recall the scar on your father's palm, though you never talked to me about its source. So tell me now – who treated it, and how was it that the hand was saved?"

"It was his daughter who saved his hand," Elisabeth said.

"But you were a child then."

"Was I?"

"Oh Elisabeth – can you please stop playing these games with me? I am truly impressed with what you've done here – your achievement. In truth, I'm impressed with you, Elisabeth – with who you are, with who you've become." When Elisabeth said nothing, Alex continued: "And it seems to me, given Daniel's disappearance, that at a time like this we need to be able to call upon one another – to count upon one another, you and I – for *his* sake. I *am* truly concerned about him, yet you seem not to believe me, and to take delight in mocking my concern."

"Oh, I believe you, Alex. Despite my what – my antic disposition? – I'm worried too. Maybe this is the way I cover up – my way of protecting myself from reality, from pain. Who knows? Of course I'm worried, and I'll do anything to help, if only someone will tell me what to do that might prove useful."

"Then you'll call me or Detective Kelly first thing if you learn anything – if you recall anything – even if it seems of no consequence?"

"Of course," Elisabeth said. "But my father *has* no phone. He didn't believe in phones."

"I remember," Alex said.

"If I think of anything, though – I do admit I was in shock, seeing you and the other two men here – I'll go downstairs and telephone from the Square."

"Thank you," Alex said. "And of course, the instant I have any news, I'll find a way to let you know. You'll be staying here, yes?"

"Yes."

"But tell me more about your father's hand. *You* performed the surgery – ?"

"It was hardly surgery," Elisabeth said. "It started with a blister – from work: he'd been shoveling all day – something he hadn't done for a while – in broiling weather, and the blister became infected, and then, though he soaked it each night and applied ointments, the hand kept puffing up. It was like a magic show – his fingers were like a clown's – like colored balloons, and inflating to twice their size, and then beginning to turn colors: red, blue, yellow, green."

"And you cut him?"

"I watched the band of color move down from his hand, past his wrist and towards the elbow, and then one evening – a Sunday, I believe – he told me we didn't have either time or choice."

"Of course not," Alex said.

"He sharpened a knife, washed his hand and put it on a wooden board. He drank some whiskey, drew a line on his palm with one of my drawing pencils – purple, I recall – that smudged because his palm was still wet, and told me not to be afraid and to cut deeply and quickly along the line. I was eight years old and, in truth, I wasn't frightened somehow."

"Not at all?"

"I don't believe so. What I recall is that I was *fascinated* – an intimation of my vocation? – and eager to see what was going on below the skin." Elisabeth shrugged. "At least that's the way I remember what happened, or the way I choose to remember. I did as he said, and when I made the cut – the knife went in with surprising ease, as if into a ripe melon – what was below spurted into the air – a geyser-like stream of it – some of it splashing onto my blouse."

"And then?"

"Then he howled and drank more whiskey," Elisabeth said.

"I think he cursed me too, but I didn't understand the words – they were probably in Polish – and he said he was sorry – not for the cursing, but for what he'd asked me to do. He spread the cut open, squeezed out more of the infected matter, poured something into the wound, took a roll of gauze and an awl, and began to stuff a long ribbon of the gauze into the wound with the awl. Every night for a while, when he'd pull the gauze out, all covered with pus and blood, I'd be astonished to see that so much of it could fit inside the hand. In my memory it was several feet long."

"He was very fortunate, as you must realize now."

"What he was afraid of, of course, was that he might lose his hand, and if he lost his hand, he'd lose his job, and if he lost his job, how would he support the two of us?" Elisabeth paused. "Most of all, I realize now, he was afraid of losing me."

Alex nodded. "I recall your telling me that he lived, perpetually, in fear of the courts."

"He was afraid they'd separate us – that they'd take me away from him because he'd be deemed incompetent – incompetent because he was indigent. He'd be declared a destitute one-armed Jew. And there was also the fact that he wasn't a citizen yet – he didn't become naturalized until after America entered the war – so his fears weren't irrational."

"The immigration service has never been fond of Jews," Alex said.

Elisabeth felt the room turn slightly, as though she'd been drinking champagne without having first eaten. She was enjoying telling the story to Alex – eliciting his admiration and astonishment, sensing his discomfort – more than was good for her, she knew.

"So tell me," she asked, "how is your family?"

"They're fine, and I thank you for asking. The little one, Noah, has a cold – but nothing serious, and – I should have mentioned it before – Sonya sends her warm regards, of course, and her sympathy, given what you're going through. And tomorrow – I know I've asked you before, and said that you have a standing invitation with us – still, I extend the invitation again, for you to join us in the evening for the Sabbath meal. Perhaps, by then, we will have found Daniel and we can celebrate our reunion. Whether yes or no, it would be good for us to be together at a time like this."

"I think not," Elisabeth said. She took two steps towards Alex, reached past him, turned the doorknob, and stepped away. Alex was only a few inches from her, and she noticed that his lower lip was trembling slightly. For a brief instant she found herself wishing he might tell her what a beautiful and fascinating woman she was – that he would try to embrace her – to kiss her? – so that she would have the chance to reject him.

Alex stepped into the hallway. In a single swift gesture, he removed his *yarmulke* and replaced it with a round fur hat.

"I don't believe you," he said.

"Excuse me?"

"I don't believe you," Alex said again. "I believe you know where Daniel is."

❖ ❖ ❖

Elisabeth covered the drawing – a child's heart in which the ductus arteriosis, necessary to channel blood from the heart to the lungs, was nearly obliterated – tacking tissue to the heavy cardboard to which she had previously tacked the drawing paper. She had only to add lettering, for the names of things, work in some additional highlights, and she would be able to send the drawing to Baltimore.

She picked up the sketches that had so intrigued Alex, and placed them on the table. Instead of looking at them, however, she first looked out the window so that, thinking of her father, she would be able to imagine, beyond the apartment houses across the street – as in a painting – fields, houses, roads, and farmland she had never seen. On a hazy day, she knew, distant hills and trees would appear less distinct and detailed, with softer contrasts. They would also be suffused with nearly indistinct tones of blue. Were she to paint the scene she was looking at through the window, she would reserve the darker darks and lighter lights for objects nearer the eye – the table, the buildings across the street, the telephone poles, the window itself.

What Professor Brödel had taught her – what proved so wonderfully useful now, though in reverse – was how to apply landscape technique to medical illustration: how to view the open cavity of the body as if one were viewing a natural scene, and to do so as if from an aerial perspective – as if there were, in this human landscape, even when discrete body parts touched one another, distinct and changeable atmospheres in which these parts lived. In her cutaway drawing of the child's heart, she cast slight shadows over the nearer objects – the tubular openings of the carotid, subclavian, and pulmonary arteries, and of the edges of the pericardial sac that encased the heart – so that the middle distance, where she had built up contrasting tones of dark and light, and where, fatally, the ductus was gone, became the focal point.

She would do the same with her drawings of subway trains, tunnels, sewers, and caves. She recalled again – though she had not made this connection before – that more than thirty years ago she had thought of the deep trenches in which her father worked as wounds that had been cut into the body of the earth where he and the other workers spent their days.

Since her return from Baltimore, she had made more than two dozen pencil sketches – mostly quick line drawings, without much shading and in no particular order – of empty tunnels, of city streets carved open, of sewers and water mains and gas mains, and of subway lines and stations seen in various stages of construction and from various perspectives: from the street above, before the hollows in the ground had been covered over, and from below, where the workers were. She had sketched two of the rooms that had been hers – alcoves of timbers and rock where she drew pictures and played house – and had shown them to Daniel. She made one sketch of a tunnel with, on the same page, a cutaway drawing that revealed, as in the inset for the illustration she was preparing for Doctor Taussig, wirings and duct work of an electrical system like those her father had worked on.

It was when she was drawing this picture that she had remembered her father's infected hand: the complex web of tendons, nerves, veins, cartilage, and muscle – and of the time, on the way home from work, he had shown her the new blisters that came from shoveling rocks and dirt all day. All the blisters except for one, an eighth of an inch below the little finger of his right hand, had healed swiftly.

Elisabeth stared at the drawing, and then at her own hands, as if, by staring long enough, the answer to the familiar question – how and when did I do this? – might reveal itself.

Then the other question was there: What was she going to do about Daniel?

She knew that Detective Kelly or one of his men would now be following her, and that even if she stayed away from Doctor Bloch's apartment for a while, they were bound to find out about him. Daniel would be expecting her, and she had to see him, or find a way to explain her absence without making him panic. But how much could she ask of Doctor Bloch, she wondered.

Her questions to Detective Kelly had been direct: What was being done to locate her father? What about the man who'd been seen wandering in the subway tunnels – had anyone seen him again? Had anyone, in and around Bantra, seen Daniel, or a boy who resembled him? Had the police checked trains and buses, or talked with bus drivers and train conductors . . . ?

Without apologizing, she had let Alex and Detective Kelly know that she had told Daniel about the surgery being planned for him, and that she had promised him she would do everything in her power to stop it from happening. She told them what she had told Doctor Ogilvie – that she had retained legal counsel, and she also told them that she had told Daniel about her own father's disappearance, and that until her father was found, she was going to live in his apartment.

Though she had pretended surprise at Alex's parting remark – that he believed she knew where Daniel was – the remark had not upset her. Despite his confident manner, Alex could not be sure he was right. More important, she counted on the fact that Daniel's safety would be his primary concern. What she wanted to say to him, and in a way she might have done years before, was this: Don't you see that a mother and a father are, like our memories of them when they're gone, illusions, and that there's no protection? Don't you see that there's only love and worry?

Within a day, Alex would be observing the Sabbath, and so, while Detective Kelly and others might continue the search for Daniel, for a twenty-four hour period – from sundown Friday until sundown Saturday – he wouldn't be with them. He would spend the day in prayer and in study, in synagogue and at home, and this would give Elisabeth time to figure out what it was she would do next.

For the moment, she would stay on in her father's apartment and work at her drawings, and when she was done, she would telephone Doctor Bloch and speak with him and with Daniel. She looked through her sketches and picked up one she had been making of the subway system's power house. She had visited the power house with her father several times, and had been able to impress her teacher and classmates with her drawings of it, and with the fact her father had given her – that, with its six enormous chimneys, all in a row, that took up an entire city block – it lay between West 58th and West 59th Streets, and 10th and 11th Avenues – this plant was capable of generating more electrical power than any facility ever built in the history of the world.

The day before, she had completed the sketch on the right side of a sheet – as she would have done for a medical illustration – and now she folded the sheet in half and pressed down with her thumbnail on the reverse side of the paper, rubbing firmly but not so firmly that she created heat, towards the free border. When she opened the paper and looked at the transfer, the reversal – what had been to the left was now to the right, and what had been to the right was now to the left – made the sketch appear to be a new drawing altogether.

She went over a few of the lighter lines with carbon pencil, corrected the angle of one of the chimneys – the reversal, as with anatomical drawings, allowed her to see mistakes of proportion, misleading contours, or errors of scale – and then, turning the sketch over, she marked a horizontal line on the reverse of this negative and re-transferred the sketch to a fresh sheet of paper.

She recalled the one time her father had arranged a visit for her inside the power house, and how impossible it had seemed, looking up at the gigantic turbines and pumping apparatuses – at engines, pipes, alternators, boilers – that the six brick chimneys, rising from the roof of the building, could be higher than the machinery inside the building. Outside, the chimneys themselves were square at their base, and then octagonal, after which, about fifty feet in the air, they became circular. Each chimney had served two of the power house's twelve boilers, and each had risen directly from the roof – there were no brickwork supports within the power house – to a height of more than two hundred feet.

She laid the sketch on her father's bed, and picked up the drawing of the man in the forest. The man, his face hidden from view, was hunched over from the weight of a large sack he carried on his back. Around him trees were bare, the moon and stars bright, yet the man, laboring under his load, walked in shadows. Ahead of him was a hill heavy with boulders, and there was no snow, and no road. In the top left corner of the picture,

Elisabeth now drew a narrow horizontal box, and in this box she penciled in words: **SOMEWHERE IN POLAND, 1893.**

Along the curve of the man's near shoulder she picked out tiny patches of pure white with her scratcher blade, after which she made more carbon dust – what Professor Brödel called 'the sauce' – and, with a sable brush, began layering in soft, dark tones that gave shape and weight to the man's torso. She worked on, without thoughts of Daniel or Alex, Detective Kelly, Mister Tompkins, or Doctor Bloch, and without thoughts of food – she was never hungry while she worked, though she could be ravenous afterwards – and she was soon pleased to see that even though the near and far objects – trees, rocks, stars – were bolder and more distinct than the figure of the man, and even though the man, in shadows, seemed almost to merge with the landscape, *he* was what your eye was immediately drawn to. What was soft, subdued, and nearly lost, by the very fact of being so, seemed to reverse the usual effect and to give the man's figure a stark quality she hadn't expected to see.

So: it wasn't the landscape of a place she had or hadn't ever seen, in Poland or in America, that she wanted to sketch, she realized, but the landscape of her father's mind. Of course. To enter his mind, and thereby to imagine what he might have thought and felt on the journey he took before she was born, and on all the days and nights of his life since then, served not only to make him a presence at her side once again, but served more palpably to make possible the pleasure of entering worlds that were, in prospect – in their topography and their weather, in their dangers and joys – as exquisite as they were mysterious.

Because the drawing was not the one she had intended to draw, it seemed much better than any drawing she would have believed herself capable of, and so, encouraged by what she had done, she found herself imagining other drawings of her father that might follow from this one – on the coast of the Black Sea, on a ship in the Atlantic, on the streets of New York. In one of the drawings, she saw, her father was standing beside her mother, and by the light in his eyes it was clear that he was a happy young man, and when Elisabeth saw this she also saw what she would do next.

She put on her coat and left the apartment. In Westchester Square, she went into a candy store and, in the phone booth at the rear, she telephoned Doctor Bloch and invited him to go to Alex's home for dinner with her the following night. But what about Daniel? he asked. Doctor Bloch was not to say *anything* to Daniel, she said. When they were together – he should call for her at her father's apartment at four-thirty so they could arrive at Doctor Landau's before sundown – she would explain everything. In the meantime, she thanked him for caring for Daniel, and asked him to put Daniel on the phone. She wanted to explain to her son that she and Doctor Bloch would be going to an early dinner together the following evening – that she wouldn't be able to see him during the day on Friday due to her work schedule, but that if he were still awake when she and Doctor Bloch came home from dinner, she would see him then.

NINE

From the Journal of Doctor Eduard Bloch
December 20, 1940

After Miss Rofman informed her former husband, Doctor Landau, whom I met for the first time yesterday evening, when we celebrated a Sabbath meal in his home, that I had, when a young physician, been Adolf Hitler's doctor, he responded by interrogating me in a most aggressive manner, so as to make me feel that my experience of more than three decades ago was somehow a personal affront to him.

Since I was a dinner guest in his home – his wife and children were at the table with us – I responded by offering factual information concerning Hitler and his family during the years in which I knew them. But the more calmly I spoke – relating, for example, the story of Frau Hitler's death – the more intense did Doctor Landau's hostility become. Miss Rofman, sensing the effort it was taking for me to remain civil, came to my aid, stating that, as far as she knew, I did not count among my diagnostic skills the ability to foretell a patient's *political* future, and adding quickly, before Doctor Landau could reply in kind, that I was writing a memoir about this period of my life.

I corrected her by saying that what I was writing was not a memoir in the true sense of that word, since what I was writing was not primarily about me, but simply my recollections of the young Adolf Hitler as I knew him, and I added that if Doctor Landau wished, I could, when I was done, present him with a copy of what I had written.

Lest Doctor Landau think I was oblivious to the danger Hitler and Germany presented, much less apologetic for the vile acts the German nation had been committing against our own people, I paraphrased for him remarks I recalled from Heinrich Heine, remarks made when he was living in exile in France, about how at some time in the future a drama would be enacted in Germany compared to which the French revolution would seem a harmless idyll.

I made these remarks in German, in part to shield the Landau children from such dark considerations, and I also recited, from memory, the well-known passage wherein Heine declares that though the German thunder may roll slowly at first, still it will come, and when we hear it roar, as it has never roared before in the history of the world, we will know that this thunder has reached its target. When I went on to say that I feared we were living in a time in which Heine's prophecy was coming true, I saw that, like a schoolboy eager to show his teacher that he agreed with him, Doctor Landau was nodding vigorously.

Heine, he exclaimed, was his favorite author – and did I know that Heine was also Albert Einstein's favorite author? I did, I answered, and at this point Doctor Landau raised his glass and made an extravagant toast to Einstein and to Heine, after which he toasted me, remarking on the fact that I too, like Heine and Einstein, was in exile from a Germany I doubtless loved.

I am, I said, Austrian.

Ah yes, he said, but is not the recent transformation taking place in the German nation – of which your nation is now part – the cause of a certain sadness I sense in you?

Whereupon, having posed this question – to which I nodded my assent – he went on to state that it was Heine's genius to understand that love of freedom is a dungeon flower. For just as we recognize spring's inner essence first in winter, so it is that one most intensely recognizes freedom's worth in prison. Just so did love for the German fatherland arise at Germany's frontier, and – more acutely, he wrote – did it arise from a place of exile where, perforce, one had to gaze helplessly upon Germany's misfortune.

Heine's words provoked in me an impulse to tell Doctor Landau of my desire to write to Hitler – to try to persuade him of the mistake he was making, and of all that we, his Jewish compatriots, could do to make Germany – a Germany in which Austria was a free and independent entity – a great and noble nation. Having been born less than a century ago, Germany was a child among nations, while we, the Jews, had a long, rich history from which our fellow citizens might draw – and were, moreover, in possession – witness Heine and Einstein! – of the culture and the mental powers that could bring true glory to Germany. We were a miniscule part of the German nation, to be sure – less than one percent of its population – yet deemed so powerful that *all* the evils that beset Germany were being attributed to us.

If, therefore, counting on the regard I believed he still felt toward me, I were able to have Hitler's attention for a short while, perhaps I might convince him that within this inordinate power he ascribed to us was a force that could be used for the good of the German people. Before I could formulate such thoughts in any coherent way, however, Doctor Landau asked if I knew Doctor Einstein personally.

I said that I did not, whereupon Miss Rofman asked Doctor Landau if he was familiar with Doctor Einstein's views on war – of how Doctor Einstein believed that the psychological roots of war were biologically founded in the aggressive character of the male animal.

Yes, Doctor Landau said, and added that in Doctor Einstein's view it was patriotism that was the source of *all* evil. He then asked if I agreed with such notions, as surely, he knew, Elisabeth did, and when I said that in fact I did, for I had experienced war first-hand, he said that like Doctor Einstein and Elisabeth, I was, in such matters, deluded by a touching but naïve idealism.

War, Doctor Landau declared, quoting Bismarck, is the natural state of mankind, whereupon he launched into a disquisition on the Jewish view of war, and of the Almighty. Although Elisabeth had warned me that Doctor Landau was prone to hold forth in these ways, and in an often tiresome manner, I found his views of great interest.

For a Jew to believe in the notion of an omnipotent God who had chosen us for good and worthy ends was quite foolish, Doctor Landau declared, the prime example being the destruction of the Holy Temple, which our God had allowed to occur not once, but twice. And for a Jew to believe in loving and forgiving our enemies was equally absurd. Forget Mister Hitler for the moment, Doctor Landau said, and look at the history of Christianity. Christianity had posited itself as the religion of love, which by inference had made us, for nearly two millennia, the religion of hate. But when, before or after Christ, had love and forgiveness ever triumphed? Forget the Crusades, the Inquisition, and the Expulsions, but consider, to begin with, our own myths. God forgave us the building of the golden calf in the desert, for example, but not before He had first killed some five or six thousand of our worshippers.

What our God is interested in was ever the same, Doctor Landau stated.

And what is that? I asked.

Blood, he replied, at which point Sonya, Doctor Landau's wife, stood and declared that it was time to put the children to bed.

But we haven't *finished*, Noah, the youngest child, said.

Hearing his son's protest, Doctor Landau's manner softened. He told Noah that we would *all* chant the *Birchat Hamazon* – the blessings after the meal – but only at the conclusion of our discussion. In the meantime, the children were at liberty to leave the table. He would call them back when it was time for dessert, and for the prayers that would end the meal.

Sonya, an attractive woman who is a good deal younger than Doctor Landau – and by an amount, I found myself noting, at least equal to the distance in years between myself and Miss Rofman – yet one whose steadfast gaze had already told me that, like Miss Rofman, she was not a woman whose essential mode was one of submissiveness – now addressed her husband in German, calling him a thoughtless *Hehrkopf* – a numbskull – yet doing so with an ice-cold, bewitching smile. She left with the children, and as she did, Miss Rofman declared that she too would take her leave. The eldest child, Hannah, seeing Miss Rofman stand, went to her and offered her hand, which Miss Rofman took.

As soon as the women and children were gone, Doctor Landau poured more wine for the two of us, and said that although he had not calculated his remarks in order to encourage the women to leave us alone, still he was glad his words had had this effect, for he had been hoping to have a word with me privately about Daniel and Miss Rofman.

But before he came to that, he trusted I would allow him to finish the discussion we had been engaged in, and he quoted from the *Book of Leviticus* the passage in which God, after stating that the life of the flesh is in the blood, and that He has given blood to us upon the altar, declares that He has done so in order that we might, with blood, make atonement for our souls.

This was, of course, Doctor Landau stated, one of the sources of certain laws concerning the eating of meat – the Jewish laws of *kashruth* – and of the specific adjuration to drain all blood from animals that were to be eaten.

Isn't it obvious, though, he said then, leaning toward me, that God forbade us eating the blood of animals because He wanted to reserve this to Himself? And in this, was our God so different from other Gods of the time, all of whom, to appease their wrath and satisfy their appetites, demanded the ritual slaying of first-born males?

I am not well versed in such matters, I said.

All religions begin in sacrifice, Doctor Landau went on. We feed them so that they might feed us, yes? Even Jesus himself, you see, is part of this – a first-born son sacrificed to appease the vanity of a bloodthirsty God. And it is much the same with the sacrifice demanded of the father of us all – Abraham, the first Jew – when God tells him to take his beloved son, Isaac, to the mountains, and to bind him, and to offer him as a sacrifice.

As soon as Doctor Landau said this, what had been a latent suspicion – that all his words were mere preface to his true subject – became patent knowledge. I started to protest – found myself on the point of asking if Daniel too was to be sacrificed – when Doctor Landau put up a hand, indicating I should wait before speaking, and then recited words in Hebrew, which words, when he translated them, were familiar enough: God's warning to the Children of Israel that, since the life of all flesh was in the blood, they eat no blood of flesh lest, eternally, they be cut off from God.

Why are you telling me these things? I asked.

Because, he said, I see that you have influence with Elisabeth, and therefore can be of help concerning Daniel. I trust you will hear me out.

He spoke softly now, his voice free of rant and of vanity. It was as if all the bombast that had preceded these few simple sentences had been for show – to get my attention, to allow us this private moment, to empty his own mind of everything extraneous.

Please, I said, indicating by this single word that he might tell me what he wanted to tell me.

You are a father, yes?

Yes.

Then I speak to you father to father and man to man, he said. But you have also become close with Elisabeth, whose charms, it is clear, have not been lost on you.

We are friends, I said.

Doctor Landau raised his eyebrows in a manner that, though indicating skepticism, was in no way supercilious. Of course, he said. Elisabeth is a most unique and loving woman, one endowed with a good and true heart. Like you, she is also an idealist – yet when it comes to our son, she is as fierce, shrewd, and manipulative a woman as exists on the face of this earth. There is nothing she will not do if she believes what she is doing is for the benefit and protection of Daniel.

Of course, I said. She is his mother.

But in her inordinate passion, Doctor Landau continued, she is greatly deluded and capable of enormous harm.

I do not understand, I said.

Perhaps not, Doctor Landau said. As we might put it were we speaking in Yiddish: There are mothers… and then there are mothers. And Elisabeth is, or rather, is obsessed with becoming, the mother she never had.

We all have mothers, I said.

Doctor Landau laughed. True enough, Doctor Bloch, he said. True enough. Just so with Mister Hitler, as you have begun to explain, yes?

I did not laugh with him, but instead found myself thinking, for the first time since my arrival in his home, of the news with which Elisabeth had greeted me when I had called upon her a few hours earlier.

I have received news of my father! she exclaimed as soon as I entered the apartment, and so happy was she to give me this news that she embraced me and held me close, her cheek against mine. But the news, she quickly explained, had come in the most surprising way.

This is what happened: She had returned home after sending off several sketches to Baltimore, only to enter the bedroom and find that there was a note on top of her drawings. She assumed at first that either Detective Kelly or Mister Tompkins had intruded upon her again, but then saw that the note was in her father's handwriting.

In it he apologized for his delay in writing – he had had to attend to matters of health – said that he liked the new drawings very much, and that she was not to worry about him.

When I was a girl, she told me, and he left for work before I awoke, he would often leave notes for me – they might be in my school lunchbox, or under my pillow, or in the cookie jar, or in the icebox. It was a game we played: I left drawings, he left notes. And so when I read his note, I was delighted – worried about his health, of course – but mostly delighted. Clearly, she said, he had waited to write until he could truthfully state that there was no cause for concern.

Her face, while telling me this, was unusually flushed, her cheeks alive with a ruddy, plum-like color, and then suddenly she let go of my hand and seemed, inwardly, to collapse.

And I was very frightened, she said. She turned away from me at this point and, without explanation, put a napkin over her head, lit two candles, covered her eyes with her hands, chanted a blessing in Hebrew, after which, taking her hands away from her face and seeing the candles lit – as if, magically, someone else had performed this act – she wished me a good Sabbath, and placed soft kisses on each of my cheeks. Next, and with an admirable economy of movement, she removed the candles from the counter to the sink, lifted her coat from the back of the kitchen chair, and handed it to me.

While I helped her on with her coat, she inquired about Daniel. I told her that Daniel had seemed quite calm – busy with his own drawings, and in the composition of a letter to Doctor Einstein – that he was eager to see his mother, and had several times made me promise that if he fell asleep during the evening, we were – 'absolutely absolutely' were his words – to wake him when we returned home.

Miss Rofman did not, before we left, show me the note from her father. But we were in haste, not wanting to arrive at Doctor Landau's after sundown – and, too, I did not think to ask, so startled was I by the news and, in truth, so nervous in her presence, this nervousness intensified by the embrace she had so freely given me. On the journey from her father's apartment to Doctor Landau's home, she took my arm in a firm and natural manner, and when she talked with me about her father, she would at times tug lightly on my coat-sleeve for emphasis.

May I digress for a moment? Doctor Landau asked, and quickly continued: The Sabbath, as you must be aware, is a day of rest, a day of prayer, and also a day of study. It is a day when we say to ourselves – to our family and friends, as tonight – stop! We do not concern ourselves with the rest of the world, whether for good or – as with your Mister Hitler – for evil. But we do concern ourselves with thoughts and reflections about such things as they relate to matters, often ineffable, that can be said to transcend the passing moment.

And the thoughts with me on this Sabbath, he continued, are of Daniel, for whose life I am frightened. Despite his condition and his history, Daniel remains an exceptionally bright and complex child, full of hopes and dreams not so different from those of any sensitive young man his age. I have been privy to these youthful hopes and dreams, and so I will say this to you, not to be dramatic, but to set words down on record – as you, I gather, set down your words about young Hitler – and what I say is this: that I would trade all of this – my home, my career, my wealth, my position – if I could return my son to safety.

Having said this, Doctor Landau stood and went to the fireplace. I said nothing.

But do you know what else? he said after a short while. I would not trade my wife's life, or our children's lives – or my own life! – for his. And that, you see, is the difference between me and his mother.

He came to me now, sat by my side, and covered my right hand with his own.

Elisabeth, you see, is the one who believes in blood and sacrifice, he said. I do not.

Certainly I have every hope you will find your son, and that you will find him in good health, I said. But again, I must ask why you tell me such things.

Doctor Bloch, he said, let us be honest with each other. I am certain that Elisabeth knows where Daniel is and, having met you and being able to intuit your place in her life, I suspect that you do too. It is also probable that she has helped him in his so-called escape – this adventure that has put him in such jeopardy.

He pressed down upon my hand, then spoke again: I will not attempt to *convince* you of such things. How persuade another – even when the other is the very object of one's passion – of the truth of one's words and one's heart? I love Daniel as I love no other being on earth, and I will do whatever I can to protect and save him. And I know – as surely as I know we are in this room together, and no matter what Elisabeth has said to you and no matter the fantasies that motivate her – that Daniel is in grave danger.

He is lost, I said.

No, Doctor Landau said. Not at all. He has been *seduced.* He has been seduced away from the path upon which he was moving because of his mother's obsessions, and also because her will is stronger than his.

And stronger than yours? I asked.

Oh yes, he said. Certainly. Which is, you see, why I am frightened.

At this point he lifted his hand from mine and held it in the air between us, so that I might see that his own was trembling. He returned to his side of the table.

But it is the Sabbath, and before supper I searched out a

midrash I am fond of and want to pass on to you – a parable, if you will, that lies at the heart of what I ask you to consider, and that I hope will lead you to actions that can be of assistance to my son, and perhaps, too, to his mother.

The *midrash* itself is quite short, Doctor Landau continued. It refers to one of the most disturbing tales in the Bible – the story of Abraham's first wife, Hagar, and her son, Ishmael, who was Abraham's first-born son – and speaks of the moment in which Abraham, prodded by his wife, Sarah, banishes Hagar and Ishmael, sending them into the desert without enough water to ensure their survival. The ethical questions our rabbis ask are many: how can Abraham, our patriarch, commit such a heinous act? How can Sarah, our matriarch, initiate such an awful series of events? And what are we to learn *from* the story?

What interests me above all, though, especially when I consider my son's life, is the passage in which, facing certain death in the desert, Hagar places her child under some bushes and, as the Bible tells us, walks an arrow's length away. She does this so that she will not have to watch him die.

The *midrash*? A single line from Rabbi Dosa that states, simply, that this was the first time Hagar ever released Ishmael. And by this Rabbi Dosa means to tell us that, since it was the first time she put Ishmael down, she had been carrying him around with her all of his days. And remember that Ishmael is by this time at least twelve years old.

There is, it happens, some justification for this view in the text itself, for one of the verses tells us that Abraham set all the provisions upon Hagar's shoulders along with the boy. But why, we ask, would Hagar be carrying her twelve-year-old son through the desert, and not letting him walk? And the answer, implied by our rabbi, is that she does so because she has always done so – because, that is, she has *never* put him down.

Doctor Landau paused. You will bear with me a while longer? he asked.

I nodded.

Let us consider, then, who Ishmael is. He was conceived for one reason only: to give Abraham an heir, and so provide continuity for the familial line. According to other commentaries, Hagar enjoyed her status, and bragged to Sarah, who did not have a son, that *her* son would father a great nation.

But then, as we know, a surprising thing happens. Hagar does not lose her son. An angel hears Ishmael's cries, saves him, gives him a blessing, and prophecies that he *will* become the patriarch of a great nation.

In my understanding of the story, however, this cannot happen until Hagar puts him down – until she releases him – until she sees him not as an appendage whom she must carry her whole life long, but as an independent human being with an identity of his own.

And in giving us a *midrash* about Ishmael, Rabbi Dosa is really telling us about the *Akidah* – the story of Abraham's willingness to sacrifice Isaac. Most times we read this story as symbolic and forget that while we read it, we feel not that it is a parable or mystical text, but a real story – a horrific, abhorrent, cruel tale in which a father sets out to kill his son.

And he does so, I believe – that is to say, God tells Abraham to give him up and do so – to give up the dreams and hopes of the Jewish people, for by this time Ishmael as well as Abraham's servant, Eliezer, have been rejected as possible heirs of Israel, and by this time too we know that Isaac is the miracle child of a couple that has been barren for sixty years – in order to remind him of a simple thing: that no one owns another human being.

We belong to God, however arbitrary, imperfect, and cruel He may be, and God is telling us that to worship a child – to keep him too close to us, to inhabit his life with our dreams and fears – to carry him always – is to sin, and is akin to the worshipping of idols.

By giving Ishmael back his life, and by ordering Abraham to

sacrifice his child, God is reminding us that we must be prepared to let go not only of our children, but of *all* our beloveds, whether young or old – and this, my dear Doctor Bloch, is what Daniel's mother, herself let go at far too tender an age, cannot do.

In the silence that followed, I found no words with which to reply, for, of course, anything I might have said would have betrayed the trust Daniel and Elisabeth had placed in me.

While Doctor Landau let the silence hang between us in the air of the room, and while I considered the story he had told me – more accurately put, his interpretation of the story – I found, although I did not for a moment believe that Miss Rofman meant harm to her son, that neither could I dismiss the implications of Doctor Landau's story.

The sounds of Doctor Landau's children laughing and playing on the other side of the door seemed suddenly closer, and when I saw Doctor Landau glance their way, a faint, loving smile on his lips, I tried to imagine what this home had been like when he, Daniel, and Miss Rofman had lived here together, which imaginings led to considerations of what Miss Rofman's life had been like in the years since she had left Doctor Landau and, more exactly, of what her life had been like on those evenings when she had celebrated the Sabbath alone.

Never having visited her dwelling in Baltimore, however, I could not *see* her doing this in a home that was uniquely hers, and so I found my mind wandering again – in exile from the moment I was living in? – and I was soon picturing the Berlin train station, and imagining Doctor Einstein standing there, his good friend Fritz Haber at his side. Doctor Einstein's first marriage was about to end – his wife, Mileva, had already left him – and with cause – and his two sons, whom he believed he would never see again, were on a train and were leaving. Doctor Einstein was weeping, and Haber, a great scientist in his own right, was comforting him. Without Haber at his side, Doctor Einstein later said, he would not have been able to endure the experience.

Was I to be that kind of friend to Miss Rofman?

It was at this moment that I recalled something else: that Doctor Einstein had also had a daughter, that he had been separated from his wife when the daughter was born, and that the daughter had disappeared soon after her birth, this disappearance shrouded in mystery. Had she died? Had they given her away? On this subject neither Doctor Einstein nor his former wife had ever spoken.

I am not interested in blood, Doctor Landau was saying. Elisabeth may have told you about the procedure that Doctor Ogilvie, the Director of the Institution where my son lives, has considered – *ill*-considered, in my view – for Daniel, and of course I am opposed to it. But Elisabeth chooses not to believe me. In this way, you see, she can hold on to her world-view – to the bitterness and anger that she thinks will serve Daniel just as, or so she believes, it has served her.

I cannot believe for a minute that what you say has merit, I began. Elisabeth is –

Is what? A good and loving mother? An intelligent and caring woman protecting her son? Doctor Landau laughed. Oh yes – you think you know her, don't you, Doctor Bloch? You think you do. But you do not. Believe me. And now, my friend, he said, sitting down beside me once more and gripping my arm tightly, tell me about young Hitler – tell me everything you know.

❖ ❖ ❖

As soon as Miss Rofman and I entered my apartment, I became aware of a distinct and foul odor. Its source, Miss Rofman perceived immediately, was Daniel, who, while sitting on my couch and listening to the radio, which was blasting incomprehensible shrill voices that were suffused with static, had soiled himself.

She woke Daniel by shaking his shoulder and whispering into

his ear. He mumbled something, rubbed his eyes, pushed Miss Rofman away. Then he sat up, and when she told him what to do and why – that he had had an accident, that he was to stand and to lean upon her, and that he was to go with her to the bathroom where she would wash him and change his clothes – he did what she said. Slumped over and with his arm around her shoulder, he walked with his mother to the bathroom, where they stayed for a considerable time.

It was while they were there that I found myself recalling the other occasion upon which I had seen Hitler's half-sister, Maria Anna. Perhaps it was the memory I had had a few hours before, concerning Doctor Einstein's daughter that spurred this recollection, or perhaps it was the memory of the conversation I had with Doctor Landau during which, telling him what I knew of the Hitler family, I had, on instinct, made a decision *not* to mention Maria Anna.

In any event, what I am hearing now, while Daniel and his mother are asleep in the living room – since Daniel has his own cot, I offered to sleep on my couch so that Miss Rofman could use my bed, but, like her son, she refused the offer – is Doctor Landau's voice, saying to me, as if it were a supreme confidence, that, like me, he too was a doctor and that therefore his mission in life was to *restore* life.

He said this to me in what I perceived as a disturbing non-sequitur, for I can discern nothing in what I had been saying that would logically have led to his statement. We had been talking not about Hitler's childhood, but about his present position of power and of how it had affected and might yet affect Jews. In particular, Doctor Landau wanted to know about my experience of the *Reichkristallnacht*, where mobs of hooligans, along with police and soldiers of the Reich, had murdered scores of our people, and had burned and destroyed a large amount of Jewish property – synagogues, homes, and businesses – and to what degree I believed Hitler was responsible for these events.

Although I answered Doctor Landau's questions as fully as I was able, I confess that I was at the same time preoccupied with Miss Rofman's behavior – in particular, with the impression she seemed to wish to convey to her former husband concerning the possibility that her relationship with me might be one of a romantic nature.

By this time, Doctor Landau and I were alone again – we had finished dinner and the prayers that followed dinner (I found the rituals surrounding the Sabbath meal to be surprisingly affecting, and was especially moved by the enthusiasm and wonder they elicited in the children), and Miss Rofman had accepted Sonya's invitation to accompany her while Sonya prepared the children for sleep. When Miss Rofman left the room this time, however, she stopped and whispered in my ear that we would return to my apartment very soon, and she did this loudly enough for Doctor Landau to hear her words. At the same time, and while touching the back of my hand with her own, she leaned upon me, her bosom pressed against my shoulder. Was she, I wondered, being genuine, or, more likely, was she using me in order to somehow conceal her true plans?

What I said to Doctor Landau in response to his inquiries about *Reichkristallnacht* was that there had been few incidents in Linz of the kind reported from Vienna, Berlin, and other German cities. I had become aware, of course, of the wanton destruction of Jewish life and property that followed upon Hitler's rise to power, but what I was led to believe, as were those with whom I talked about such matters, was that it was Joseph Goebbels, Hitler's Minister of Propaganda, who had encouraged the unfolding of these events. In point of fact, I noted, Hitler had publicly condemned them, although in my opinion he had done so not because he wanted to befriend Jews or bank the fires of anti-Semitism, which of course he did not, but primarily for reasons of domestic *realpolitik*.

How ask sacrifices of the German people, with all the costs

and deprivations involved in the rapid rearmament of the nation – in addition to severe food and coal shortages, longer working hours, and higher taxes, we were even commanded to save things such as empty toothpaste tubes – yet permit the gross destruction of valuable property? What could ordinary, hard-working Germans think, no matter their hatred of Jews, when they would see precious goods thrown into the streets while members of the police and Nazi Party rejoiced? Moreover, in order, perhaps, to create an image for himself as a statesman and man of peace, Hitler had several times intervened directly when the Nazi Party had plundered Jewish businesses and attacked Jews, and had publicly declared these acts illegal. More specifically, he had issued orders that the SS, upon whom he depended more than upon any other unit of his regime, was forbidden to participate in such vulgar 'demonstrations.'

Doctor Landau, who was well-informed on these matters, did not dispute my facts. Nevertheless, he told me that what I was saying was nonsense. Hitler knew of and controlled *everything* that happened in his government, he contended, especially when it pertained to Jews. Still, Doctor Landau did not criticize me for wanting, as he put it, 'to believe the best of others,' nor did he have any desire to debate matters with me. What interested him more, he said, were issues both larger: the question of evil – and smaller: Hitler's personal habits.

On the latter I could comment knowledgeably, and to his queries I offered the information that yes, it was indeed true that Hitler, despite his obvious love of the grand and theatrical ceremonies that celebrated his person and his power, remained, in his private life, a curiosity. He kept no regular working hours, slept late in the mornings, watched moving pictures virtually every evening (and favored, it was rumored, American cowboy films), and lived this way in part, I believed, because he continued, as he had when a boy, to think of himself first and last as an artist.

As to his personal habits, I could confirm the following: Hitler did not smoke (and was promulgating policies that would serve to induce our entire nation to cease smoking), he did not drink alcoholic beverages (not even, to celebrate military victories, champagne), he did not eat meat (he preferred vegetables and greens, due in part to his ongoing stomach problems and what appears to have become a morbid fear of cancer), and he had never, as far as I knew, courted women or been comfortable with them in intimate settings (though he could affect gallantry on public occasions). This strange mixture in him of great public self-confidence, monk-like asceticism, artistic yearnings, and childlike fears – compensated for by his famously ferocious 'mad dog' temper – was, I agreed, curious, but more curious, from my perspective – explicable perhaps, but still unfathomable – was that the man he was had metamorphosed from the quiet, well-mannered boy I had known.

It was my saying this to Doctor Landau – thoughts hardly original or profound, that brought to mind Maria Anna, and that called up from memory the second, and last time I saw her. It was, I realize now, because I believed mentioning Maria Anna's existence might bring our conversation back to Daniel in ways for which I felt ill-prepared, that, earlier in the day, I had chosen not to mention her to Doctor Landau.

In order, however, to hold true to my pledge to set down in writing all I know about Hitler from my personal experience of him, I will here describe what happened the second time I saw her. And because Doctor Landau will be among those to whom I will present these recollections, and therefore will learn of her, I am made conscious of a curiosity in my own behavior I had not previously noticed: of how wary I often am of saying certain things aloud to others, yet of how safe I feel when I am writing these same things down on paper.

The difference as to why this is so would seem fairly obvious: much as children fear the dark, so I fear the unknown, and, in particular, the thoughts and feelings that an *unedited* conversation

– some idle remark! – might evoke. Such a tendency to what has become a new and doubtless excessively ruminative habit of introspection was unknown to me before I met Miss Rofman and embarked on this enterprise. And here again I am put in mind of remarks made by Doctor Einstein, for just as he found that his love of science could lift him from the vale of tears that was his life, and transport him to quiet spheres – impersonal and without rebuke and complaint – and just as he has often talked of the tension that exists in his life between the need for solitude and the desire for companionship, so do I find that I have come to take great and singular pleasure from setting down my thoughts and recollections in solitude, and that I do so in a way that I like to imagine is not unlike the way Doctor Einstein takes his solitary scientific pleasures.

It is thus, for example, less confusing, and more gratifying, for me to record the way in which Doctor Landau talked about Miss Rofman than it was for me to hear the words themselves.

You should know, Doctor Landau had whispered in a conspiratorial way shortly before our departure – Sonya was across the hallway helping Miss Rofman on with her coat – that Elisabeth has always had a special fondness for doctors. When I did not respond, he went on to say that Miss Rofman had had a penchant for doctors in the way some women had a penchant for violinists or hunchbacks.

Although his remark was surely intended to unnerve me, it did not succeed, and it did not succeed because even in that moment I knew that I would, before the day ended, have occasion to reconsider the moment we were experiencing. More than this, I sensed even then some of the pleasure it would give me, as now, to set down the incident and to review it in the privacy of my imagination, after which I would be able to choose what, of these writings, I will show to others, and what I will not.

Just so, then, am I remembering Maria Anna, as she looked on an early autumn afternoon – this was in the year 1919, several months after the Armistice had been signed at Versailles – when I was walking in the forest to the north of Linz. It was a Thursday afternoon, the one afternoon of the week other than Sunday when I did not keep regular hours in my surgery. I had walked along the Danube for a while, then crossed over on the bridge one would take to arrive at the Hitler residence, after which I made my way into the woods that lay below Bestling Mountain. There are many trails one might take through these woods, and I chose a footpath that would, after about twenty minutes, open out into a meadow of which I was, at this time of year, especially fond, for it was composed of wild grasses that were, in their varying autumnal shades of green, rust, and aubergine, especially beautiful.

What I loved also about this time of year was that, the leaves beginning to fall from the trees, one could now see more of the landscape – the hills, rocks, trees, and flowering shrubs that were ever, in their quietude, a balm to my heart.

Rarely on these Thursday afternoon walks – this was not so on Sundays – did I meet another soul, and so I was surprised, as I neared the meadow, to hear loud giggling and shouting, as of schoolchildren who were rejoicing because they had given themselves an illegitimate holiday. When the shouting became shrieking of an alarming kind – a woman's voice – I hurried forward only to see that the voice was Maria Anna's. She was skipping and leaping across the meadow while simultaneously shrieking with what seemed not terror but sheer ecstasy. Adolf was with her, and while she leapt about he would bend over and pluck up clumps of grasses and flowers, then race to his sister, stop her, bow to her in a mock-chivalrous manner, and present her with the bouquets, which, once received, she would hurl into the air so that they showered down upon the two of them.

So occupied were they with their games that while I stood at the edge of the meadow I was invisible to them. On young Adolf's face there was a look of incandescent happiness of a kind I had never before seen. He had his favorite ivory-handled walking stick with him, and when Maria Anna stopped dancing about, he would parade in front of her in what I can only describe as foppish ways, striking elaborate poses, singing to her, and twirling the cane – throwing it in the air and catching it – as if he were a performer in a music hall. Watching him, I was, like Maria Anna, enchanted, and was made aware again, as he gesticulated, of something I had first noticed when he was a young boy: the unique, somewhat feminine quality of his hands, and, as he charmed his sister, their exquisite expressiveness. Had I not known that he and Maria Anna were brother and sister I would have taken them for young lovers, but in the very instant that this thought entered my mind, Anna Maria screamed and threw herself upon the ground as if struck by a seizure, after which she continued to howl dolefully.

I moved forward at once, but when I saw that young Adolf had lifted his sister's skirts, and that this gesture had, instantaneously, a calming effect upon her, I moved no further. The air was still, the sounds of birds suddenly absent. The only thing I heard was young Adolf's voice as he talked to his sister in the gentle way he had talked when they were in my office several years earlier.

Maria Anna put her wrist in her mouth and sucked on it even as, submitting to her brother's ministrations, she let her head fall back upon the grass. Not an attractive woman in the least, in this moment she looked nearly beatific. Young Adolf was on his knees before her, and was quite intent upon the act he was performing, and what he was doing, I soon realized – I could not avert my eyes, much as I knew this would be the more proper course of action (and when I saw what he was doing, I nearly gave my presence away with a shriek of my own, so great was my astonishment) – was changing her diaper.

I retreated into the forest, and when I was once again safely hidden from view, I saw that they were walking hand in hand, Maria Anna's head upon her brother's shoulder, his mouth close to her ear (there had, I now realized, as in a *déjà vu*, been two large safety pins protruding from his mouth moments before). To judge from her response, he talked to her in a constant stream of what must have been loving sentiments. The only individual word I could make out from either of them, in fact, came from Maria Anna, who, every half minute or so would tilt her head back and shout *"Wolf! My Wolf!"* (Her cries reminded me that "Wolf" was Hitler's favorite nickname, the one used by his young friends when he was growing up in Linz.)

Hitler's sister is 'crying wolf,' I thought to myself, *and unseen, I am the only one who knows this is so.*

What such a predictable thought brought to mind, even as I made my way back through the woods towards home, was *Daniel's* flight through the woods following upon his escape from the Home. It also brought to mind the words Daniel had used to describe this flight: If I could have continued to run through the forest forever I would have been an extremely happy young man, he had said. And then: Can you understand that? I said that I thought I could, and recited for him an old saying I recalled from my childhood – that one makes a road by walking on it.

I had thought this adage would please Daniel by its appositeness, but instead he frowned and said he did not understand what I meant. What *he* meant, he said, was that he loved running through the woods more than he liked the rest of the journey to New York City – more than the ride in the limousine, or on the train, or in the subway. What he loved was racing through snow, climbing over rocks, scaring off birds and small animals, cracking the ice of shallow streambeds with his shoes, and knowing all the while that he was evading capture and captivity.

That had been a *true* adventure, whereas having to stay in my apartment and being forbidden to go outside was only, like the Home – he stated this as if it were a mere and inoffensive fact – another kind of prison.

Before he went to sleep this evening – after his mother had washed and changed him and he was lying on his cot under a blanket – of a sudden he sat up, and said to his mother: Would you please talk to me about my grandfather? You used to tell me stories about him all the time and you haven't done so since we arrived in New York. Miss Rofman said that it was too late, but she did offer the information that she had had word from his grandfather, who would be returning home soon. He might, in fact, she said, already be there.

I don't think so, Daniel said, shaking his head sideways. What I think is that he's decided to live in the subways that he helped build. That's why he has disappeared.

Then he once again asked his mother to tell him about his grandfather, and about what it had been like, when she was a girl, to go to work with him while he was building the subway lines.

She said again that it was late, but that if he promised to go sleep, in the morning she would tell him about his grandfather.

Okay then, Daniel said, and he lay back down, and pulled the blanket to his chin. Then he turned to me. There are more than six hundred miles of subway tracks in New York City, he exclaimed brightly, and you can ride them forever for only a nickel. Did you know that?

I said that I did not.

I believe that a person could live in the subways forever, and they would *never* find you, that's how vast the system is, he said. They used to march circus elephants to their destination by walking them through the underground subways. Did you know *that*?

I did not, I said.

What I think, he said then, is that the subways are like the forest.

And what I think, Miss Rofman said, is that you are overtired, after which she told him that she had been sketching some pictures of what the subways were like during their construction, and that in the morning she would go to her father's apartment and retrieve these sketches so she could show them to him.

But how, I wondered, could she do this without giving away the fact that my home was her son's place of hiding? How, given the information Doctor Landau had imparted to me, could I allow him to stay here much longer without endangering him? And how, given my conversations with Miss Rofman *and* with Doctor Landau, was I to know who to believe?

It was only then – when I had posed the salient question – that it occurred to me that Miss Rofman *wanted* Doctor Landau and the others to believe that she had spent the night with me. Thus did I wonder: Were we able to find a safer place for Daniel, would Miss Rofman, out of a desire to appear consistent – or out of desire itself – continue to reside with me?

But I did not pursue this line of thinking. Rather, I concentrated on Daniel's situation, and decided that in the morning I would tell Miss Rofman that Doctor Landau had voiced suspicions to me, that I thought Daniel was in danger of being discovered, and that it was imperative that we find a new home for him. What led me to this line of reasoning more than the dangers of the present situation – or, rather, what made the dangers immediate – was a look of concern I saw on Miss Rofman's face when she turned away from her son, the look, in this unguarded moment, revealing that she was troubled in the extreme.

I thought of an obvious solution – of speaking with my daughter Gertrude and her husband (they are childless) about taking Daniel in, but then I thought too of my conversation with Doctor Landau, and of the likelihood that he and Detective Kelly would have assigned people to trace my movements.

In order not to worry Miss Rofman any more than was necessary, and in order not to commit myself to a hastily conceived plan that would increase danger, I said nothing aloud. But to come up with an effective plan, I knew, I had to reflect carefully upon my conversation with Doctor Landau so as to gauge the authenticity – and sincerity – of what he had told me.

So: in order to give Miss Rofman privacy, I said good night to Daniel and excused myself, after which I came to my bedroom and began setting down these words. But by the time, perhaps a half-hour ago, that, realizing I had not said good night to Miss Rofman, I returned to the living room, all lights were out, and both Miss Rofman and her son were fast asleep. From my doorway I could see Miss Rofman lying on the couch, under the blanket I had left for her. She was sleeping on her side quite peacefully, I was pleased to see, and a guttural but light and pleasant sound of snoring was rising from her open mouth.

TEN

What Doctor Bloch tried to explain to Doctor Landau, he had told Elisabeth on their way home, was that there were lies which a person, or a people, knew to be lies, but without which a person, or a people, would perish. The German and Austrian peoples might, for example, make an outward show of love for Hitler and his regime despite what their better selves knew and felt. There was a special, and rare, German word for this – *Lebenslüge* – which, loosely translated, Doctor Bloch said, meant 'the lie that is life-giving,' and he wondered if Elisabeth knew the word.

Elisabeth said that she had heard the word, but she chose not to correct Doctor Bloch – not to tell him that the word was Norwegian in its origin, not German. And now, in a panic as she knocked on Doctor Bloch's bedroom door a second time, the word was pounding inside her head as if it had fists.

Daniel was gone, his cot empty. If Doctor Bloch was also gone, did that mean that they'd gone off together, and had they, the night before, secretly *planned* to go off together? But if they had, how did Doctor Bloch expect to ensure Daniel's safety – to protect him?

The sound of the ocean was in her ears – blood rushing there – and she forced herself to take deep breaths, warned herself not to act on impulse. If Doctor Bloch wasn't there, she would dress and go out to look for Daniel. But where would she look?

And if Alex's men – Detective Kelly, or Mister Tompkins, or men they hired – were on duty . . . ?

It occurred to her that Daniel and Doctor Bloch might have slipped out of the apartment earlier in the morning and were simply taking a long walk in the neighborhood of the kind the doctor enjoyed. Maybe Doctor Bloch, who took pride in the ways he was educating himself about the Bronx and its history, was telling Daniel about the Lindbergh child and Bruno Hauptmann, or about famous individuals who had lived in the Bronx: Anne Hutchinson, or Edgar Allen Poe. Did Daniel know that Poe had written "Annabel Lee" while living in the Bronx? he might ask. Had Daniel ever read the poem and if so had he been required to set it to heart?

Lebenslüge. The word was there again, and though Elisabeth was bothered by the irritating way it made its presence felt, it came to her attached to a memory that was itself pleasant and comforting. Elisabeth had learned the word from Ulla, the woman who had kept house for her father when Elisabeth was a child. Ulla had been born in Norway, of German-Jewish parents who emigrated to Norway before coming to the United States, and Elisabeth had first heard the word on a day when Elisabeth's father was getting ready to leave for a job interview.

Ulla had wished him good luck and then, when her father had asked about the suit he was wearing – was it not too shabby? – Ulla had told him the suit was handsome, and that he looked distinguished in it.

But you *lied*! Elisabeth cried as soon as her father was gone. You *lied*! You told me the suit was *ugly*!

Ulla had laughed. It was true that Ulla had called the jacket ugly when she was patching it the day before, and that she had said it was a shame that Elisabeth's father, who was such a handsome man, had to wear an inferior garment.

Elisabeth had continued to protest – to cry out that Ulla had lied, and that one was *never* supposed to lie – and that was when

Ulla had used the word, and told Elisabeth what it meant, after which she had added, softly, as if it were the most obvious truth in the world: Oh my dear Elisabeth, we often lie to the people we love.

On their way home from Alex's house, Doctor Bloch had also asked if Elisabeth thought it was a good idea to tell Daniel the story of Anne Hutchinson: of how Anne Hutchinson had been banished from the Massachusetts Bay Colony for her beliefs – that the individual could experience God's grace *without* the need for church or religion – and of how she and five of her six children were murdered by American Indians while they were living in the Bronx. Elisabeth had said that she saw no reason to keep such stories from Daniel. Maybe, then, at this very moment, Doctor Bloch was taking Daniel to the place, near Pelham Bay Park, where Anne Hutchinson's short-lived settlement had been established. Perhaps when Daniel heard the story . . . .

Elisabeth knocked on Doctor Bloch's door again.

"Bitte," Doctor Bloch said, opening his door and lifting a white stocking cap from his head. He wished Elisabeth a good morning, apologized for being slow in answering the door, and asked if she would like him to make coffee for them. Elisabeth had obviously woken him from a deep sleep – he wore a white terry cloth robe, whose belt he was still tying, over red and blue striped pajamas – but obviously too, to judge from his smile, he was not unhappy or embarrassed to be greeting her in his nightclothes.

"Is Daniel with you?" Elisabeth demanded. "*Is* he – ?"

"Why no, my child. Why would he be with me?"

Elisabeth heard herself cry out, and then she was raising both fists in the air and watching Doctor Bloch step backwards, as if frightened she was going to strike him.

"Damn!" she cried and, turning away from Doctor Bloch, she pounded the air with her fists.

Doctor Bloch asked no questions but, touching Elisabeth's

shoulder lightly, moved past her and made a quick survey of the living room, kitchen, and bathroom. He went to the front door, where he discovered what Elisabeth had already discovered: that it was not locked.

He returned to his bedroom, opened a window, and looked out onto the fire escape. When he came back into the living room, he went directly to the fireplace – he seemed reassured to find the postcard Hitler had sent him still in its place on the mantel – after which, with what seemed to her excessive calm, he took a cigarette from the cigarette box on the table beside his easy chair, and lit it.

"He is not here," he stated.

"I *know* that," Elisabeth said. She looked down, half-expecting to see her rage, like blood, gliding down her legs and pooling on the carpet. She heard pounding again, inside her head, and pictured herself in the hospital's morgue in Baltimore, where she was selecting a cadaver to use for anatomical drawings, after which, having chosen one, she saw herself, hammer in hand, nailing the cadaver to a table. Although she felt weak, she moved towards the bathroom, determined to wash, to change into street clothes, and to go out in search of Daniel.

"I will make coffee," Doctor Bloch said.

"Maybe Daniel's gone to my father's house," Elisabeth said.

"Perhaps," Doctor Bloch said. "I will make coffee."

"Yes," Elisabeth said. "Coffee. Please. But what of my son?"

"Perhaps tea would be preferable to coffee," Doctor Bloch said. "You are in a high state of anxiety, and not without cause. You should lie down and take deep breaths – in and out, in and out, yes? – and allow me to take care of things. Your judgment, at this time, is not what it would ordinarily be."

"Do you *hear* me – ?" Elisabeth asked. "Have you heard *anything* I've said. What of my *son*, Doctor Bloch – what of my *son*?"

"Of course," Doctor Bloch said. "I am well aware of the

situation, and of why you are upset. Since it is difficult for a woman like you to be faced with a situation about which you can do nothing, you feel profoundly helpless. You are a woman who is used to doing things well – to accomplishing things in a competent and expeditious manner, to being able to make things work, yes? – to being able to fix things if they are in need of fixing."

"And I'm a woman who doesn't like to be told who I am, or what I feel," Elisabeth said.

"Of course not," Doctor Bloch said. "I did not mean to presume – only to observe. As to Daniel, however, let me say this: he is, I expect, more capable than you allow. He is at least as eager to survive, and not to return to the institution in Maryland, as you are to have him here with you in New York."

"But I work in Baltimore – that's where my home is. That's where – "

"No matter. You are here now, and what you wish for, it seems clear to me, is that Daniel might reside with you permanently."

"Sometimes I do," Elisabeth admitted. "How deny it? But if Daniel and I lived together I know I couldn't do for him what would need to be done – not on a daily basis, that is. I just – " Elisabeth felt tears begin to well in her eyes. "I didn't mean to snap at you before," she said. "It's just that I'm frightened. I know I haven't thought this through very well – that I've been remiss, but when I did what I did, all I knew was that I couldn't leave him at the mercy of their decisions and their power. Can you understand that?"

"There is no need to explain yourself. You are a brave and loving woman. You are also experiencing shock, which is understandable. You are quite pale, you know. You should lie down please."

Elisabeth sat on the couch and watched as Doctor Bloch began to fold Daniel's clothes and linens.

"What are you *doing* – ?" she asked. "And *why*? Why *now*? Do you think my son will *never* return?"

"He will return," Doctor Bloch said. "What I was doing was thinking of Detective Kelly and that Negro man from the institution whose name I forget – "

"Mister Tompkins."

"Mister Tompkins, yes – I was thinking they might come by to inquire – to investigate – and that, therefore, we should be prudent. Were Daniel here, I would not allow them entry, of course. Since he is not here, however, I suggest that we be more than prudent and use your son's absence to our advantage."

"I'm afraid you've lost me," Elisabeth said. "Or maybe I'm the one who's lost. Maybe I'm lost and – bravo for me, I suppose – I've managed to become lost all by myself and without anyone else's help. What do *you* think, Doctor Bloch?"

"As I said, what I think is that you should lie down. I think you are experiencing a mild case of shock, and that therefore you should do as I say and let me attend to things."

"Shock would seem an accurate diagnosis," Elisabeth said. "If I were in my right mind, I'd probably concur. But I'm also getting reassurances from you that are hardly reassuring. More *Lebenslüge*?"

"Not at all," Doctor Bloch said. "Oh not at all, Miss Rofman. In such a serious situation, I would not humor you or condescend. You should know that I respect you too much for that."

"Do you think what I want from you is *respect*? Do you think I'm looking to have you flatter me?"

"Of course not," Doctor Bloch said. "Your lack of a shallow sentimentality in such matters is one of your more admirable qualities." He glanced at the stack of linens and clothes he held in his arms. "So: I will put these away – I will fold away Daniel's bed also – and you will lie down, please, and then we will consider what we are to do."

But where could Daniel go? she wanted to ask as soon as Doctor Bloch left the room. And if Daniel returned, where could she go *with* him? Until she could figure out a way to secure his safety, who else would be willing to take him in?

When she told Alex and Doctor Ogilvie that she had retained a lawyer, she had been bluffing, but maybe there was a way that a court or a judge *would* grant Daniel the protection she was seeking. Maybe, despite the fact of Daniel coming into his majority, a friendly, sensitive judge would give Elisabeth rights concerning Daniel's well-being that would provide reliable safeguards. Or – why hadn't this occurred to her until now? – maybe Antoinette Lanana's parents, who had invited her to visit them several times, would be willing to take Daniel in. Who would ever think of looking for Daniel in *their* home? Their gratitude to Elisabeth seemed boundless. After all, she was the woman who had *not* saved their daughter's life, wasn't she? Perhaps, in exchange for keeping Daniel, she could bring them a drawing of their daughter's heart.

"What I believe," Doctor Bloch was saying, "is that although your son may be troubled, he is not stupid, and that his instinct for survival is quite robust. Through the years I have encountered a number of children like him – and there were some young soldiers I treated during the war, for example, with whom he shares significant characteristics."

Elisabeth went to the window. She was about to tell Doctor Bloch about Antoinette's parents when the obvious occurred to her for the first time – that Antoinette's parents did not live in New York City. 'Just a minor oversight,' she heard herself explaining to Doctor Bloch.

"There's a man across the street who's looking up at your apartment," she said. "The same man was there earlier this morning before I woke you."

"I am not surprised," Doctor Bloch said. "If he is one of Detective Kelly's men, this could prove fortuitous. Would you draw the blinds closed, please? In that way, those outside may believe that we are hiding something, and they may therefore decide it is a good time to visit us."

The shrill blast of the tea kettle startled Elisabeth.

"I will make your tea," Doctor Bloch said.

Elisabeth let her forehead rest against the window. When she stared at the man across the street, he looked away. She drew the blinds closed. Then, without removing blanket, sheets, or pillow, she lay down on the couch and closed her eyes.

❖ ❖ ❖

Excuse me," Doctor Bloch said.

He stood above her while setting down a tray of food – rolls, butter, jams, crescent-shaped cookies, tea, coffee, milk, and sugar – on the table next to the couch.

"Yes?" Dazed, she looked around, saw that Daniel's cot was gone.

"You need not move," Doctor Bloch said, and he reached under the pillow where Elisabeth's head lay.

"It is as I thought," he said, withdrawing a piece of paper and handing it to Elisabeth. "Your son has left you a note."

Elisabeth sat up. "How did you know?" she asked.

"How did I know?" Doctor Bloch said, and answered his own question: "I said to myself: If I were Daniel, what would *I* do? This is a way of thinking – of understanding others – that has often proven useful to me, both with patients and with friends. So I asked the question, and this led to my remembering your story about the exchanges of messages between you and your father. Next, from Daniel's question last night, and your promise to talk with him about your father this morning, I made the further assumption that you have probably told him of these exchanges."

Elisabeth unfolded the note.

Dear Mother and Doctor Bloch:

Thank you for the hospitality. I have many things to do today in the world outside but do not worry about me for I will be very careful in both my going out and my coming back.

Yours sincerely, Daniel Landau.

Elisabeth showed the note to Doctor Bloch.

"I believe him," Doctor Bloch said. He poured tea for Elisabeth. "It is in his nature to be as careful as he is sometimes impetuous. So now we will wait, yes? Now we will worry less."

"Maybe," Elisabeth said, and then: "Thank you for being so patient with me."

Elisabeth realized that Doctor Bloch had changed from his night clothes – she was still in her nightgown – and was wearing a brown wool three-piece suit.

"I should change clothes," she said.

"No," Doctor Bloch said. "I suggest that you stay as you are. If they come in search of Daniel, it would be good for them to find you like this."

"Because – ?" Elisabeth asked.

"Because it will cause them to infer certain things about our relationship," he said.

"What things?" Elisabeth asked, and saw that her question caused color to rise in Doctor Bloch's cheeks.

"That there is, let us say, a certain intimacy between us," Doctor Bloch said.

"But there *is* a certain intimacy," Elisabeth said. "There is a friendship – one I've come to value greatly. Why would my being in my nightgown make a difference?"

"My dear child," Doctor Bloch said, "you are clearly determined to embarrass me, and clearly, too, you are succeeding. It would be indiscreet of me to say more than I have said."

Elisabeth sipped her tea, bit into a cookie. "I didn't realize how hungry I was," she said. "Was I asleep for a long time?"

"No. Perhaps twenty minutes."

"You look especially handsome this morning, you know," she said. When Doctor Bloch touched a corner of his moustache, and returned her gaze steadily, she felt heat rise to her own cheeks. "I didn't mean to embarrass you before."

"You are being less than truthful with me," Doctor Bloch said. "It is obvious that you take great pleasure in embarrassing me."

"Is that a bad thing?"

"Not at all."

"Lebenslüge?" she asked.

"Not exactly," Doctor Bloch said, "although it is pleasurable to have you trifle with my feelings in this manner. It confirms what I have, from the first, suspected – that you have the capacity to be quite playful."

"Another of my *admirable* qualities?"

"Admirable, yes, and also a source of delight," Doctor Bloch said, "for you are a most attractive woman, in my opinion, and in all positive senses of that word."

"Now you're embarrassing *me*, Doctor Bloch."

"Good!" Doctor Bloch exclaimed. "At last! Excellent! I will consider that one of my finer recent accomplishments."

Elisabeth placed Daniel's note on her pillow. "I didn't know I was going to say that earlier – " she offered " – that I find you handsome."

"And you have already revised that evaluation, I see," Doctor Bloch said. "What you said before was that I looked especially handsome *this morning*."

"I like the tie you're wearing," Elisabeth said. "I haven't seen it before."

"It is a gift from my daughter, Gertrude. I am gratified to have you notice it."

Elisabeth reached out and took Doctor Bloch's hand in her own, and was surprised, given his age, at how smooth his skin was. "You've been very kind to me," she said. "To me and to my son. Why?"

Doctor Bloch put a hand on top of hers. "To that question, I will reply in a proverbial Jewish manner, and ask: 'Why not?'"

Doctor Bloch lifted her hand, as if he were going to press it against his lips, then reconsidered. "You are passing through a most intense period of turmoil in your life," he said, "and I am glad – honored – to be your friend, and to know that you have chosen to rely on me. Given the turmoil, however – your understandable upset and anxiety concerning your son – I am not convinced that you can trust your more personal feelings at a time like this."

"They are unlikely feelings," Elisabeth said, and as Doctor Bloch moved to take his hands away, Elisabeth held onto one of them and, closing her eyes, let her cheek rest against it momentarily.

"Would you do something for me?" she asked. "Would you tell me that everything will be all right?"

"Of course," Doctor Bloch said, but when he did not do what she asked, she let go of his hand. She stood and, as she moved towards the window, hoping she might see Daniel walking along the street, there was a loud knocking at the door.

"You will stay where you are, please," Doctor Bloch said. "In this instance, the maxim about one picture being worth a thousand words will work in our favor. Seeing you here in your present state of dress will tell them all we want them to know."

Doctor Bloch opened the door, but instead of finding either Detective Kelly or Mister Tompkins there, a disheveled man with blackened face, bent over and trembling, reached forward in a gesture of supplication. He had a bright red scarf wrapped around his head, and wore a winter coat that was too small for him.

"Alms for the poor?" he said. "I beg of you. Alms for the poor?"

Doctor Bloch took a step backwards. "I do not understand, please. Why would you need arms?"

The man tore off his scarf, and stepped into the apartment.

"Daniel!" Elisabeth exclaimed.

"Surprise!" Daniel shouted. *"Surprise!"*

Elisabeth tried to embrace Daniel, but he moved away from her.

"I did it, I did it!" he cried. "I fooled you. I fooled you. Admit it – !"

"Yes. And I don't want you to ever fool me or do anything like this again," Elisabeth said. "Do you understand? Do you *hear* me?"

"But shh," Daniel said, a finger to his lips. "I made a discovery while I was out there. I made a discovery about the future. Do you want to know what my discovery is?"

Saying this, he collapsed onto the couch, grabbed a pillow and clutched it to his chest.

"You are wearing my coat," Doctor Bloch said. "I do not recall granting you permission to take it."

"But I brought it back in the same size," Daniel said, and began laughing. "I brought it back in the same size."

Elisabeth stood over him. "Don't you *ever*, *ever* do anything like that again. Do you hear me? You had me scared to death. What if – " she hesitated " – what if the others had found you, had recognized you?"

"But they didn't," Daniel replied. "And do you know why? Because I'm too clever for them. So here's my question for the morning: Do you want to know what I discovered?"

"No," Elisabeth said. "What I want is for you to promise you'll never do anything like this again."

"And if I don't promise, what will you do – take me back to the Home?" Daniel asked. "Or if it's a *real* punishment you're after, take me to my *father's* house?" Daniel shook his head sideways. "Fat chance of that!"

Elisabeth felt a hand on her arm, and heard Doctor Bloch speaking to her softly, in German. When Doctor Bloch touched her arm a second time, she pulled away, told him to leave her alone. To her surprise, and with a strength she had not imagined he possessed, he moved her aside, and spoke to Daniel.

"You will stand up at once, young man, and apologize to your mother."

"But – "

"There will be no *buts*," Doctor Bloch declared. "You will do as I say."

"Who's going to make me?"

"If I have to, I will," Doctor Bloch said.

"You and what army?" Daniel replied.

Doctor Bloch lowered his voice. "You will please to do as I say," he said. "I will not ask you again."

Daniel sat up. "I'm sorry, I guess," he said. "But I had a *really* good time."

"You will stand up and you will not employ any *buts*," Doctor Bloch said. "You will please to do as I say and make a proper apology to your mother, and you will do it now."

Daniel stood and faced his mother. "I'm sorry."

"What are you sorry for?" Doctor Bloch asked.

"I'm sorry I made you worried," Daniel said.

"Very good," Doctor Bloch said. "Now, you will please to take off my coat, wash your face, and then we will talk about this incident together."

"What if they followed him?" Elisabeth began. "What if – ?"

"If anyone comes to the apartment," Doctor Bloch said to Daniel, "you will please to go into my bedroom, and stand behind the door. I will not *allow* anyone entry. Should they force their way in, however, you will step into the bedroom closet very quietly, and make yourself invisible. Is that clear?"

Daniel's eyes brightened. "Oh yes!" he said, and then: "*Now* can I tell you what I found?"

"Only after you tell me that you understand what you are to do, and only after you wash your face," Doctor Bloch said. "It is coal that you have applied to blacken it, yes?"

"Yes."

"Would you like me to help you wash the coal off?" Elisabeth asked.

"He will do that himself," Doctor Bloch said. "Is that not so, Daniel?"

"*Then* can I tell you about what I discovered?"

"Yes," Doctor Bloch said.

"Okay. Then I say thank you very much, Doctor Eduard Bloch!" Daniel declared, and he took off Doctor Bloch's coat and handed it to him.

"Thank *you*," Elisabeth said when Daniel had closed the bathroom door behind him.

"You should sit," Doctor Bloch said, "and you should have something strong to drink that will restore your color. When I serve Daniel his breakfast, I will put some *schnapps* in your tea. Sit, please."

"Then everything *will* be all right?" Elisabeth laughed. "I used to ask Alex that question, especially when everything was going well – when we were happy. 'Everything will be all right, won't it?' I'd say to him. Or: 'Tell me everything will be all right.'"

"I have met Doctor Landau, which makes it apparent to me why the two of you were greatly attracted to each other," Doctor Bloch said. "You are both handsome, intelligent individuals who are prone to take pleasure from this mode of discourse – from such ironies."

"Maybe," Elisabeth said. "Strange, though. When I'd ask the question, Alex would often say that of course things would be all right – they would be all right because our pleasures gave God a reason to exist."

"Doctor Landau is, I judge from our evening together, a man of considerable religious conviction."

"In his own way, yes. But why did God exist and watch over *us*? I'd ask. Because life was absurd, he would reply. Because life was meaningless. *That* was why Alex chose to believe in God, and that was why everything would be all right even after it had *been* all right."

"But isn't such a way of thinking itself absurd?" Doctor Bloch asked.

"Of course," Elisabeth said. "As Alex himself would be quick to admit." She paused. "It surprises me that you'd understand that about us – about how Alex's mind works."

"The sentiment expressed, however – the belief in God – is *not* an absurd one for Doctor Landau, I suspect – thus his use of an ironic mode of expression. It is a sentiment I can understand."

"One you share?"

"I do not think in such terms," Doctor Bloch said. "I am, in point of fact, as little interested in God as I suspect God is in me, were such a being to exist. Nor am I interested in Doctor Landau's philosophical-religious games. What I am interested in is you, and in Daniel, and in whether or not Doctor Landau might himself be outside at this moment with others. And I am interested in finding out what our young man has discovered during his adventure this morning."

"But you must have some thoughts about this – some feelings about what I'm telling you, and about why I feel free to do so."

"You misperceive me, I think," Doctor Bloch said. "Although, as you know, I am a cousin to the author Mister Franz Kafka, I myself have never coveted irony. Moreover, I am not like your former husband in that I do not often think, either in an ironic *or* a playful manner, of ultimate matters – of God or of no God, or of the existence or non-existence of evil. To call Hitler evil, for example, as many, Doctor Landau included, do – and here he was, I believe, speaking *without* irony – is of what use? How does it change the ways in which we are called upon to act?"

"I don't know," Elisabeth said. "But – "

"There will be no *buts*," Daniel declared, coming out of the bathroom, his face bright red. "Am I clean enough yet? You can examine me now if you want, both of you. I scrubbed *really* hard."

❖ ❖ ❖

Elisabeth kept her eyes on the cast iron slabs of metal that were the object of Daniel's obsession. When she crossed from one side of a street to another, she tried to walk close to manhole covers so that when she returned to Doctor Bloch's apartment, she could tell Daniel about the ones she had seen, and compare them with those he had drawn.

What amazed her most were not Daniel's drafting skills, which had always been considerable, but his memory: his ability to conjure up manhole covers he had seen during his walk in such incredible detail. While she and Doctor Bloch had been drinking tea and talking quietly about what they might do if anyone showed up, Daniel had sat at Doctor Bloch's desk in the bedroom, working steadily and with great concentration at his drawings. Within an hour, he had sketched a half dozen different manhole covers, which, he said, represented only a *fraction* of those he'd seen.

The fact that he could sit still for such an extended period of time – that he wasn't restless in the way he usually was – heartened Elisabeth. When she commented on this, Doctor Bloch was not surprised. Daniel had a great capacity for concentration when he found objects worthy of his attention, Doctor Bloch said. In Doctor Bloch's experience, it was, in fact, a characteristic of young men with Daniel's condition to be both obsessive and perseverative, and, therefore, to be capable often of remarkable achievements.

Although Doctor Bloch did not place any particular value on Daniel's passion for these street coverings, he was encouraged by the effort with which Daniel was acting on it. This was a quality he would with the years and with proper guidance, Doctor Bloch was convinced, be able to apply to other worldly tasks.

What Daniel had discovered was the endless variety of vents, grills, grates, maintenance covers, and manhole covers that were embedded in the sidewalks, gutters, and streets of the city. How could it be, he asked, that he'd never noticed them before? They were *everywhere*, dozens of them on any one street, and they were, he realized once he began figuring out how to decipher their markings – their letterings, symbols, and designs – entryways to vast subterranean systems that provided the essentials of daily living: water, gas, coal, electricity, telephones, telegraphs, drains, and sewers. Many of them were worn down and had been half-swallowed up by new sidewalk or roadwork, and some had dates on them – the earliest one Daniel found was from 1836 – and if you wanted to, he said, you could probably figure out the whole history of the city from these pieces of metal. How, he asked, could anyone walk in the city and *not* notice them?

They came in different sizes and shapes – circles, squares, hexagons, rectangles – and in a great variety of designs: in zigzag patterns, checkerboard patterns, pebble-grain patterns, waffle patterns; in designs that imitated starbursts, sunbursts, fish scales, snowflakes, flowers, and honeycombs; in chevrons and diamond treads and basket-weave designs, and in different styles of lettering – lower case and upper case, plain and Gothic. And after Daniel, nearly breathless from describing what he had seen, had said he intended to draw as many of them as he could remember, he had paused, and added, quietly: I think they're really beautiful.

What enchanted Daniel more than the beauty of these objects, though, he had gone on to say, his voice trembling with his excitement, was something else: their *future*. What if, several hundred years from how, he asked, *everything* on earth was destroyed – all the people, and all the buildings, bridges, factories, subways, tunnels, automobiles, ships, airports, and airplanes – and what if the only things left were bombed-out streets, and the only things on these streets were these pieces of metal? And what if aliens from outer space, descending on our planet, came upon them? What would they understand about us, and about what we were like, and why these objects had existed? What would they *think*?

And what do *you* think? Daniel asked.

Doctor Bloch, quoting Rilke's advice to his young poet – to have patience with everything unresolved and to try to love the questions themselves – had said that he found Daniel's questions testimony to the richness of his imagination.

But I asked you a question because I want *answers*, Daniel had responded. I already *thought* of the questions. I want *answers*. I asked the questions because I want *answers*.

Maybe, Elisabeth had said, they would think these objects were religious in some way.

Yes! Daniel had exclaimed, and he had slapped his thigh with his hand several times. *Yes! Yes! Yes!* That's exactly what I thought too. But what *kind* of religion, do you think?

Jewish, of course, Elisabeth had said.

Jewish?! Jewish manhole covers?!

Much more *grounded*, Elisabeth had said. More *embedded* in the here and now, don't you think? As my father used to say: We Jews believe in this world – let the *goyim* believe in the next. Although there were the Marranos, of course, who in order to practice our religion . . . .

And I think you're joking with me, right? Daniel had said then, his head tilted to the side. Oh I know you when you get this way, Mother! You're being *fanciful*, aren't you?

Elisabeth had said that yes, she was being fanciful, but maybe if Daniel found a manhole cover in the form of the tablets of the law, or of the Holy Book itself . . . .

Daniel had laughed, and lowered his voice. But do you know what else I thought about while I was walking around? he had asked. I thought about the underground railroad that slaves used for escaping to freedom – through tunnels and sewers and swamps, and hiding in attics and cellars and chimneys, and sleeping in cow poop – and I thought about my own escape and how I may have to be hidden the way they were, and go from place to place in order to stay ahead of those who would do me harm, and so I figured out that if my enemies get too close to me, I could crawl down through one of these openings in the street and live underground. So what do you think of that idea?

I think it's terrible, Elisabeth had said.

But *why*? Daniel had protested. I could bring food and water with me, and I could be in a different place every day – and maybe find other people living down there who would know how to get what we needed in order to survive. I think it could be a *great* adventure. I mean, just *think* about it, Mother!

What I think about are the dangers, Elisabeth said. I think of the darkness, and of the cold, and of the rats.

Rats!? Daniel exclaimed, and Elisabeth immediately regretted what she had said since for Daniel the possibility of finding rats only made the prospect of hiding below ground more enticing.

When I went to work with my father, we'd see them all the time, she said, some of them as large as small dogs. They ran in packs usually, and the men would shoot them. Sometimes they'd roast them and eat them, which made them very sick.

But I'd be *careful*, Mother, Daniel said. I promise. Maybe I could carry pieces of cheese with me, to pacify the rats, and I could put on disguises the way I did this morning.

So the *rats* wouldn't recognize you? Elisabeth asked.

Daniel laughed. *Which* rats? he asked, and laughed harder, after which he repeated what he had said about how clever and careful he would be. So just you think about *that*, all right? he said.

Oh yes, Elisabeth said. I will. And she thought: I'm also thinking of what it is I'm going to do next. Just promise me you won't go below ground until I return, all right? she said aloud.

Return from where?

I'll be leaving for my father's apartment soon, she said. I want to retrieve some drawings and supplies – the drawings I promised to show you – and also to get some other drawings, to send to Baltimore, and to find out what they want me to work on next.

And I'm going there as soon as I can, she thought, in order to lead the others away.

Perhaps, she said, on my way there and back, I'll find some of the same manhole covers you found.

Daniel said that he would keep on drawing while she was gone and that when he had enough drawings, maybe he'd make up a story to go with them. It could be set in the twenty-fourth or twenty-fifth century, and when he was done maybe he'd send the story and the drawings to Doctor Einstein and get *his* opinion.

❖ ❖ ❖

Now, leaving Westchester Square – the air was balmy, the streets gleaming from melted snow – Elisabeth stopped to study a manhole cover she found especially handsome – three thin concentric circles surrounding a basket-weave pattern, the word *STEAM* inscribed along the curve of the outermost circle.

She had not looked behind during her walk, but she was confident that at least one of Alex's men – Detective Kelly, or Mister Tompkins – had been following her. She turned the corner – her father's apartment house was at the far end of the street – and came upon a crowd that was blocking the sidewalk. On a stool by the curbstone, his horse and cart tethered to a lamp post, a knife grinder was pedaling away at his machine, sparks spraying from his grinding wheel while men and women, holding knives or carrying them in cloth and paper sacks, waited.

In order to get around the crowd, Elisabeth walked out into the street, and as she passed the horse – an ageing dapple-gray, without blinders – she reached up and stroked its neck. Accustomed to having people touch it, she knew, children especially, the horse did not seem to mind, or even to notice her. Its neck was warm, and its body heat reminded her of the time she and her father, having climbed up from a subway trench at the end of a workday, had come upon a horse – also a dapple-gray – lying on its side in the street.

It was a winter day like this one, she remembered, and steam rose from the horse's body even though, as she would later realize, the horse was already dead. She had wanted to get close to the horse – to touch it – but her father had tugged on her so hard that her mitten had come off in his hand. He had pulled her away roughly, commanded her not to look back, and on their way home he wouldn't answer her questions about why the horse was lying down, or why people were crowding around it, or why the men close to the horse seemed so agitated and angry.

It was only later on, reconstructing the scene in her mind, that she realized that the men closest to the horse, some of them climbing onto it as if it were a small hill, were carving chunks of meat from its body. In her memory, not only was steam rising from the horse's body and spraying from its nostrils, but the horse itself – the same thing sometimes happened with people after their hearts stopped beating – had been twitching violently in spasms.

❖ ❖ ❖

So lost was Elisabeth in her drawing that when she went into the kitchen to make another cup of tea for herself, she was surprised to discover, from the clock above the refrigerator, that it was nearly three in the afternoon and that she had been working for more than a half dozen hours.

Arriving at her father's apartment in the morning, she had found a letter from Doctor Taussig waiting for her on the table in the bedroom, left there, she knew, by her father – his way of assuring her that all was well. In the letter, Doctor Taussig wrote that she was beginning to see a solution to the problem of the blue babies – to see the kind of surgical procedure that held promise of success in saving their lives. Experiments on dogs, which were conducted mostly by Doctor Taussig's associate, Vivian Thomas, a black man who, though not a physician, was as brilliant and innovative as any of the staff surgeons, had been going well, Doctor Taussig reported, and several dogs upon whom they had performed the procedure had now lived for more than three years following their surgeries.

During embryonic life, Elisabeth knew, the blood of the fetus received its oxygen directly from the mother. For this to happen – for the circulation to bypass the lungs – each child had a duct called the ductus arteriosus which shunted the blood from the pulmonary artery directly into the aorta. Once the child was born, however, since the ductus was no longer needed, it closed; it did so, in fact, the instant the infant drew in its first breaths. The solution that Doctor Taussig was proposing for the blue babies – what had worked with the dogs – was to reproduce the embryonic experience by creating a ductus surgically that would divert the blue blood around the narrowed or closed pulmonary artery and directly into the lungs. Doctor Taussig had asked Elisabeth to prepare drawings of children's hearts that illustrated the procedure she was considering. Her idea was to join together the end of one of the heart's arteries – the subclavial or innominate arteries were the prime candidates – to one of the pulmonary arteries surgically, as they had with the dogs, thereby allowing the lungs to receive enough oxygen to keep the child alive. In those infants with malformations of the heart who did not survive, Elisabeth knew, it was never the malformation itself that proved fatal, but the lack of circulation to the lungs. Provided there was adequate circulation to the lungs, there were many gross malformations of the heart that were compatible with life.

Doctor Taussig had written in detail about the specific procedure she was contemplating, and had included several of her own rudimentary sketches. She hoped that Elisabeth had had news of her father – how much more distressing than even the most terrible news *not knowing* could sometimes be – and if Elisabeth could have some preliminary drawings to her within, a week – or, failing that, by the first of the year, now less than two weeks away – she would be grateful. Would Elisabeth please telephone her collect and let her know if she had time to prepare the drawings? If not, Doctor Taussig could probably impose on Professor Brödel or one of his advanced students to do them. She did not, of course, mean to press Elisabeth, given her father's disappearance; still, she wanted Elisabeth to know how much she valued her skills. In the months to come, and once her family situation was resolved, she trusted that Elisabeth would also have time to prepare illustrations for a book she had been working on – *Congenital Malformations of the Heart* – that they had already spoken about.

Elisabeth had removed two of the children's hearts from the jars of formaldehyde she had obtained at Bellevue Hospital, and had begun a dissection of one of them on her father's bread board, cutting away the pericardial sac, then carefully dissecting from the heart an innominate artery. Since there was a right aortic arch in the child in whom this heart had once lived, the innominate artery was directed to the left, and Elisabeth knew that this meant it could be anastomosed – joined – to the side of the left pulmonary artery. She believed this would be the most efficient choice because although the subclavian artery by its size – the diameter of its internal lumen – may have seemed the ideal artery, and the one Vivian Thomas had most often used in dogs, the innominate artery had the advantage of being more nearly the size of the pulmonary artery to which it would be attached.

The heart itself was an inch and a half in breadth at its broadest section and less than an inch in thickness, and weighed perhaps two to three ounces. It was probably the heart of a child who had died before the age of two, and from its size and its well articulated blood vessels, Elisabeth assumed it had belonged to a girl. Boys' hearts, like those of men, were generally larger than those of girls or women. The average weight of an adult man's heart, she knew, was from ten to twelve ounces while the average weight of a woman's was slightly less. And yet, in proportion to the whole body, it turned out that men's hearts were smaller than women's. This was a fact she would remember to share with Daniel – and without commenting on its metaphorical implications – the kind of fact she knew he loved.

Although she had not eaten since early morning, she was not hungry – she felt alert and energized – and it made her happy to know that while she was working in her father's apartment on her drawings, Daniel would be working in Doctor Bloch's apartment on his drawings. It gave her pleasure, too, while she worked, to feel her father's presence – his invisible collaboration – and she found that she had stopped questioning why it was he had gone away and had not returned, except to leave things for her – there was a fresh bottle of milk in the icebox, a new jar of apricot jam on the kitchen counter. She wondered if he had *any idea* of what had been going on – of Daniel's escape from the Home, or of how she and Daniel had taken up residence with Doctor Bloch – and of why it was best if he continued to stay away. Given Alex's way of thinking, he would believe it was no coincidence that Elisabeth's father and Daniel had disappeared at the same time – a way of thinking that would, Elisabeth believed, serve her and Daniel well.

Lost in his own drawings, though, would Daniel be thinking of her now? Would he have any sense of *her* life: of how peaceful she felt when she was drawing? She wondered too: In the way that her drawings of a person's internal organs often seemed more real to her than human flesh, were Daniel's drawings of the manhole covers becoming more real to him than the covers themselves?

Elisabeth wanted to return to Doctor Bloch's apartment while there was still available light, so that she and Daniel could compare drawings. She picked up several of the rough sketches she had set down on her father's bed – those she had made before starting on the assignment for Doctor Taussig: her father laying cable alongside railroad tracks, her father climbing a ladder and coming upon the dead horse, her father glaring at the men who were cutting up the dead horse, her father washing his hands at the kitchen sink.

One of the major reasons people were going to love the new subway, her father had told her, was that trains would replace horses and make the city streets more civilized. Did Elisabeth know about the City Beautiful Movement? Did she realize what great progress would occur if the subway system became the city's principal mode of transportation? Could she calculate the quantities of horse manure that now fouled the streets on any given day? Although she had giggled at the question, she recalled, her father had remained serious.

Each day, each horse – and the city had thousands of them, he told her – deposited an average of ten pounds of manure on the streets, and when this manure was not collected and hauled off by muck carts – themselves pulled by horses! – it created enormous aesthetic, sanitary, and health problems.

Pleased with the way she had captured her father's expression – grave and intelligent – Elisabeth slipped this sketch, along with the others, into her portfolio. Her father had always been a thoughtful man, with firmly held, often eccentric views. She had never seen him back down during an argument, and had often witnessed other men succumb to the force with which he held his views, and to the orderly, logical way he presented them. For the elevated subway structures, she had heard him frequently propose to his co-workers the idea of eliminating trains and tracks altogether and substituting perpetually moving platforms that would traverse the entire city. These platforms, powered by gigantic engines housed below ground, would be carried on friction wheels and would move up and down Broadway at ten to twelve miles an hour.

Her father had told her that it might someday even be possible for a citizen of New York City to live out his entire adult life without ever going outdoors. This imaginary man, he said, might awaken in the Ansonia Hotel, for example, at Broadway and 73rd Street, a building that would be completed in the year of the subway's opening, and he would ride down in an elevator to an underpass that would connect him with a subway that would take him to an elevator that would deliver him to his office. During the day, he would move about solely by elevator and subway, stopping at underground shops – a newspaper stand, a florist shop, a café – for his needs, and returning to his apartment in the evening, all without ever having felt the direct rays of the sun. Elisabeth remembered her father telling her about this man, but she could not recall if he had done so in order to celebrate such a life, or if he had intended it as one of his cautionary tales.

What she wanted to do in passing on such stories to Daniel, was, mainly, to amuse him. And she wanted to do this, she knew, so that once Daniel was calm enough to *hear* what she was telling him, she could impress upon him not how exotic the world she had known with her father was, but how foul and dangerous it had been.

My father's world, she heard herself telling Daniel, was a world of rats and shit. It was a world that reeked of misery, loss, and loneliness. She wanted to say this to Daniel because, in his fascination with the manhole covers and with his grandfather's life – his enchantment with subterranean worlds – she sensed that he was believing what she had sometimes believed when she was a child: that the world below ground that others regarded as hellish, was somehow better – more noble, glorious, and heavenly – than the world above.

While she often thought the happiest days of her life had been spent below ground, she had come to realize that her nostalgia for these days had frequently served to keep her from remembering just how unhappy and lonely she had been. What happiness she had felt probably came from the fact of proximity – from being near her father. Once they were below ground and he was working, however, she had been isolated and left to her own devices. What had made those days and years bearable, she had concluded, was the capacity for being – Daniel's word came to mind – fanciful: her father's ability to transform the world he lived in by conjuring up an imaginary world that might someday come into being, and her ability to transform the world by drawing pictures that made it appear better than it was.

She believed it was much the same for Daniel at the Home, for though he lived with other children there, she sensed that he felt as isolated among them as she had been when she was playing in the spaces her father found for her. She sensed, too, that it was Daniel's imagination – his willingness to fantasize futures for himself, and, as with his escape from the Home, to act on them – that, if it didn't prove lethal, would ultimately prove to be his salvation.

But what if, she found herself musing, Doctor Bloch could, with his nephew's help, obtain part-time physician's work in Baltimore or in Washington? If Doctor Bloch moved there, and if she brought Daniel back to Baltimore with her once it was safe to do so, could the three of them set up house and live together the way they were doing now?

She set the two hearts she had been using as models – one entire, one dissected – back into their jars of formaldehyde. The strong chemical odor, ordinarily a reminder of mortality, seemed distinctly pleasant now, and reminded her of how eager she was to return to Johns Hopkins and to her studio. She pictured herself bringing Daniel with her – introducing him to Doctor

Taussig, Professor Brödel, Vivian Thomas. She pictured taking him with her to the children's ward, where she might suggest that he sketch portraits of some of the children . . . .

On her way back to Doctor Bloch's apartment, she would stop in Westchester Square and telephone Doctor Taussig to tell her that she expected to complete the sketches within ten days. Doctor Taussig was a woman whose life had become, for Elisabeth, more than exemplary. Doctor Taussig had never married or had children, yet neither her life nor her person seemed diminished in any way by the absence of these experiences. A woman in whom intelligence, independence, and kindness were joined in equal measure, Doctor Taussig was devoted to her work, and to the children whose lives were in her care, with a quiet passion Elisabeth found inspiring. Elisabeth also believed, and with a hopefulness that sometimes overwhelmed her, that Doctor Taussig's dreams *would* come true, and that the work she was doing would someday bear precious fruit for thousands of children and their families.

Although Doctor Taussig was two or three years younger than Elisabeth, Elisabeth realized that she thought of her as being several years older. Perhaps, it occurred to her, she could introduce Doctor Taussig to Doctor Bloch – they were both physicians, and were both solitary, kindly, scholarly individuals who would have much in common, and who might enjoy one another's company.

As soon as the thought entered her mind, though, she rejected it. She preferred, she realized at once – and she smiled at the thought – to reserve Doctor Bloch for herself. And why not? He was a wonderful influence on Daniel. He was intelligent, generous, handsome, and, in his formal Germanic way, charming. She felt a measure of comfort in his presence that she had never known with Alex, and perhaps this feeling of comfort – a feeling grounded in the knowledge that here was a man who both adored her *and* could care for her – was preferable to the conventional romantic feelings that, in her experience with Alex, and with men she had known before and after Alex, she had sometimes craved excessively. But of what use, she asked – the words, she knew, echoing those Doctor Bloch had used with respect to evil – was romance? How could it change the ways in which we were called upon to *act*?

Elisabeth looked at a sketch she had made earlier in the day: four men sitting around a fire in a subway alcove, roasting meat on wire skewers. She could fairly smell again the sweet fragrance of the roasting meat. She had sketched a portrait of one of these men – he was Portuguese – and in return he had offered her a piece of the meat, which had been sweeter in her mouth than its fragrance had been in her nostrils.

What they had been roasting, she later learned – her father told her this so that she would never again accept food from a worker without asking his permission first – were not rats, but kittens.

Elisabeth wondered if she should show the drawing to Daniel.

She placed the portfolio on a chair in the kitchen, then lifted her coat from the chair's back. It was only now, when she was ready to leave, that she became aware that the soft persistent tapping sound she had been hearing for a while and that she had assumed was coming from the radiators – air trapped in rising steam – was coming from the front door.

She put on her coat and went to the door, hoping she would find Detective Kelly or Mister Tompkins there, or even – sublime thought – Doctor Ogilvie himself. Instead, she found herself looking into the face of a middle-aged woman.

"Yes?" she asked. "May I help you?"

"I am Gertrude Kren, Doctor Bloch's daughter," the woman said. "You must be Elisabeth. May I come in? I would like to talk with you about my father."

ELEVEN

From the Journal of Doctor Eduard Bloch
December 22, 1940

I will write now of the outrageous accusations being leveled at me concerning my alleged responsibility for Adolf Hitler's hatred and persecution of Jews. That these allegations, made known to me by my nephew, Doctor John Kafka, who has communicated them to my daughter Gertrude Kren, are being made primarily by Jews, makes them all the more despicable. And that among those most prominent in promulgating these accusations are physicians – in specific, several psychoanalysts and followers of Doctor Sigmund Freud – is, for both Jews and physicians, a disgrace.

Although it is not my intention to here defend myself in the particulars, neither can I, with honor, ignore these public attacks on my person. Therefore, I will summarize for the reader the specious speculations that have been used to castigate me, trusting that their intrinsic absurdity will be sufficient defense, after which I will go on to elucidate several matters brought to mind by these accusations that may prove of more germane use in our understanding of the German dictator, and of his peculiar obsession with Jews. I will also make known for the first time some privileged information that has reached me concerning actions taking place within Germany, actions sanctioned and performed by physicians, which, in their deadly issue, especially with respect to children, make what is being done to me seem less than trivial.

But first, the contentions leveled against me, as made known to me by Doctor John Kafka: that in the many efforts to understand Adolf Hitler, individuals have been publishing papers in learned journals and giving public lectures in which they set forth the following argument – that Adolf Hitler's conscious and unconscious attitudes towards me, the Jewish doctor of his childhood, were diametrically opposed; that he was unaware of this conflict; that this conflict came into being and was intensified during the time of his mother's dying of breast cancer and my caring for her; and that this conflict was the primary source of his obsession, hatred, and persecution of Jews.

How do they arrive at such a conclusion? They do so, first, by using Doctor Freud's Oedipus theory, a theory that often, when properly (and figuratively) understood, has clinical validity as an aid in interpreting particular neuroses and psychoses, but which, when used in an irresponsibly speculative manner, becomes, in effect, what a lumberman's axe would be in the hands of a skilled surgeon.

They claim, correctly, that Hitler feared and despised his father while loving and revering his mother. But, one might respond, to how many might such a description apply? It is surely true, as I have indicated previously, that young Adolf's love for his mother was intense in the extreme. Again, however, I note the obvious – that Frau Hitler was herself a loving, dedicated mother who had *earned* the devotion of her son. Would these esteemed doctors want young people *not* to reciprocate in kind the nurturing love of a mother or a father?

They go on to describe Hitler's overwhelming and quasi-hysterical horror of sexual relations between Jews and Germans. Although Hitler dwelt at length, in many public utterances, on Jewish criminality in the fields of politics, economics, and culture, and on the menace of International Jewry, never did he become more overwrought than when speaking or writing about the sexual aspects of the problem. These, he often said, posed the danger of infecting and destroying the racial foundations of the Reich, and would lead to the "blood poisoning" of the German nation. For Adolf Hitler we Jews were, at various times, bacilli, bacteria, poisons, and cancers, all of which threatened to destroy some chimerical "purity" of the German race. To bolster their argument, my accusers cite sections of *Mein Kampf*, in particular, Hitler's description of "a dark haired man" (a Jew) defiling a blond girl (an innocent, virginal Aryan) in an incestuous and diabolical manner.

These individuals also elaborate upon Hitler's alleged incestuous feelings not only towards his sisters, but towards his half-sister, Angela's daughter and namesake, Angela Raubal, known as 'Geli,' who, although his niece, and nineteen years younger than he, was, according to them, his paramour. While living in Hitler's Munich apartment, and under clouded circumstances, I note, this poor woman shot and killed herself with Hitler's revolver, thereby sending a guilt-ridden Hitler, two years before his ascendancy to the position of Reich Chancellor, into a near-suicidal state of being.

They employ these and other postulations to give substance to what they diagnose in Hitler as an unresolved Oedipus complex, after which they utilize this diagnosis – *in absentia!* – to posit emotions they *imagine* Hitler experienced, and what they see as his confused, conflicted feelings towards me at the time of his mother's dying.

They assert that Frau Hitler's death reinforced young Adolf's considerable feelings of guilt, and that he unconsciously placed the blame for her illness, suffering, and death upon himself. But what son, a sensible person might object, would not feel helpless, and, therefore, guilty, in the ordinary sense of that word, when witness to the slow, agonizing death of a beloved parent? At this point – I here summarize several lengthy papers and arguments, although, I trust, not in an unfair, reductive manner – they will often cite a theory of Doctor Freud's daughter, Anna – one called "identification with the aggressor" – and will use it to explain how in his extreme state of grief, Hitler, now fearing madness, defended himself from feelings that were unbearable by internalizing criticism and externalizing his imagined offense. The mechanism of identification with the aggressor, thereby, they assert, is supplemented by yet another hypothetical and defensive measure: the projection of guilt.

This is the point at which they introduce my person into their imagined drama. They claim that Frau Hitler's intimacy with me – a Jewish doctor – was conducive in Adolf Hitler's psychopathology to a confusion of the doctor and Jew with his father. While *consciously* imbued with gratitude towards his Jewish doctor, they conclude, young Adolf *unconsciously* made this doctor into the incestuous poisoning murderer of his mother. Moreover, they posit a projection of his hatred of the lascivious, aggressive father onto the Jewish doctor, and speculate rather extravagantly about the fantasies young Adolf might have entertained concerning his mother's cancerous, surgically treated breasts, fantasies that abound with brutality, aggression, and mutilation.

The defense mechanisms of his ego, they declare, had succeeded in dissociating it thoroughly from its original source of conflict. Thus, they continue, not only did the Jew become an incestuous, blood poisoning murderer, but the very concept of incest came, subtly, to change its meaning: from intercourse between the parents, and between the Jewish doctor and Frau Hitler, it came to signify the ultimate horror of intercourse between Jews and Germans. Their proof? That Hitler once declared Jewry to be a cancer on the breast of Germany!

It is as if those who subscribe to this fairy tale believe that the price paid for the special privileges bestowed upon a Jewish doctor who did his best once upon a time to care for a dying woman is nothing less than the suffering now being experienced by untold thousands of Jews in Germany, Austria, and other occupied territories.

In addition, my nephew informs me that one of my accusers has gone so far as to speculate on the amount of iodoform gauze (the standard treatment for the condition in that era) I utilized to treat Frau Hitler's breast cancer. He next compiles statistical tables which imply that I employed excessive amounts in order, first, to be cruel to the poor woman, and second – how like a Jew, this man, himself a Jew, seems to be saying – for monetary gain!

I have several times considered answering these allegations in a public manner, yet I remain steadfast in my decision not to do so, and not, thereby, to lend them additional legitimacy, by my recollection of one of my father's favorite sayings: A fool may throw a stone into the water, my father taught, that ten wise men cannot recover.

Still, I can not and will not deny that these accusations have stirred up a distinctive noise in my bowels. More importantly, they have also stirred up several recollections concerning Adolf Hitler that may prove of interest to those with a genuine desire to understand this man.

Let me also state that I would not want to have my bitterness concerning the use to which these theories have been put lead one to believe that I would not, in appropriate circumstances, employ some of them myself. Reaction-formation, for example – that unconscious defense mechanism whereby a person develops a socialized attitude or interest that is the direct antithesis of some infantile wish or impulse, and a mechanism that lies at the heart of their base accusations – can often prove a quite useful way of understanding human behavior. Any competent country doctor, and I am proud to count myself among them, will understand the process whereby, unable to face a difficult situation with, let us say, a disabled child, a mother may suppress her true emotions and substitute for them false but saving emotions. Such a mother, for example, who feels cursed because her infant is abnormal, in order to bear her overwhelming feelings of disappointment, guilt, and anger, may compensate by inwardly dissociating from these feelings while outwardly expressing love and gratitude for the child she unconsciously hates. Thus, the disabled and despised child – her curse – becomes the wonderful and beloved child – her greatest treasure.

That Adolf Hitler might have borne me some conscious or unconscious measure of ill will because his mother suffered while in my care is surely possible; but that his gratitude to me for the comfort and solace I gave to her is a mask for a hatred so large that it was capable of spawning the Nuremberg Laws, *Kristallnacht*, and numerous other acts of brutality, expropriation, deportation, and murder that he and his barbarous regime have perpetrated against the Jewish population, would seem laughable were not the charges as lamentable as the situation from which they derive.

These thoughts come to mind with particular urgency this evening because earlier today my daughter, Gertrude, brought me renewed proof – copies of lectures – that those who disseminate such views will not relent in their efforts to disparage me – and even, it seems, to file papers that seek my expulsion from the United States.

Here, however, with mention of my daughter, Gertrude, and before I proceed to set down, briefly, the random recollections concerning Adolf Hitler I have alluded to, along with, more importantly, the medical information I have been privy to, I will pause, and happily so, to record several other events that have transpired today. I have never been one to believe in cosmological influences, yet on this day of the winter solstice, when the sun appears to stand still in the heavens, so does my life appear to stand still here on earth, for I feel that I have been living in a singular moment which, although occurring several hours ago, persists into the present – beyond time somehow

– and enables me to feel at one with Faust's great longing, and, *mirabile dictu*, with its fulfillment: to be able to say to the passing moment: *Stay!*

Here is what happened.

When Miss Rofman returned to my apartment this afternoon, she was, to my surprise, accompanied by my daughter, Gertrude. Gertrude, who can be headstrong in ways others do not often find congenial, had, it seemed, and without prior notification, taken the liberty of visiting Miss Rofman while Miss Rofman was working in her father's apartment.

Although both women were exceedingly gracious in one another's company, and sensitive to young Daniel's presence, it was their very excess of politeness that made me sensitive to a definite and palpable tension that hovered in the air between them.

My daughter said nothing of what had transpired, only that she was pleased to have at last met this woman about whom she had heard so much. Once Gertrude departed, however, it did not take long before Miss Rofman informed me of what had happened.

She did so, in fact, within a few seconds of Gertrude's leave-taking, when, gesturing to the large bag of food and sundries my daughter had brought for me, I made light with Miss Rofman about Gertrude's concern for my well-being, and added that she was at times perhaps something of an over-protective daughter towards an ageing father. To this remark, Miss Rofman said a simple but bold *'Oh yes!'* – and in these two words lay, I knew at once, a tale.

And the tale, which Miss Rofman told without prompting, began with this information: that Gertrude had gone to visit Miss Rofman by herself expressly to talk with her about me.

She believes I am leading you on, Miss Rofman stated.

Leading me on? I said.

She believes, dear doctor, Miss Rofman said, that I have cast a spell over you.

I do not understand.

Don't play the innocent with me, Miss Rofman replied. Clearly you are taken with me in ways that are not lost upon your daughter.

I value our friendship enormously, I stated.

Do you really? Miss Rofman said, and at this point, resting her chin upon her hand, she gave me the gift of a smile that I can only describe as bewitching. I was truly at a loss for words, which seemed to please Miss Rofman, though within a few seconds I recovered enough to be able to say that Gertrude was perhaps being excessively solicitous of my well-being.

Solicitous? Miss Rofman said. Not jealous?

Why would she be jealous? I replied. After all, she is my daughter, and you . . . .

Precisely, Miss Rofman said, after which she began to give me what I took to be a verbatim account of the conversation that had taken place between them – an exchange wherein my daughter accused Miss Rofman not merely of trying to seduce me, but of taking advantage of me in a way that could do me permanent harm. Ever her blunt and frank self, Gertrude declared that, inasmuch as it would provide an entertaining diversion for a lonely man living in a strange land, a dalliance – her exact word – might be a salutary event in my life. In fact, Miss Rofman said, my daughter all but recommended it!

This declaration was immediately followed, however, by a series of statements that were equally direct but considerably less companionable.

Your daughter told me that I should beware of starting that which I did not intend to finish, Miss Rofman said. She told me that she would not object to a dalliance, but that she deemed *you* constitutionally incapable of one. She believes, it seems, that you are incapable, as she put it, of giving your body to another without at the same time throwing in your soul.

Oh dear, I said.

She told me, Miss Rofman continued, that you had experienced a good deal of loss in recent times, and that I dare not underestimate the cost to your generous heart that my behavior might exact. She told me that you had often in your life been attracted to women much younger than yourself, and that she had no quarrel with this, except that she believed you were unaware that your expectations of these younger women were usually unrealistic, and that you too often, thinking you were the exploiter, wound up being the exploited. She asked me many questions, to none of which she seemed to require answers. She asked if my intentions were honorable, and if I felt myself worthy of a man of your accomplishments and character. She asked if I expected you to play the role of father to my son. She asked if I intended to take up permanent residence in New York City, or – her words – to 'leave you in the lurch.' She told me that if I hurt you in any substantial way, I would have her to reckon with and that I would pay dearly. And finally, she advised me to be more honest with you than with myself.

Whatever did she mean by that? I asked.

This, Miss Rofman said, and having spoken this solitary word, she came towards me – I was in my easy chair, she was sitting on the couch (Daniel was in the bedroom, drawing) – and quite resolutely took the cigarette I was smoking from my mouth, set it down in an ashtray, caressed my cheek lightly with the back of her hand, bent down, and kissed me lightly on the lips.

More exactly, she let her lips graze across mine with a tenderness that, I thought, would have made angels weep. And this became the Faustian moment that, though passing in the briefest moment, has seemed to last forever.

Then she was, once more, sitting across from me on the couch.

I am not your daughter, she said.

That is quite clear, I said, although in the forthright way in which you express yourself, I must say that you are not *unlike* my daughter.

Well, Miss Rofman said, she certainly was forthright.

In truth, so intoxicated was I by what had happened that I do not remember exactly what we said to each other after this. What I do recall, however, is that while we talked – I found myself telling Miss Rofman how, as a young girl, Gertrude had always been headstrong and independent – the only thing I could see was Miss Rofman's mouth. While I stared at her, transfixed by the movement of her lips and tongue, the rest of her face, as well as her person, were obscured in a kind of shimmering, gelatinous haze.

What was most strange was that when she spoke – like a surreal moment that might have taken place in one of my cousin's more impenetrable stories? – her words seemed disconnected from her mouth and person in the way that her mouth seemed disconnected from her face, and her face from her body. They seemed to have almost physical weight as they traversed the narrow space that lay between us. How could this be?

We talked on at some length: she told me of the drawings she was making concerning possible remedies for the Tetralogy of Fallot, and of those deformities in children's hearts which led to cyanosis – to that telltale mulberry color one sees in these children – and I reciprocated by recounting, as they came to mind, items concerning Adolf Hitler. Did Miss Rofman know, for example, that Hitler's art dealer in Vienna, with whom he was quite friendly and upon whom he depended mightily, was a Jew by the name of Joseph Neumann? Did she know that, in private, Hitler wore reading glasses? Did she know that he was intending, according to some, to send all those German and Austrian Jews who had not yet emigrated from Germany, to Madagascar? Did she know that when he visited Linz following the *Anschluss* he spoke of his great love for our city and of someday making it, and not Vienna, the capital of Austria?

I expressed my own love for Linz, and the wish that at some time in the future, when the dark times we were living in had passed, I might have the pleasure of showing its unique riches to Miss Rofman. I was grateful indeed to be living in the United States, I added, and I had found much to admire within the limited landscape, urban and rural, to which I had so far been exposed. Still, I said, gesturing towards the window and what lay beyond, although the hills are very beautiful, they are not mine.

Miss Rofman did not react directly to this statement, but instead – as if to make equal our exchange, and to acknowledge her understanding of the feelings that lay below my spoken words – she asked if I would like to see some of the work she had done earlier in the day. I said that I would, and she proceeded, on the kitchen table, to open her portfolio and to show me drawings she was preparing for Doctor Taussig.

Why they are splendid! I declared. I am astonished.

Astonished? she said. Did you think I lacked talent?

No, I answered. Of course not. But I was not prepared for such a high level of excellence.

What *were* you prepared for? she asked, to which I replied, and in a way I trusted would not be lost upon her, that nothing in life had prepared me for the moment in which I found myself living.

She laughed then, a guttural laugh of such pure, exquisite delight, that, for the first time since she had touched my lips with hers, I found my heart easing somewhat, and found also that a strong wave of laughter was now rising up from inside me.

You really *are* a truly gallant and honorable man, aren't you? she said.

Probably, I replied.

Probably?! she laughed. And you are also quite the romantic – more romantic, perhaps, than even I am – or, rather, than I have sometimes been.

It is, I suspect, my cultural heritage, I said. I am doubtless very German in this. We are a romantic people, as you know, and I use the term in its historical sense. Think of our composers and our poets – of Beethoven, Schubert, and Brahms – of Rilke, Schilling, Heine, Goethe, and –

You are also a very funny man, she said. Did you know that?

No, I said, and she seemed to find this response even funnier than what I had previously said. No, I said again. Nobody has ever accused me of being a funny man.

Well, then, she said, I am proud to be the first, whereupon, her palm pressed against her mouth, she began giggling as if she were a schoolgirl.

It was at this point that Daniel came into the kitchen. He asked what his mother was laughing about, and when Miss Rofman tried to explain – 'It's just that Doctor Bloch turns out to be a very funny man,' she said – Daniel seemed puzzled.

It is not so, I said, and I call upon my father as witness, for when I was a boy he often would say to me, 'Eduard, you're not funny . . . you're funny *looking*!'

At this remark, Daniel slapped at his thigh and roared with laughter. As soon as he leaned forward and saw the drawing that lay upon the kitchen table, however, he stopped.

Wow! he exclaimed. You're *really* good, mother. And then: That's a child's heart, isn't it?

Miss Rofman said that yes, it was a drawing of a child's heart, and Daniel said that of course you couldn't open up a child and cut out the heart just because you wanted to draw it, so that must have meant that the child this heart belonged to was already dead, and that somebody had cut out the child's heart, and that somebody else had split it in two. Was he correct?

Miss Rofman replied that he was correct, but before she could say anything else – I do not think she would have informed him that *she* was the one who had performed the dissection – Daniel became agitated.

His breathing was quick and shallow, and when he stood, he began opening and closing his hands while raising and lowering them in the air repetitively, after which, his body trembling, he turned away from us as if to try to gain control of his bodily movements. When he turned back to us, his face was quite red, and he glared at his mother in a way that made me frightened he might strike her. Miss Rofman did not show fear, however – nor did she show concern for the safety of her drawings – and so I did not act upon my impulse to step between the two of them.

What concerned me above all, then as now, was not the heart that had so disoriented Daniel – Miss Rofman's drawing of it, that is – but *Daniel's* heart, for I had come to know this boy during the several days we had spent together, and despite the brief duration of our acquaintance, what I had concluded was that whenever Daniel felt anything, he felt it intensely, and that it was not, as others might have believed, that he was the way he was because he was *disconnected* from ordinary and natural feelings, but because he was, perhaps, too *deeply* connected to them.

So profoundly did he feel things, I believed, that he could rarely find a viable way of expressing his feelings, many of which frightened him, and some of which overwhelmed him. I refer, in particular, to his great and fierce love for his mother, and his equally great dependence upon her – and, thus, his inevitable resentment of her – along with the corollary to these feelings: those intensely ambivalent emotions he bore towards his father.

I had considered saying to Miss Rofman at a propitious time that I believed many of the mannerisms others found to be alarming in Daniel – those anomalies and eccentricities of behavior that set him apart from children deemed normal – were nothing else but adaptations he had made to the confusions and fears that lay within, and that, in their way, enabled him in those moments when he felt most overwhelmed, to survive what he would not otherwise have been able to bear or to understand. His outward agitation, that is, was only the manifest sign of his inner turmoil, and of a tenderness of heart that I would count rare not only in children, but in any of us.

Thus, my instinctive sense that what so unnerved him when he looked at his mother's drawing were the intense feelings he experienced towards the child who had died – an unknown child with whom he immediately identified – 'merged' might be a more accurate word – and which feelings, in their enormity, had the effect of rendering him helpless, immobile, and angry.

Whenever he felt inwardly overpowered (and terrified) in this way, that is, he reacted outwardly with a rage that was equally overpowering (and terrifying).

I wondered: Was Miss Rofman thinking thoughts similar to mine? Did her understanding of Daniel – why he was the way he was – lie at the heart of her intense love for him, or were her feelings merely those *any* mother might feel in the presence of her wounded child?

Daniel approached his mother again. Do you still have the heart? he asked quietly. The *real* heart?

Yes, Miss Rofman replied.

May I see it?

Yes, she said, and from the large leather bag she had brought with her from her father's apartment, she took out a small jar and set it on the table beside her drawing. Daniel bent over and stared into the jar, but he did not touch it. I could smell the faint, caustic tendrils of formaldehyde that emanated from the jar, and this, stimulating an olfactory memory of iodoform gauze, and of the strong disinfectant hospital odor it gave off, made me think of Klara Hitler as she had been during her final days, lying in bed with a serene expression on her face, when, the iodoform gauze failing to provide release from pain, I had begun using morphine.

I'm crying, Daniel said, yet when I looked into his eyes I

saw no tears.

Yes, Miss Rofman said, and saying this, she reached towards him, at which gesture Daniel moved back a step.

I'm crying, he said again. There were still no tears in his eyes, however, and his voice was without affect.

Then he turned and left us, and this was the moment when I determined that I would do what I am about to do now: to write about that information, given to me shortly before I left Linz, which information was, today, jarred loose from a room of memory which I have clearly neglected and, to my shame, nearly forgotten.

I should not have tried to touch him, Miss Rofman said.

I disagree, I said.

Miss Rofman smiled a smile that was bittersweet. She reached across the table and caressed my cheek with her hand.

All right, she said. Yes.

Gently, she touched my cheek again, and when I closed my eyes and sighed, she said something I could not deny: that she had had the sense for some time that all she had to do to get me to do anything she wanted would be to touch me.

I would not disagree, I said.

I'm hungry, she said then. Are you hungry too? I haven't eaten all day – not since breakfast. Can we eat now?

And so she put away her drawings and we prepared a meal together – lamb chops, spinach, baked potatoes – and we did so, for the most part, in silence. Two remarks she made, however, rekindled in me the feelings – and hopes – that her kiss had ignited. At one point, while I was at the sink washing the spinach and she stood beside me slicing garlic, she touched the back of my neck. 'Domestic bliss, yes?' she said.

And a while later, shortly before we summoned Daniel from the bedroom to come and eat with us, touching my ear with her lips, she whispered that she was hungry for me too.

Now, hearing her voice again, I will put aside the memory of the hunger I felt – and feel! – for this woman in order to write of those less personal matters about which I have been remiss. Daniel's reaction to seeing the child's heart certainly had its effect upon me, and upon what I am about to disclose. But I wonder: Had I not experienced the kiss that Miss Rofman so tenderly bestowed upon me, would I have been so affected by Daniel, and would his circumstances and behavior have impelled me to be reminded of what I will here set down – those revelations that I should have disclosed to the appropriate authorities long before this?

No matter. Although the hour is late, I am not without energy. I feel more alert, in fact, than I have all day – thus, my intention: to complete the transcription of these memories and speculations within the next two to three days, to separate out from them all that is personal, and to confer with my daughter and nephew about the most effective way to make my writings available to those who can most usefully gain from them.

Hunger. I begin with this word – hearing once more, as I do, Miss Rofman's voice in my ear – for it is this word that has set loose from the well of memory inside me several hitherto forgotten remembrances of the young Hitler.

As I have previously noted, Adolf Hitler was a gaunt, frail young man, somewhat isolated and withdrawn, with sallow cheeks like his mother's, and – except when expressing emotion towards his mother or caring for Maria Anna – a perpetually dour expression. This dour expression was the outward sign of the chronic stomach distress that afflicted him. The source of this distress was doubtless psychological to some degree – I could find no somatic causes for what ailed him – and on these causes we might speculate infinitely (and fruitlessly); more to the task at hand, however, I will report on a specific interaction I had with him, one which was as close as we ever came to a confrontation, and which, to my mind, and only in retrospect, would seem revealing.

After I had, one day, examined Adolf and listened to his familiar complaints, I talked with him about the necessity of altering his eating habits. In his passion for vegetarianism – he was perhaps fifteen or sixteen years old at the time – he had recently begun to spurn *all* meat. If he did not like beef, I strongly urged, he might at the least add some poultry or fish to his diet.

'But that, Doctor Bloch, would be a sign of weakness,' he stated, to which I countered with the obvious observation that when it came to weakness – to that physical weakness I was remarking in him, along with the symptoms of intestinal distress of which he had spoken – it was the very *absence* of meat in his diet that we needed to correct. At this point, pulling himself up to his full height and fixing me with a most intense gaze, he declared – and these are his exact words – 'To do so, Doctor Bloch, would represent the surrender of will.'

In the moment, since I assumed that this young man's obsession, like other childhood and adolescent phases, would pass, I did not argue with him. As is well known, however, his belief in vegetarianism not only did not fade, but has grown more fervent with the years, a fervor matched by his near fanatical beliefs in the need to avoid the evils of alcohol and cigarettes.

To the memory of our talk about diet, I will add a minor recollection, that of visiting the Hitler home some three or four days before Klara's death. On this day I found him in the kitchen wearing his mother's apron and kerchief. It was with great pride (and, despite performing a woman's task while dressed as a woman, without embarrassment) that he showed me the dinner he had prepared for her – baked custard, and vegetables he had cooked so that they were soft and easily palatable: mashed potatoes, summer squash, carrots, and turnips. His well-known vegetarianism, thus, unlike his anti-Semitism, I can affirm, existed during his early years.

When I see again the young man beatifically happy to be preparing his mother's food, or standing tall and asserting that it would be weakness to eat meat, and when I think of how, across the years, he has denied himself pleasures not only in his diet, but with respect to alcohol and cigarettes (and, I suspect, women), it occurs to me that there may be a connection – and the connection I speak of is purely conjectural, a result of the kind of imaginative flight I have not, throughout most of my life, especially as a physician, been in the habit of making – between the young Adolf I knew – that fairly ordinary, polite, fragile, and somewhat feminine young man – and the man who now rules not only Germany and Austria, but much of Western Europe.

What lies at the source of much of his lust for power, I suggest – a suggestion, admittedly fanciful, that one may dismiss in the way I dismiss the theorizing of those who lay upon me the burden for Adolf Hitler's anti-Semitism – was present in the moment when he responded to the suggestion that he add meat to his diet. His insatiable lust for power, that is, would seem to be at one with the zealotry of his eating habits, and is surely connected to his lifelong complaints of intestinal distress.

What we have here, in short, is a common example of a man who, literally and figuratively, is insatiable – who can never have enough because, first, he continues to deny himself what is essential, and second (and this I have seen an untold number of times in those patients who presented with stomach ailments of unknown origin) because he is a man who quite literally is and has been eating himself up alive.

The familiar metaphor, in this instance, I submit, has a rather ordinary physical manifestation. Hitler, however, has become no ordinary man, no matter the unremarkable quality of the person he was as a boy and young man. And it is in the words he chose on that day so many years ago – when he talked about not surrendering his will – that we might discern something of the man he has become. Here I am, of course, thinking of the constant oratorical appeals that lie at the center of what we might (charitably) call his philosophy. I refer to his praise of and belief in the *triumph* of the will.

To this belief he attaches a rather shallow Social-Darwinist notion of struggle, one in which not only do the strong prevail and the weak fail, but wherein the strong have the natural right – the duty! – not only to govern and subjugate the weak, but to do away with them.

So: we have arrived at what I have learned, and what I have not seen reported in any public form of communication, and will report here.

Three days before I departed from Linz and began the journey that has brought me to the United States, I received a letter from a physician with whom I had worked for a fortnight during the Great War. Brief though our acquaintance was, there was an affinity between us – stimulated doubtless by the conditions under which we met, where we worked, under tragically inadequate circumstances, to try to save the lives of brave young men – that has resulted in an enduring friendship. (In order to shield my friend from reprisals, I will not here rehearse either our wartime experiences as physicians, or provide other data that might identify him to the authorities.)

In this letter, my friend, himself a Quarter-Jew on his paternal grandfather's side, learning of the special status Hitler had accorded me and fearing that his own status and protestations might lead to his incarceration, or worse, informed me of the following: that Adolf Hitler had himself signed an order – a rare occurrence, for Hitler generally protects himself in such matters by assigning to others official responsibility for acts that might receive public disapproval, whether domestic or international – giving to physicians the right, at their discretion, *to eliminate the incurably sick*.

According to Hitler's directive, not only are those adjudged incurably sick to be granted "mercy-death," but physicians are charged, forthwith, with the duty to see to "the destruction of life not worth living" *(Vernichtung lebensunewerten Lebens)*. This, my friend wrote, is clearly, for tens of thousands of individuals, an open-ended death sentence, and one that goes well beyond the government's previous policy, under which it ordered the sterilization of individuals declared mentally retarded, feeble-minded, or insane.

And chief among those deemed to be living "lives not worth living," my friend disclosed, are children. This program of racial hygiene, which will be surely justified, when no longer a secret by the usual Nazi rationale about those, unlike pure Aryans, who are "not born to life" – by an appeal to eternal laws of Nature's absolute order *(Gesetzmassigkert)* that help nature to its "right," or by the necessity for the Reich not to "waste" money needed for survival on "useless" human beings – will surely, too, be opposed, as sterilization was, by many brave citizens, physicians and church leaders chief among them.

The situation has, however, in my opinion, become too grave for mere protest. My friend writes that he has seen documents indicating that since February of this year more than ten thousand children have been put to death, usually with injections of the barbiturate Luminal and that, in order for hospitals, doctors, and nursing staff to be better deployed for the war effort, entire mental asylums (in Grafaneck, Haamar, Bernburg, Brandenburg, Hartheim, and Sonnenstein) have been purged of their patients, the patients either shot by SS squads or done away with by carbon monoxide gas administered by the patients' very own doctors.

Shortly after Hitler's seizure of power, Doctor Albert Einstein, vowing never to return to Germany until conditions changed, called for a worldwide moral intervention against the excesses of Hitlerism. The response of the government, as is well known, was to burn his books, confiscate his property, and revoke his citizenship. Oh that the world had, a half dozen years ago, listened more attentively to Doctor Einstein! And oh that I myself had understood the dangers as Doctor Einstein did. Still, it is my hope that by disseminating this information I may begin to repay the singular privileges I have received. I direct my words, in particular, to leaders of the government of the United States, which alone has the power to set things aright, that they might swiftly consider the necessity of going *beyond* moral intervention in order to quell those actions of the German government that are both murderous in themselves and an outrage against all that is human and civilized. Nor is it beyond possibility, were these outrages made known to the German people, that they might themselves rise up and say to their government: Stop – you may not do this in our name!

I trust this entreaty will seem neither too pious nor too vain. When I first set pen to paper I did not know I would, for those who have beseeched me to tell them what I know of Adolf Hitler, inform them of what I had learned from my friend. Nor, having destroyed his letters, do I know how I might verify his revelations. Worst of all, it is difficult to know what I might do, beyond providing witness, to alter the situation.

Still, I will persist. Once I have put these writings in proper order, I will confer with my nephew and daughter, and with the Office of Strategic Services in Washington, D. C., which was the first organization to contact me after my arrival on these shores, and I will continue to hope that my own good fortune might be of help in transforming the fortunes of those whom fate has treated less kindly.

I fear the hour is late, however, and… and what? And as soon as I write these words, I am aware that the energy and joy I felt but a short time ago, when recalling happier moments of the day, are gone. Writing the above – putting into frangible locutions the most awful news – returns me, I realize, to who I truly am – an elderly man far from home: alone, helpless, spent.

How strange, to have felt a few moments ago that I, an ageing

Austro-Jewish doctor living in a small one-bedroom apartment in New York City's Bronx region, might, due to the vagaries of my life as a physician, be not only close to the center of a supreme world-historical moment, but that I might be able to have some influence *upon* that moment.

And, too, what is stranger still: that while I was setting down information that might help thousands of children (all unknown and invisible to me: abstractions!) afflicted with conditions akin to the condition that plagues young Daniel (were he living in Germany, he might already be both sterilized *and* dead), I have been aware that Daniel might agree with those who possess the power and the will to do him ultimate harm.

I refer not to Daniel's father, or to the administrators at the institution where Daniel has been living, but to others, on this side of the Atlantic, whose beliefs, alas, are not so different from those of Adolf Hitler and his accomplices, and I refer to people on these shores because it is Daniel himself who has made them, and their extreme beliefs – their distortions of the good that a well informed and humane program of eugenics can accomplish – known to me. They are, it seems – Colonel Lindbergh, alas, and the French-born Nobel-prize winning Doctor Alexis Carrell chief among them – his heroes.

And they are his heroes, he has explained to me, with enthusiasm, because they are scientists who are perfecting mechanisms – a mechanical heart, along with a perfusion pump to keep human tissue and organs alive indefinitely – that will eventually help teach people how to live forever, and who also – what has inspired Daniel above all – have issued public statements that declare it the right of the strong to determine who among the weak and disabled shall or shall not live.

Surely one can perceive the pathos in Daniel's desire to identify himself with such doctrines. Yet surely, too, one's heart must die a little to hear *him* espouse such views. Even as I express such sentiments in writing, however, and even as my own will to persevere begins to falter – even as I, like the melancholy and lonely young man I once was, feel myself grow tired and forlorn, at the same time I cannot, out of habit, do other than to urge myself to move from the abstract and the speculative to the concrete and the real.

Miss Rofman has graciously accepted my renewed invitation to visit one of the German taverns in the Throg's Neck section of the Bronx tomorrow evening, and if I do not do so before then, I will use the occasion of our being alone to discuss with her what it is that might – that must! – now be done for her as well as for her son.

I intend also, given the possibility of intimacy that has presented itself, to inquire about several matters of which I am naturally curious but have been reluctant to address: what it is she knows about her father's whereabouts, for I have the distinct impression, due to her lack of expressed concern about his disappearance, that she knows more than she has let on; what, if anything, she remembers about her mother; and why it is she has remained unmarried in the years that have passed since her separation and divorce from Doctor Landau.

TWELVE

Would Professor Brödel and his friends have filled the large room with music, laughter, and cigar smoke, Elisabeth wondered. Would Mister Mencken have held forth on his hatred for President Roosevelt, a man he considered more despicable than Adolf Hitler? Would Mister Mencken, Professor Brödel, and the other members of their Saturday Night Club have chanted German student songs, swilled down mugs of beer, and stood on tables to proclaim their love of the Fatherland?

She and Doctor Bloch were seated near a window in Manfred's Tavern, and in the distance, across Long Island Sound, she could make out faint pinpoints of light. They came from City Island, but were the island not there, she would not have been able to discern the horizon – to distinguish the blackness of the water from the blackness of the sky.

It felt wonderful to be in a place where she had never been before – to be *somewhere else* – and to feel pleasantly light-headed. She was enjoying, in particular, the acute physical awareness she had of her tongue: the feathery ways it touched her teeth when she spoke – the soothing ways it pressed against the soft upper palate behind her teeth.

"Forgive me," she said. "I was daydreaming – or rather, night-dreaming, yes? Where was I?"

"You were telling me about your father," Doctor Bloch said. "You were describing the ceremonies that accompanied the opening day of the New York City subway system."

"Of course," Elisabeth said. "So I was."

She looked through the window again, where there were no boats moving through the water, then looked around the large dining room. The waiters, in black tuxedos, and the serving girls, in brightly colored peasant dresses, stood silently at their stations. Nobody was playing on the upright piano that sat by a far wall. Nobody was singing. Nobody was arguing, laughing, or making loud, elaborate toasts. She counted: only three tables in the room were occupied.

"I remember noise," Elisabeth said. "I remember sounds. I remember that ships in the harbor were blowing their horns, that church bells were ringing, that people were blowing on noisemakers as if it were New Year's Eve, and that I rode high up on my father's shoulders through the thickest crowds I'd ever seen. My father had bought me a tin whistle and an American flag and I kept waving the flag and blowing on my whistle, and whenever I saw another child on someone's shoulders, I'd cry out 'Hurray! Hurray! The subways are opening! The subways are opening!'

"I'd never seen so many people – so many *happy* people – before in my life. There were thousands of us walking across Brooklyn Bridge – it seemed the whole *world* was gathering to celebrate what my father and the other workers had accomplished, and . . . ." Elisabeth paused. "I felt wonderful – magnificent, really."

"I imagine so," Doctor Bloch said. "I wish I could have been there with you. You must have been a very beautiful child."

"I was, oh I was," Elisabeth said. "And the day was beautiful too – a clear, splendid day in late October. A perfect day."

"Optima dies . . . prima fugit," Doctor Bloch said, and translated: "The best days are the first to leave. That is Virgil."

"Oh I know *that*," Elisabeth said. "Willa Cather used it as an epigraph to *My Ántonia*. It was my favorite book when I was in high school. Have you read it?"

"I have not."

"I'll get you a copy then. No, I'll give you mine. I'm surprised your uncle didn't send it to you. It's about your people, you see – about Bohemian immigrants who came to America and made their lives here. They journeyed out west to Nebraska where they became farmers and where – I remember this from the book – when the wind swept across fields of wheat, the fields resembled the sea."

"I would like to read that book and to see those fields."

"And would you like to go to Nebraska with me?"

"I hardly think the time is propitious for such an adventure."

"Shh," Elisabeth said, a finger to her lips. "You take me too seriously sometimes. So: let me tell you more about the day I was remembering. I was blowing on my whistle, yes?"

"You were blowing on your whistle, yes."

"Well, every man, woman, and child in the city was supposed to blow a whistle or a horn, or ring a bell," Elisabeth said. "'It is commanded to make noise today,' my father announced before we left home. And when we came to the other side of the bridge and arrived at City Hall, there was a band playing, and thousands more people. People were setting off firecrackers, and there were lots of speeches, and at exactly two o'clock the fireworks began, and even though it was the middle of the day, they were spectacular, and they fired off huge canons from the roof of the Pulitzer Building.

"After that, my father and I walked around the city together visiting subway stations. He had gotten tickets for us – they were called 'Belmont passes,' named for the man who'd paid for the building of the subways, a man my father despised – a Jew who became an Episcopalian – and we were able to get tours at a lot of the stations, and at each station I'd ask if *this* was one he'd worked on, and if *this* was a place where I'd been with him, and I let go of my usual shyness and talked to anyone and everyone.

'My father built the subway – did you know that?' I'd say. 'My father built *this* subway station – did you know that?' And every time I talked to someone this way, he'd laugh."

While she spoke, Elisabeth found herself staring at tiny brown patches on the back of Doctor Bloch's hand – liver spots – and imagining that, as if on a map, they represented a chain of small islands. She saw herself at the window of her father's apartment, and imagined that she was looking out, not at snow-covered power lines and roofs, but at the rolling sea. She wondered: were she to draw more pictures for her father and show them to him – of the opening day celebrations, of men he'd worked with, of the imagined ship on which he'd come to America – would this free him to talk about those parts of his life he still kept in darkness?

She looked around the tavern at Christmas decorations and at trees laden with candles and ornaments – tinsel, ribbons, lights, stars, candy canes – then reached across the table, took Doctor Bloch's hand, pressed her lips to his palm.

"I feel celebratory tonight," she said. "I can't remember when I last felt this way."

"Yet you are also, I sense, experiencing a certain sadness," Doctor Bloch said.

"That too," Elisabeth said.

"Do you know where your father is now?" Doctor Bloch asked.

Elisabeth let go of Doctor Bloch's hand. "No."

"You believe he is still alive – yes?"

"Oh yes – I'm certain he is. He's left several notes for me in the apartment. Did I tell you that?"

Doctor Bloch shook his head sideways.

"I probably should have told you sooner," Elisabeth said.

"I am not surprised to learn of this. And you will, I trust, forgive my bluntness, for I find no other way to address the issue of his disappearance, but why is it, do you think, that he has gone away and is in hiding?"

"So that you and I could meet, perhaps?" Elisabeth said. She drank the last of her wine. Doctor Bloch was asking if she wanted more wine, if she would like coffee or tea, dessert, or an after-dinner drink – and while he spoke, she found herself concentrating on the movements of his tongue.

The tongue, she reminded herself, consisted of symmetrical halves separated by a fibrous septum, each half composed of muscular fibers arranged in non-symmetrical patterns, the fibers containing masses of interposed fat that were fed by a large number of vessels and nerves. The tongue also contained mucous and serous glands, and the mucous glands, she remembered, were uniquely similar to the labial glands. Could this, she mused, be yet another proof of what doctors and professors often referred to as 'the wisdom of the body?'

"You are not being serious with me," Doctor Bloch said.

"*Au contraire*, my dear doctor," Elisabeth said, and she leaned forward, beckoning with her index finger for him to come closer. When he did, she kissed him, letting her mouth linger on his, letting her tongue touch his teeth through the narrow opening between his lips. He tasted of wine, potatoes, and tobacco.

Exactly how long had it been since she'd known a man? Had Doctor Taussig *ever* known a man? Did Professor Brödel sometimes make advances on his female students, and if so, why hadn't he suggested a liaison with her? And were Doctor Bloch to reciprocate the advances she was making, how and where, given Daniel's presence, could they fulfill their desires? These, she decided, were the truly essential questions, though should she voice them, she was not optimistic concerning Doctor Bloch's ability to be of much assistance in answering them.

In the aftermath of the kiss, Elisabeth saw, Doctor Bloch had apparently decided to remain silent, and so she talked on about the opening day of the subway system, describing for him her first impressions of the City Hall station, with its marvelous skylights of leaded glass and tiled Romanesque vaults – and of the Astor Place station, her favorite not only because of the magnificent cast-iron and glass kiosk through which one entered it, but because of the lovely enameled bas-relief beavers, there to remind riders that John Jacob Astor had first made his fortune in the fur trade.

"Tell me, Doctor Bloch," she said. "Wouldn't you like to take me away from all this?"

"I would."

"I thought so. But where might we go, do you think – to Vienna? Paris? Rome?"

"I hardly think we can visit such places at this time."

"Warsaw then? Prague? Amsterdam? Berlin?"

"Baltimore seems more inviting, and more possible."

Elisabeth sighed. "Well, wherever we went, we would take Daniel with us. That's understood, of course."

"Of course."

"I wonder, though – to return to your questions about my father: Do you think it's possible that he's living in the subways – in one of the tunnels, or in an abandoned station?" she asked. "I used to think of the stations, tunnels, and caves below ground as heavenly places."

"Heavenly?"

"Most people think of worlds below ground – subways and sewers – as being like the underworld, but I never did. In Jewish mythology the underworld is neither heavenly *nor* hellish. It's just the place you go to when you die – a place where there are no masters and no slaves, where people are very much the way they were when alive, except that they're all waiting around listlessly, like people in old age homes."

"Then we should definitely not go there," Doctor Bloch said. "It *has* occurred to me, however, to wonder if your father might have taken himself there – to the subway tunnels. From what you have told me, they were once home to him."

"Maybe," Elisabeth said. "I was thinking more of Daniel – of his obsession with the street coverings and where they lead, and of his fascination with his grandfather's life."

When she had first talked with Alex about times she'd spent with her father below ground, and of how those were among the happiest hours of her life, Alex had gone on at length about the Jewish concept of the underworld. Nobody really *wanted* to go to the Jewish underworld, he explained, because you only went there if you died. And before the idea of an afterlife was invented, *nobody* wanted to die, for if you died you went *down there*, where there was no torment, of course, since without a heaven there was no hell, but where there was no bliss either. Once Christians invented the idea of an afterlife, however – and contrary to what most people thought, in the beginning the rabbis had taken up the idea of an afterlife with zeal – the idea of an underworld had disappeared. Unlike the world below ground that she and her father had known, however – a world teeming with *life* – the underworld in Jewish lore was essentially a lifeless place in which God simply had no interest.

"I was eight years old – eight years and a few months – on the day the subways opened," Elisabeth said. "But I was younger than that during the years my father worked building them."

"You are quite worried about Daniel, aren't you?" Doctor Bloch said. "That he might want to go down there on his own."

"In search of my father?"

"That was my thought."

"It's occurred to me."

"And are you also worried, I sense, because, to pursue our pleasures, you and I have left him alone in the apartment."

"Oh not at all," Elisabeth said quickly. "Not at all." She lowered her voice. "What I was thinking was this: perhaps Daniel's right, and my father *has* gone there – into the subways – and taken a *woman* with him. My father's a very handsome man who's known many women. Have I told you this about him before? Am I talking too much?"

"The answer to both questions is no."

"Good," Elisabeth said. "Once, I remember, returning home early from school, I found him with Ulla – Ulla was our housekeeper, after my mother died – in what I'd later understand to have been a compromising situation. She was a married woman, but I never met her husband, and only one of her four children. That was Grete, who was my age – Ulla would bring her to our apartment sometimes so I'd have someone to play with. And sometimes back then, I'd imagine that she hadn't died – my mother, that is, not Ulla – but that she'd abandoned us, and that my father had *invented* the story of her death because this was his way of protecting me."

Elisabeth looked through the window and imagined she saw Daniel walking towards her across the water, smiling mischievously and carrying a large manhole cover, like an umbrella, above his head. She remembered that there were men called swamp angels – fugitives from the law for whom the sewers and subway tunnels were like biblical cities of refuge – and how, the first time her father pointed one of these men out to her, she had asked him where the man's wings were.

"And sometimes I imagined she was a prisoner somewhere – in a jail, in a lunatic asylum, in a locked room where my father brought her food every day to keep her alive," Elisabeth said. "Sometimes I imagined that she'd died, not from tuberculosis, but during childbirth, and that the child had lived, and that my father gave the child away or sold it to another family."

Sometimes, she told Doctor Bloch, when she was out walking in her neighborhood – to or from school, or to or from a friend's house – she had imagined that on *that very day* a woman was going to stop her on the street and reveal to her that *she* was her mother. Sometimes she imagined the woman as old and poor – consumptive, rheumatic – and sometimes she imagined her as a wealthy woman who dressed the way she had dressed when she was first married to Alex – the way Sonya dressed now – in silks and jewels and furs . . . .

"You were a most imaginative child clearly," Doctor Bloch said.

"I was that," Elisabeth said, "though I don't believe such daydreams are unusual for someone who doesn't have a mother."

"But, my dear child, you *did* have a mother. We all have mothers."

"Please do not call me your child."

"It was a figure of speech."

"My father would never talk with me about her," Elisabeth said, turning away from Doctor Bloch but staring at his reflection in the window. She pictured him beside her, on the train to Baltimore – pictured introducing him to Doctor Taussig, Doctor Blalock, Professor Brödel, and Vivian Thomas, and pictured showing him around the hospital and her studio. But where was Daniel? Had he stayed behind in New York? Had she left him alone in her Baltimore apartment? Or was he still outside, walking on water but moving eastward, away from her?

She saw herself walking arm in arm along Broadway with Doctor Bloch, from the hospital and towards her apartment, then inviting him in, serving him wine, taking him into her bedroom. His touch, she knew, would be gentle, and it occurred to her suddenly, and in a way that was not unpleasant, that the hands that might soon be caressing her were the same hands that had once touched Adolf Hitler's private parts.

What an extraordinary idea, and how much more extraordinary that I'm having it, she thought, and that I'm not embarrassed to be having it, or to be imagining intimacies with this man. Doctor Bloch *was* an intelligent and sensitive man – dutiful, measured in word and action, and with exquisitely proper manners. Still, Elisabeth felt certain that passion burned beneath his exterior

– a rich, roiling world of thought, emotion, and sensuality that – why deny it? – she wanted to arouse so that she could experience its heat. She wanted to *know* him – to stroll along the pathways of his mind, to hear him tell her about his early years, his war experiences, his romances, his marriage . . . .

"He kept no photographs of her that I ever found," Elisabeth said, "and I've never been able to remember her face. Sometimes at night, though, I tell myself that I can remember the sounds she made when she coughed – that I can see the blood-spotted pieces of cloth she used. But these are, after all, conventional notions that might be the stuff of anyone's fantasies. They don't necessarily come from my particular experience."

"Did you ever attempt to draw her picture – ?" Doctor Bloch asked " – to draw the mother you do *not* remember?"

"No."

Elisabeth stood, put a hand on the table to steady herself.

"Although they're not without merit, your questions are irritating," she said. "What you should do instead of asking questions is to think about answering the question I asked before."

"About taking you away from all this?"

Elisabeth smiled. "In our brief acquaintance," she said, "I have never known you to be an unintelligent man."

She put a hand on Doctor Bloch's shoulder – did he have feathered wings below his jacket and shirt that, as her guardian angel, he was commanded to keep hidden from view? – bent down as if to kiss him, but instead ran a finger across his lips, then took the corner of his moustache between thumb and forefinger, and twirled it.

❖ ❖ ❖

In the restroom, an elderly woman in a black and white maid's uniform stood, curtsied, and handed Elisabeth a warm towel. She spoke to Elisabeth in German, telling her that her name was

Frau Giesler, that she hoped Elisabeth was enjoying her evening at Manfred's Tavern, and that she wished Elisabeth all good things for the holidays.

Elisabeth thanked Frau Giesler even while she was concluding that it had been exactly two years and three months since she had last known a man, and Doctor Thomas Jefferson Ogden had been that man – that *lucky* man. Although she knew she was a bit unsteady on her feet, and that she had to concentrate in order not to slur words when she spoke, the fact that she could calculate accurately reassured her.

Tom Ogden had been visiting at Johns Hopkins for half a year from Harvard Medical School in order to study new techniques for ear surgery that were being developed by Samuel Crowe and Tom Cullen. Ogden was a married man with several children – three? four? – she couldn't recall – who claimed that he and his wife had an arrangement: they remained married, but no longer shared a bed. He had been well-educated – a Classics scholar during his undergraduate years – urbane, witty, and physically fit. *Their* arrangement had lasted the better part of four months, and when they parted – should she admire herself for this, or see it as a failing? – she had had no regrets, little sense of loss.

In the mirror above the sink, Elisabeth was surprised to see that the woman who stared back at her – a woman with short black hair and an attractive birthmark at the tip of her nose – looked radiant and youthful. Turning away, she noticed several photographs propped against the wall at one end of the marble countertop, and, thinking this would please Frau Giesler, she asked about them.

Frau Giesler said that they were photographs of her children and grandchildren: three sons, two daughters, seven grandchildren. Elisabeth pointed to a photograph of a man in military uniform. Your son? she asked, and Frau Giesler laughed and said that this was a photograph of her *husband* – Otto – who had died in Germany nine years before. They had grown up together in the city of Mannheim, and had been childhood sweethearts.

Did Elisabeth have children? Frau Giesler asked. Elisabeth said that she had a grown son, and she reached into her handbag and took out a picture of Daniel. Frau Giesler remarked on how handsome Daniel was, on how much – especially around the eyes – he resembled his mother.

Had Elisabeth been to Manfred's Tavern before? Frau Giesler asked. Were her son and husband there with her this evening? Elisabeth replied that she was familiar with the area and had visited it several times with her father, but that she hadn't been to Manfred's Tavern before. She wasn't married, she said, and had come with a friend, an Austrian physician recently arrived in America, but she hoped to bring her son with her on her next visit. She put Daniel's photo back into her handbag, excused herself, and entered one of the stalls.

When she emerged, Frau Giesler turned on a faucet, and gave Elisabeth a fresh warm towel. Wasn't it wonderful, Frau Giesler said, to be able to celebrate the Christmas season in an authentic German atmosphere?

It was, Elisabeth replied, and added that it must be gratifying for Frau Giesler to see that most of the ways in which Americans celebrated Christmas derived from German traditions. "Oh yes!" Frau Giesler responded, and brushed Elisabeth's dress lightly. Elisabeth considered the hours Frau Giesler spent by herself in a narrow room that smelled, with excessive sweetness, of lavender, and wondered how many hours Frau Giesler – mother of five and grandmother of seven – worked here. Was *this* what she had come across the ocean for?

Frau Giesler asked if Elisabeth would like to try some of the tavern's *eau de Cologne*, which, she said, really did come from Cologne. "Please," Elisabeth said, and closed her eyes while Frau Giesler lifted Elisabeth's hair and sprayed cool, fragrant mist on the back of her neck. Would Elisabeth like to try some of the tavern's hand cream, which came from Müllheim, a city in the Black Forest not far from Freiburg?

Elisabeth spread her palms upwards so that Frau Giesler could dispense cream onto her hands. She smelled violets now, and something more pungent – verbena? thyme? lily-of-the-valley? She enjoyed being pampered, and she wondered: Was Frau Giesler going to offer her a massage? A bath in black mud? A manicure? A pedicure? Was she going to invite her home for the holidays?

"You have been most kind," Elisabeth said, and she set a dollar bill on the counter beside the photographs. Without looking at the dollar bill or thanking her for it, Frau Giesler asked if Elisabeth lived in New York City, or was she merely visiting and did she intend to return to Germany when that became possible? Only Frau Giesler's eldest son, his wife, and their two children were here in America, she said. The others had stayed in Germany, where her two other sons and three of her grandchildren were now serving in the Army.

Elisabeth was about to tell Frau Giesler that she was not German, though she was gratified to find her spoken German good enough that Frau Giesler thought she was, when Frau Giesler whispered words Elisabeth was not sure she wanted to understand. She asked Frau Giesler to repeat what she said. Frau Giesler came closer and, her hand on Elisabeth's hand, said again that what made things so special at this time of year – something, as two German women, they could appreciate – was that although they were in America, here at Manfred's Tavern they could celebrate the holiday in the old way *and* in a place where they would not encounter Jews.

"But I'm Jewish," Elisabeth said.

Frau Giesler said that clearly, in addition to being gracious and beautiful, Elisabeth was also possessed of a distinctive sense of humor – a kind of German humor Americans did not often understand.

"Otto – my husband, *not* my son – had that kind of humor," Frau Giesler said. "Still, it is good to be here now – to have this work – but it will be better still, I think, when we can return home."

Elisabeth felt momentarily confused. If she insisted to Frau Giesler that she was a Jew, what, other than hostility and resentment, would be gained? Should she reach into her handbag and give Frau Giesler even *more* money? And if she did, would such a gesture be seen as profligate – would it prove to Frau Giesler that she *was*, or that she was *not*, a Jew? And were this woman to be persuaded that she had been deceived about Elisabeth's identity, what in her, or in Elisabeth – or in the world! – would change? Elisabeth considered saying that although her mother and father were Jewish, she of course was not, but she feared that such irony – *any* irony – would be lost on the woman.

More: she sensed that what she was most upset about was not the woman's anti-Semitism, which seemed common enough, but the fact that what had been a nearly perfect evening, and what, if in a woman's restroom, had just been a few moments in time that were blissfully out of time: simple, luxurious, and meaningless – had been sullied by the woman's stupidity.

For a brief instant, she imagined that her father, overhearing the conversation from the other side of a wall – from the men's restroom – was standing in the doorway, glaring at Frau Giesler. Her father, though not an observant Jew, had a pure hatred for those – August Belmont, the man who had financed the building of the subways, chief among them – who had denied or rejected their origins. In her mind, she saw her father bow to Frau Giesler, smile, then slap her hard across the cheek. The imagined sound, like that of a sapling being snapped in two, made Elisabeth wince.

"I have had too much to drink," Elisabeth said. "But you have made me sober, Frau Giesler, and for that I thank you. I am a

Jew – a *Jewess*, yes? – and I am spending a romantic evening here tonight with a dear friend – the physician of Austrian descent I mentioned before who, like me, is also a Jew."

Without waiting to see or hear Frau Giesler's reaction, Elisabeth left the restroom. There was no response, she knew, that would satisfy, though the melodramatic scene in which she had imagined her father taking part, along with an antic impulse – a fleeting desire to tell Frau Giesler who Doctor Bloch's most famous patient had been – spoke, she knew, to the intensity of her reaction.

She walked quickly through the deserted dining room only to hesitate when she saw that a man was seated at the table with Doctor Bloch, and that the man was Alex. Mister Tompkins and Detective Kelly, in dark winter coats, stood next to the table.

The four men turned towards her when she arrived at the table. Alex urged her to be seated – she refused – after which he spoke as if from a prepared speech.

"I have come to offer apologies to you and Doctor Bloch," he stated. "I regret this interruption of your evening, but it seemed imperative that I be here straightaway – certainly before the two of you returned home – in order to offer apologies personally."

Detective Kelly and Mister Tompkins inclined their heads, and said that they too offered their apologies.

"Apologies are hardly sufficient," Doctor Bloch declared. He was sitting up straight, his cheeks bright red, his eyes blazing. Were someone to cut a clean slice across the top of his head, at the hairline, Elisabeth thought – and Alex was the man capable of doing so – she expected she would see flames rise up from inside his skull.

Elisabeth said nothing. She saw that both Detective Kelly and Mister Tompkins had removed their hats, but that Alex was still wearing his fur *streimel*, probably because, ever politic, he preferred not to be seen wearing a *yarmulka* in a German restaurant. And what, she wondered, would Frau Giesler and others in the restaurant make of the presence here of a well-dressed *Negro* man?

"We have just come from Doctor Bloch's apartment, where we had reason to believe Daniel was staying," Alex said.

"You've done *what* – ?!" Elisabeth exclaimed, and felt her heart thump so loudly she feared the others could hear it.

"As I have already explained to Doctor Bloch, we had a proper search warrant – "

"But by *what* – ?"

" – and we took care not to disturb anything unduly, and to return items to their proper places," Alex continued. "What I have come here to do is to report what you already know: that Daniel was not there, nor was there any evidence that he had ever been there. My suspicions were in error, and so I regret our violation of your privacy and your trust."

Although her heart continued to pound wildly, Elisabeth feigned a calm, indignant response.

"As well you should," she said, "though there was little trust left to be violated."

"Be that as it may, we are left with the problem of Daniel's whereabouts," Alex said. "What I think, therefore, is that you and I should now consider – "

"What I think is that you should leave," Elisabeth said.

She moved to Doctor Bloch's side and, while she rested a hand upon his shoulder, felt a surge of pride in Daniel – that he had, once again, evaded capture.

"I hope you will both forgive me so that we can cooperate more effectively," Alex said. "Let me explain: We – Detective Kelly and his men, and I, along with Mister Tompkins – had reason to believe Daniel might be staying with you, and given this assumption, we decided to wait until the two of you were gone. We concluded that this would be the most discrete way to determine if our suspicions were correct. Obviously, they were not. We should not have doubted your word, of course, and again we ask your forgiveness."

"There is, sir, no forgiveness for unforgivable acts," Doctor Bloch declared.

"That may well be," Alex said. "I'll depend, therefore, on your generosity."

"If you do so, you err," Doctor Bloch said. "Forgiveness, in my opinion, is, as you Americans might put it, distinctly overrated. As one who prides himself on knowledge of Jewish history and traditions, you especially should know that Jews do not put the value on forgiveness that, say," Doctor Bloch nodded towards Detective Kelly and Mister Tompkins "our Christian friends do. Thus, I join Miss Rofman in asking that you take your leave of us, and that you do so at once."

Elisabeth bent down, cupped her hand over Doctor Bloch's ear.

"You're my hero," she whispered.

"If, upon my return home," Doctor Bloch stated, "I find that damage has been done to my apartment, I will, I assure you, take measures."

"Let me interrupt to say that it was my idea to enter the doctor's apartment," Detective Kelly said. "Based on what we learned from the authorities in Maryland, ma'am, we're pretty sure your son isn't there. That's why it seemed wise to follow all possible leads and to do so without warning anyone who might be implicated in his disappearance. We want only what you and Doctor Landau want, after all – to see the boy returned safe and sound."

"May I add," Mister Tompkins said, "that Doctor Ogilvie has given me liberty to inform you, should you hear from Daniel and have communication with him, that the Salisbury Home will take no punitive measures against him when he returns."

"Is surgery considered a punitive measure – " Elisabeth asked " – or an ameliorative one?"

"Will you please, *please* let up on that?" Alex said. "Why

in God's name must you remain fixated on something I've already said I *agree* with you about?" Alex shrugged. "He is our *son*, Elisabeth – yours and mine, and for all our sakes, I only hope – "

Alex broke off, closed his eyes and bit down on his lip as if, Elisabeth thought, to keep tears from forming in his eyes. Was this an act, she wondered, or was he sincere? And – the more relevant question – would he know the difference?

"I assure you again," Detective Kelly said, "that we're doing our best, and that we intend no harm, either to you or to the boy. I've got five sons myself, ma'am, so I understand."

"No daughters, Detective Kelly?"

"No daughters."

"And how is your hand?"

"With all respect, ma'am, I've experienced worse and I bear you no grudge." Smiling, he turned to Doctor Bloch. "I understand, sir, that you were Adolf Hitler's doctor."

"That is true."

"I'm sorry to hear that," Detective Kelly said. "It must be a heavy burden to have saved that man's life."

"I did no such thing," Doctor Bloch said.

"That's not the information I received," Detective Kelly said. "But if you say that it isn't so, I'll take you at your word and go back to my sources and find out why they believe otherwise."

"By what right do you slander me, sir?" Doctor Bloch said.

"It's no slander to tell a doctor he saved a life, however rotten the life saved," Detective Kelly said. "I was only doing my job – trying to verify what was told to me. I was also told you may have been responsible for his mother's death."

"That is absurd," Doctor Bloch said. "These are gross distortions which I will correct in due time. I have already begun to . . . ."

Seeing that Doctor Bloch's hands were trembling, Elisabeth moved closer to him. "Shh," she said, her hand on his shoulder.

"There's no need to justify yourself to men like these."

"That's certainly true," Detective Kelly said, his brogue suddenly thicker, "for there are others, I'm told, who are going to demand answers to questions about your relationship with the German dictator pretty soon. It's also occurred to me to ask why if you *were* in any way responsible for his mother's death, he's been so generous to you?" Detective Kelly paused, and when Doctor Bloch did not respond, he continued: "I take the liberty of talking with you this way because you strike me as an honest and honorable man."

"A man like yourself?" Elisabeth said.

"The way I see things is this, Doctor," Detective Kelly said, ignoring Elisabeth's remark. "Many years ago you were put in an unenviable position, and you did your job. What choice did you have after all? Given my own line of work, I can sympathize. I inquire and I observe. I gather evidence. I do my job. I don't judge."

"But you do," Elisabeth said.

Detective Kelly reached into an inner pocket of his overcoat, withdrew a notepad, and leafed through it.

"Yes," he said, placing the notepad back in his pocket, and turning to Elisabeth. "With respect to your father, ma'am, I've been given permission to tell you that a man fitting his description has recently been seen in the tunnels beneath Riverside Park – not in the subways, as was reported earlier, but where the Penn Station railroad yards used to be. We're hoping to have some definitive news for you soon. It's also occurred to us to wonder why your son and your father disappeared at the same time. That's why I'd like to call on you tomorrow, maybe late morning – say, eleven – to ask some questions and get some additional information that might prove useful to us."

"No," Elisabeth said. She lifted her hand from Doctor Bloch's shoulder, and, leaning against him, smoothed his hair with her palm.

"Then we'll have to proceed without your cooperation, Detective Kelly said. "If you change your mind, I trust you'll let me know."

"Dear, dear Elisabeth," Alex said. "Can you please soften your heart? We are not *against* you in this. I'll say it again: I regret what we did this evening – we truly meant well, and though you might respond by saying that the road to hell is often paved with good intentions, I hope that in this instance you'll look to our mutual concern. Daniel has been missing for nearly a week now, and as desperate as he may be, I am equally desperate on his behalf. We may disagree about many things, but surely we both fear for his safety, and surely we would both agree in doubting his ability, especially in winter, to survive on his own for any length of time."

"I too am concerned," Mister Tompkins said, "and concur with Doctor Landau's opinion of your son's abilities. In my experience of the boy, I – "

"Do not, please, talk to me of your experience of my son," Elisabeth said, and when she did, Doctor Bloch reached up, took her hand in his.

Alex stepped away. "I may have erred," he said. Then, his eyes fixed on Elisabeth and Doctor Bloch, he smiled mischievously. "But as you will recall – a saying that was your invention, I believe – to err is human, to *sin* divine."

Feeling an urge to strike Alex across the face but sensing the pleasure he might take from the act, Elisabeth did nothing. Doctor Bloch, however, was already standing and glaring at Alex. Elisabeth slipped her arm into his.

"How dare you talk to Miss Rofman in this manner," Doctor Bloch said. "How *dare* you!"

"Pistols at dawn, my good doctor?" Alex replied, after which, he inclined his head in a gesture of farewell, turned, and with Mister Tompkins and Detective Kelly following, left the tavern.

THIRTEEN

From the Journal of Doctor Eduard Bloch
December 26, 1940

One of Adolf Hitler's first acts as Chancellor of the Reich was to secretly raise the wages of female ballet dancers by 300 percent in order to save them from the threat of lives of prostitution. I mention this fact, which came to me on good authority – a patient, now in retirement, who had been a Director of the Vienna Opera House – because I have become aware, in America, of the tendency of many to talk of Adolf Hitler as 'evil,' as if with this one word to dismiss the man and all that he is and represents – as if, were he gone – had he never existed! – all would be well.

To call Hitler evil, in my opinion, is of little *utility*. What we need to do instead – thus my modest contribution concerning the interactions I had with him during his early years – is to see him clearly. In this way we may hope to enable those who must engage and confront him to do so with a greater possibility of curbing his ambitions and his power.

To that end, I have faithfully recorded my memories of the young Adolf Hilter, even when they seem profoundly inconsequential, and I here record a final recollection, that of an incident so strange that doubtless I had ceased, in part of me, to believe it ever occurred. That this is so – that the incident itself had, in my mind, become non-existent – is, as we will presently see, bound up, albeit ironically, with the curious nature of the incident itself.

The incident took place several weeks after Frau Hitler's death, when young Adolf came to my office with a most bizarre complaint: He believed he had become invisible.

At first I thought he was merely confused, and had intended to say that parts of the world were becoming invisible to *him*. I thought, that is, that he might, in grieving for his mother, be experiencing some form of hysterical blindness – a condition I encountered in several young men during the war – but he was quite insistent in saying that he feared that parts of his body – legs, arms, and hands in particular – were, in an alarming and regular way, becoming phantoms.

Awakening during the night, for example, and raising one of his arms in the air, he had been able, he claimed, to pass the other arm directly through the raised arm as if it were not there. When he took walks in the woods surrounding Linz – that beloved forest in which, he said feelingly, dwelt our spirit, our ideals, our past, our poetry, and our truth – and, sitting with his back against a tree, meditated on his mother's life and all that she had done for him and meant to him, he would suddenly find his right hand moving downwards of its own accord and slicing through a part of one of his legs as if the leg were not there.

I showed no least skepticism, and assured him that, since everything that took place in my office was confidential, he need not be embarrassed about such disclosures. But could he, I asked, repeat the experience in my presence?

Not if you are watching me, he replied.

How then, I asked, could I make sense of his experience?

Were you to leave me alone in the room, he said, and without having anyone spy upon me, I am confident that the experience would repeat itself.

Let us see, I said, and so saying, I left the room.

When I returned several minutes later, he was sitting in the chair opposite my desk, one leg crossed over the other, exactly as he had been before I left the room.

He nodded once.

Then it has happened again?

Yes, he said. This time I was able to pass the index finger of my right hand through the palm of my left hand.

I took his hand in mine – he did not resist, and had always, in fact, during examinations, been without that physical modesty common to many young people – and examined his palm. I saw nothing unusual.

There is something else I must tell you, he said. Although the kind of transformation wherein parts of my body disappear or become transparent has been occurring frequently when I am alone, it is also true that when I have been in public spaces I have several times become invisible to others.

Three times during the previous week, he asserted, when he had been walking in the city, friends had passed him without seeing him. Furthermore, on one occasion I myself had looked straight at him without acknowledging his existence.

Did I remember going to the Opera House on Thursday afternoon to purchase tickets? he asked. I said that I did. He then told me that he had been standing to one side of the ticket office when I approached and that I had been carrying a shopping bag full of purchases, a bag that, in order to reach my billfold, I had transferred from one hand to the other. Did I recall the moment?

I said that I did.

Well, when you stopped to do this you were standing no more than two feet from me. You looked right at me yet said nothing.

I apologized for any unintended rudeness, and said that although it was of course my habit to greet him as I would greet anyone at such a moment, I did not recall seeing him.

After I said this, he remained silent for a good while, and so I began inquiring further, asking if, when he was a boy, he had, in the manner of other children, imagined that he was invisible.

He shook his head sideways.

Had he ever believed – a common childhood experience – that he had an imaginary playmate who was visible to him but invisible to others?

Again he shook his head sideways.

Had he, when in Vienna, seen any magic shows in which ladies vanished, or limbs or other body parts seemed to fly through the air, or small animals were made to disappear?

Once, he recalled, when a boy, he had seen a magic show in which a magician's head disappeared and was made to reappear, rising up from the magician's upturned hat as if it were a rabbit. But he could not recall ever seeing another show of the kind I was asking about, whether in Linz or in Vienna.

At this point I noticed that he was becoming agitated, his right hand moving up and down involuntarily, and so I suggested that we proceed to a physical examination. Perhaps in so doing we would discover a source for the unique experiences he had described.

He cooperated with the physical examination eagerly. When I auscultated his chest and back, for example, he asked, with genuine curiosity, what I was hearing, and when I looked into his eyes – half-fearing I might discover a tumor pressing upon the optic nerve, or evidence suggesting the presence of a lesion – he asked me to describe what I saw.

When the examination was over and we sat in my outer office again, I told him I found nothing that would account for his experiences. Still, to help him sleep and calm his nerves, I offered him phenobarbital. Had he of late, I then inquired, been drinking alcohol in any unusual quantities?

I do *not* drink alcohol, he declared.

He returned to my office several days later, and it was apparent at once that something had changed, and in a positive way. I did not have to do anything more than shake his hand and ask him how he was before he burst into a long monologue of what I would call rhapsodic intensity, one in which he told me that since his previous visit to my office, the experiences of invisibility had vanished, but that at night – he had been taking the phenobarbital regularly, and even confessed, while giggling, to having sometimes doubled the dosage – he had begun to be visited by famous historic personages: Joan of Arc, Napolean Bonaparte, Frederic the Great, Richard Wagner, Otto von Bismarck, the Prophet Mohammed, and Gengis Kahn prominent among them – and during these visitations, they had all, without exception, wanted to confer with him about one thing and one thing only – his diet: about why he drank no alcohol and ate no meat.

I had to work hard not to laugh aloud at these fantasies, but to my surprise I found that I had no need to restrain myself, for Adolf himself began to laugh.

I know my dreams are childish, he said, but they are also quite wonderful, don't you think?

I agreed with him and, in truth, I cannot remember another occasion when he was as relaxed and forthcoming as he was during this visit. As I have noted, he had always been a shy, isolated, and somewhat morbid young man, yet until this moment I confess that I had not been aware that he possessed anything resembling what one might call a sense of humor.

After he had recounted his dreams in lavish detail – in the way that some patients, to no seeming purpose, would begin a consultation by telling me item by item and course by course of the elegant meal they had enjoyed in a restaurant the night before – he laughed heartily.

I must be boring you, he said after a while, and I am aware you have other patients waiting, so I will tell you the primary reason for this visit. Given my recent experiences, I would like you to advise me: Do you think I would benefit from the services of an alienist?

I said that I saw no need for him to consult an alienist.

Unless, of course, he said, smiling broadly, I become invisible again!

If so, I suggested, I have no doubt but that your dreams will once again come to your rescue.

That is true, he said, and bowing and taking my hand in his – for a moment I had the distinct impression he was going to kiss the back of mine – he thanked me and took his leave.

I have presented this anecdote as accurately as I am able, not because I believe that in itself it will explain anything about Adolf Hitler that is of practical use, but simply because it occurred. Taken in conjunction with my other recollections, and with the vast fund of information doubtless gathered from other sources, both public and private, I trust that it will prove of some help to those who must actually deal, in the world of *realpolitik*, with Adolf Hitler himself.

Reviewing my relationship with the man, however, I must add, reinforces my earlier sense that although he was surely an intense and unique individual, there was nothing in his physical being, character, or history that would enable one to account for the man he has become. To put it in another way, I believe we may have here a peculiar instance in which the usual truth to which I have previously alluded – that the child is father to the man – lacks apparent validity.

It is, moreover, this very disjuncture between the young man I knew in Linz and the man who now rules Germany, Austria, and much of Europe, that compels our attention, and that draws us, if I may make bold to say so, to those mysteries of human character – of how and why we become who we are – that are forever beyond our understanding. What we may have in this man's life, then, at least to this point in time, is merely an extreme instance of a general truth.

I will also add what may seem a puzzling and perhaps arrogant statement: that the process of recalling and recounting my experiences has convinced me that it is a good thing that we can *not* understand how and why we become who we are – or why it is, to put the matter in theological terms, that God destroys the good and the wicked equally – and that the journeys of our lives, therefore, remain, whether for good or ill, unpredictable.

Would we, I wonder – despite the suffering that has resulted from this man's influence – have things any other way? I am not, of course, suggesting that I wish upon others the anguish this man has, in recent years, initiated, but it seems to me that the course of his life – the fact, that is, that a man of such authority and charisma could have risen from the unremarkable boy I knew – lamentable as its issue may be, is itself cause for wonder.

Such, then, are the musings of an ageing Austrian physician, readily dismissed or ridiculed, I am certain, but presented along with accounts of my interactions with the young Adolf Hitler, and presented without, as was my promise, concealment. I am reminded, in this regard, of a stanza from Rilke's *Stundenbuch*, which I set to heart when I was a young man of Hitler's age:

I believe in all things heretofore unuttered
My most reverent sentiments – these I wish to set free.
What none have yet dared to desire,
Will one day spring forth within me.

Should my writings in some small way alleviate the suffering that, as more nations draw near to the ongoing war, seems imminent – should they be a source of understanding, or of counsel for good – I will be grateful. Although I am not a believer in an Almighty or an Unseen Power, yet do I fervently pray that the worst fears some have as to what may ensue due to this man's ascendancy may never be realized.

About this, I myself remain hopeful, not only because it is in my nature to be optimistic, but because there does seem something distinctly unnatural in the disjuncture to which I have alluded. That the child is not, as in this instance, father to the man, would seem to go against the natural order, for it is nature's way to constantly reassert its dominion and not to permit what is *un*natural to survive for any prolonged period of time. With Doctor Einstein, therefore, I believe that the search for the absolute – the primary mission of all science – is predicated on a faith in Nature's order, which faith derives from the longing to behold that eternal harmony.

Still, I must wonder: Have I said all I wished to say and recalled all there is to recall? Is there some memory of this man, relegated to an inaccessible room of my mind, that I have been *unable* to bring to light? I hope not, and I think not. But I am aware that my senses – inflamed, aroused, satiated, confused, alarmed, and alert – are in a heightened state of awareness, and that this may account for the sanguine manner in which I have ended that portion of these writings that pertain to Adolf Hitler.

For the present, however, and in the quiet of my room, I will now reflect on those more private matters that have, in recent days, given untold joy to my heart. Outside my bedroom window, I see that the snow that began to fall on Christmas Eve continues to fall. Stray sounds arrive from the outside world as if from far-off lands. The streets below, covered in a deep, clean thickness of white, are deserted. It is well past midnight, yet I feel no fatigue. The more I write, it seems, the more I want to write.

Miss Rofman, only a few feet distant from me, is fast asleep, as she has been for several hours. Although I dearly wish I could have been able to allay her anguish concerning Daniel, yet do I acknowledge that it was this very anguish that has helped bring into being the great happiness I have known. Suffering, as the poets have taught us, can often be the seedbed of joy.

I am aware that had Miss Rofman, yesterday evening, known with certainty that Daniel *was* safe and sound, we might not have been drawn to each other with the urgency and passion that consumed us. Fear and sorrow clearly inflamed our ardor, and while I do not believe that it was primarily fear or sorrow that caused us to find and know each other in this way – that caused Miss Rofman to be kind to me in ways I never imagined possible in this life – surely her despair at the possibility that something grave had befallen her son, or might soon befall him, brought forth in her an equally overwhelming feeling: a desire for human comfort that I was, thankfully, here to provide.

Although we have exchanged neither avowals of love nor conventional words of romance, yet were we able to give to each other that solace which, though physical in its manifestation, was also, by freeing us from ordinary consciousness, the balm our souls craved.

That Miss Rofman sleeps peacefully now, her mouth open in a small, beautiful oval, gives my heart ease. The desire in me to put pen aside and simply stare at her as if, with my gaze, to will her into a deeper, more restful sleep, is compelling, but I will forego this desire and instead use these hours to record, if in an abbreviated fashion, what has transpired these past several days. For this too – the writing down of what has happened – has become precious to me: a tangible way of keeping alive those moments that have brought us to one another.

Here is what happened:

While Miss Rofman and and I were dining together in a restaurant, Daniel's father, along with a Detective Kelly and a Mister Tompkins, a Negro man employed by the Home in which Daniel resided, entered my apartment and searched it. They had expected to find Daniel, or evidence of his presence, but they found neither, whereupon they immediately made their way to the restaurant – thus confirming our suspicion that they had been shadowing our movements – interrupting our evening to apologize for having suspected us of hiding him, and for having intruded upon our privacy. They also, again, solicited our collaboration in the search for Daniel.

Miss Rofman was magnificent, for despite her fears about what had happened to Daniel, and despite a cruel remark her former husband made concerning her relationship with me, her demeanor remained calm, proud, and diffident.

The instant these men left the tavern, however, she collapsed as if something inside her had broken. We departed the restaurant several minutes later, Miss Rofman in such a state of exhaustion and near-hysteria that she had to lean on me merely to walk. Her breathing was rapid, her voice alternately weak or shrill, and during the return journey to my apartment by taxicab, she implored me with the same questions, over and over: What were we to do, and was Daniel safe, and where did I think he was, and what would happen to him, and was it her fault that he was in danger, and how would she be able to go on living without him.

When we entered my apartment, everything was, as Doctor Landau promised it would be, in order, except for one crucial element: there was no evidence that Daniel had *ever* been here. His possessions, clothing as well as toiletry articles and drawings, were gone.

I found this reassuring, and said so to Miss Rofman. If Daniel had made certain to leave no trace of himself behind, surely such resourcefulness and efficiency, along with his prescience – the intimation of his father's unannounced visit – augured well for his ability to survive on his own.

I served us each a glass of port wine to help us recover from the shocks of the evening, and, confident it would yield knowledge of Daniel's whereabouts and/or his plans, suggested we make a careful survey of the apartment.

Miss Rofman drank her wine, set down her glass and then, tears welling in her eyes, she came to me and embraced me so hungrily that I wondered if she even knew to whom she was clinging, or if I were simply the nearest warm and human body to which she might hold.

I held her close and stroked her hair. Soon, however, unable to resist, I began kissing away her tears. She continued to hold fast to me. After some time, when her heavings had subsided and her grip upon me had slackened, she raised her face to me and, with soft wet lips that tasted of salt, kissed me full on the mouth.

Then, quite calmly, she drew away.

Thank you, she said, almost as if, by allowing her to kiss me, I had rendered her a service. Her voice, like that of a schoolgirl, was soft and wistful. I think I should see about my drawings now, she added. Don't you agree?

She set her portfolio on the kitchen table, opened it, and soon discovered, with relief, that all was intact.

But what about your manuscript? she asked. Shouldn't you make sure they have not taken it, or taken anything *from* it?

I entered the bedroom – she followed – and removed my journal from the top drawer of my secretary. To assure myself that nothing was missing, I turned the pages over one at a time, and – why hadn't I foreseen this? – there, following on my description of the first time Miss Rofman had kissed me, on a page that was indistinguishable from any other page of the journal, and written in a hand that imitated my own with remarkable similitude, was a letter from Daniel.

Dear Doctor Eduard Bloch:

Because my pursuers are nearby, I have decided to take your advice – I am going to make myself invisible again (ha! ha!). Do not worry about me or try to find me. They are <u>making</u> me escape again so that when they capture me they can give themselves the right to punish me.

But their ways are known to me, and I am going to fool them. You'll see! They will never *be able to do to me what they are planning to do. And I know where the safest place in the world is in which to conceal myself too. Can you guess?*

You have been very good to me. Thank you very much.

I have decided not to write a letter to Doctor Einstein but I think that you should write a letter to Adolf Hitler if you still want to.

I hope you and my mother will be happy together.

Your friend, Daniel Landau.

I handed the letter to Miss Rofman, who was puzzled by the fact that it was addressed solely to me, and also by Daniel's wishes for our happiness.

How could he know what even we didn't know? she asked. Was he prescient about this too?

I said that I had, within these pages, written openly of my feelings for her.

But he *likes* you, Miss Rofman said. And he wants me to be happy. I know that. Why would he *not* want the two of us to care for each other?

He does, I said. Still, I am not his father, and given his age and his condition – and given my age, and the difference in *our* ages – this cannot but be confusing for him.

Miss Rofman started to protest, but I stopped her by saying that what was probably more confusing for Daniel than what I had written about *her* was what I had, in my journal, written about *him*. Although I had described Daniel with affection and admiration, and had said nothing that would be distressing to Miss Rofman or myself had someone else described her son the way I had – still, I had no doubt but that it would be troubling for him to see words on a page that confirmed that he was, in certain particulars, strikingly different from other young men.

Miss Rofman asked if she could read what I had written, and I said that I thought this was not a good idea – that she would, in her present state of anxiety, probably find *anything* I wrote problematic.

At this, she became angry and *demanded* that I give her my journal.

I refused.

There will be a time when you will be able to read it with a clear mind, I said, but that time has not yet come.

I do not want to read it with a clear mind – I want to read it with *my* mind! she responded, after which she moved to take the manuscript from me, and in so doing – and in my pulling it away from her – the pages slipped from my hand and flew into the air.

We watched them fall and scatter around us, neither of us, for a few moments, moving to pick them up.

Then Miss Rofman simply knelt down and, without saying a word, began collecting the pages – I had numbered them sequentially – and putting them back in order. I soon sat beside her, and we traded pages back and forth until, within a minute or two, we had completed our task.

If Daniel dies, she said then, very quietly, I will follow him.

I said that Daniel was not going to die, that he was a vigorous and bright young man who clearly loved life in a way not dissimilar from the way his mother did. Having said this, I started to explain what I thought would happen next, and what we might do.

It was my opinion that we should not immediately go out in search of Daniel since, first, Detective Kelly had clearly not relinquished his suspicions and would be sure to follow us, and second, because I believed that Daniel would, despite what he said in his letter, soon communicate with us again. In the meantime, we needed to get our rest – Miss Rofman was clearly spent, emotionally and physically – so that, in the morning, we might address the situation with greater clarity.

Clarity? she said, and laughed in a slightly hysterical manner. *Clarity?!* she said again. Do you desire *clarity*, my dear Doctor Bloch?

She handed the journal to me, rose from the floor, and sat on the side of my bed. She said that she agreed with me about not going out immediately. We did need our rest, and there was a snowstorm, and it was nearly midnight, and Daniel had, once again, proven himself capable of evading capture, and in a cunning way. What she wanted to do most of all, though – her true preference – was to draw: what she wanted to do most of all was to be at the table in her father's bedroom, alone, so that she could, on paper, conjure up something – a child's heart, a drilling machine, an egg, a shovel – that would seem more real than the life in which she was living.

After saying this, she began laughing again, as if she were telling herself a funny story, and I asked her what it was that she found so humorous.

She leaned down – I was still sitting on the floor – and whispered: Just this, my friend – that it's none other than Adolf Hitler himself who is responsible for bringing us together.

Then she patted the bed with the palm of her hand to indicate that she wanted me to sit beside her. Please, she said. And again: Please.

I did what she asked.

Now how, she asked a good while later, could a man others believe to be the cause of so much evil be responsible for so much good – for so much sheer happiness?

I did not answer her question, of course, but after she had fallen asleep beside me, her words returned, and although I knew that her exhaustion and her apprehension – her despair! – had surely played a part in her willingness to give herself to me so utterly, the rapture she experienced masking what I took to be an ongoing if subdued hysteria, still I was struck by the truth she had spoken of, whimsical as it seemed; that if I had not, for example, because of the war, come to settle in Linz, and if I had not become a doctor to Adolf Hitler and his family, and if Frau Hitler had not become ill with breast cancer, and if Adolf Hitler had not in his gratitude for my services granted me passage out of Austria, and if he had not also seen to it that my nephew, John Kafka, previous to this, received priority in leaving Austria, our lives would never have been joined.

In the morning, Miss Rofman showed no least embarrassment

about what had taken place between us, and acted, in fact, as if what had happened were the most natural thing in the world. We talked for a good while, exchanging stories of our lives and, especially, of our childhoods, and it occurred to me that this was perhaps the truest way in which people showed their trust in and affection for one another. At one point, after telling me of the sequence of events that followed upon her divorce from Doctor Landau and led her to take up medical illustration and relocate to Baltimore – she had moved there temporarily during Daniel's first months at the Salisbury Home, and, visiting a friend from college who was married to a physician at Johns Hopkins, had learned of Professor Brödel's work and his Institute – she suddenly began to touch and prod my face, and to do so as if she were molding clay.

What she would really prefer to do someday, she informed me, was to draw not my face, but my skull. Although she had from the first found me attractive, when she looked at me recently she often found herself imagining what lay not only below skin and hair, but below muscle, tendon, ligament, and cartilage.

I admire your bone structure enormously, she said, and I replied that she could not have paid me a greater compliment.

We talked then of cranial and facial bones, and of orbital cavities – of the occipital, parietal, frontal, temporal, sphenoid, and ethmoid bones of the cranium, and of the nasal, maxillary, lachrymal, malar, palate, inferior turbinated, vomer, and inferior maxillary bones of the face. We amused ourselves for a while – Miss Rofman moving her hands across my head as if she were a phrenologist – by seeing who could remember more comprehensively the large variety of Latinate words there were for the various parts of the skull. Miss Rofman easily surpassed me in her knowledge of anatomical terminology, and became especially tender with me – delighted by her prowess – when she was able to retrieve from the well of her memory particularly obscure terms.

Did I know that the external surface of the superior region, or vertex, was bounded by the glabella and supraorbital ridges? Did I know that the point of junction of the coronal and sagittal sutures was called the bregma, and that in the area of the parietal foramen the word *obelion* was sometimes given to that point of the sagittal suture which lay exactly opposite to the parietal foramen?

To her questions I replied with a proposal: that I bequeath to her my cadaver, so that her wish to draw my skull might one day be realized.

That would be most kind of you, she said, after which she spoke of the many possibilities for dissection that would present themselves were I, as was likely – and essential to her project – to predecease her. That we were able to be playful in this manner speaks of our ease with each other. Yet this ease, and our sudden, pronounced attachment to each other was born, I believe, of something more fundamental. It was born of the fact that while fearing the worst – a loss that might prove unbearable, for there is no language or word of which I am aware that has been invented to describe a person who has lost a child – yet did we, *because* we feared the worst, manage to find great happiness in the pleasures of life that remained.

It was, that is, as I have earlier suggested, the very possibility of loss of life – of a life more precious to her than her own, and of the hurt that accompanied this loss, along with the desire *to* hurt, which I never underestimate – that seemed to exacerbate Miss Rofman's very hunger *for* life. (Not wanting to alarm her further, I did not inform her that I had, when looking for Daniel's message, been vexed to discover that my copy of *Gray's Anatomy*, which Daniel had been studying, was gone.)

Thinking of the single-minded intensity with which Daniel would sit at the kitchen table, or at my desk in the bedroom, and draw pictures, whether of manhole covers, body parts, battleships, or warplanes, it occurs to me to note that the gratification Miss Rofman takes from her work – in the drawings *she* makes – is not unlike the pleasure I have come to take in the words I write. Her desire, for example, to draw my skull – in effect, to make tangible that hard reality which will endure after I have departed from this world – is not unlike the desire I have to make real and enduring in words on a page those events and feelings that are themselves as ephemeral as flesh.

It occurs to me also to set down this clarification: that it was not Daniel's mention of invisibility that called to mind the anecdote I have here recorded about Hitler, but rather the moment when, several days ago, fearing others might come to my apartment in search of him, I suggested, using a common figure of speech, that he "make himself invisible." I might have come to recall the incident had I not used the phrase, but using it did serve to remind me of the incident I have this night recorded.

And while it is true that at the time Adolf came to me to tell me of his experience, he was approximately the age Daniel is now, and that Daniel, like Adolf, has spoken of an experience of invisibility, though he has used the term in a far less literal way, there seems nothing else about the two young men that would cause one to elaborate on their similarities, and, thus, no useful purpose served in my noting their many differences.

In this regard, I am reminded of an amusing anecdote concerning an ancient king of Bavaria who, in a boasting mood, compared himself to Alexander the Great. In what ways, my lord, he was asked, do you resemble Alexander? To this question, the king replied: Because we both rule nations, and because in each of our nations there are rivers, and in the rivers of each of our nations there are fish.

Recalling this tale, however, I am also reminded that there is yet one way in which others might find similarities between Daniel and the young Adolf Hitler. For just as some believe that Hitler consciously thanked me, the Jew he knew and respected, for caring for his mother while unconsciously harboring great hurt and hatred towards *all* Jews, so Daniel may overtly be expressing admiration and gratitude towards me for giving him sanctuary, while unconsciously suppressing rage and resentment for my having replaced his father and somehow 'stolen' his mother's affection. I write this not because I believe it to be so, but because the accusations others have made against me have wounded me and have made me more sensitive to such possibilities than I otherwise would have been.

But now to the events of yesterday, which I will record swiftly so that, having done so, I might yet achieve some small measure of sleep before dawn.

While Miss Rofman and I ate breakfast, she talked at length about the subways and about why she believed Daniel might have chosen to hide there. She cited, again, both his fascination with the stories she had told him about her childhood and her father's work, and his obsession with the various street coverings that led to underground worlds. She also said that it had occurred to her that the journey we might soon take in searching for her father and son in the underground recesses of the city – a journey into an unknown and potentially unhappy future – would also be a journey into a half-remembered and potentially frightening past.

I responded by telling her that I vividly recalled the analogy she had made about paths of memory being, for her, like routes subway trains took, and she thanked me: for having listened attentively to her, and for not disparaging what seemed to her, patently, to be her unduly labored and lame speculations.

The truth, she said, was that to search in the subways would be futile, not only because of the dangers involved and because we had no clue as to where to begin, but because, on a moment's reflection, she was forced to acknowledge that she did not truly believe that either her father or son would do something so predictable as to go there. Neither of them, she said, were men who would, especially in a time of crisis, make an *obvious* choice.

I agreed. I said that knowing Daniel as I did, my own thought was that he would reverse things: rather than trying to escape from those, like us, who might try to follow him, what he would do would be to follow us.

But of course, Miss Rofman said.

I next suggested that I make a brief excursion from the apartment and, given the possibility Daniel might, in disguise, return, that Miss Rofman remain behind. I left soon after this conversation and, truth be told, had prevaricated somewhat, since I had no expectation Daniel would be following me.

Thus did I make my way, by foot, to the apartment house in which Miss Rofman's father lived, and stood for a while across the street, on the building's northern side, which provided the best light for drawing, looking up at what I knew to be the bedroom window next to which Miss Rofman had worked. A curtain was drawn across the window, but it was not long – ten minutes at most – before the curtain was pulled back, and a man appeared. He was quite pale, and had what appeared to be a white scarf tied around his neck. He inclined his head once, as if to indicate that he had been expecting me, and then let the curtain fall back across the window.

I entered the building and was about to start up the stairs when a door at the far end of the hallway, from the building's cellar, opened, and a dog came towards me, limping and wagging its tail. It was a Collie, quite old to judge from its clouded eyes and ragged fur. Its master, a slightly bent and very short man, jaundiced in complexion, walked behind the dog. I reached out to pet the dog, and when I did, it rose up viciously and snapped at me, nearly trapping my hand in its teeth.

"Best to leave it be," the man said, and called the dog to him.

"Of course," I said.

"Who are you, and what do you want?" the man asked.

"I am a friend of the Rofman family," I said.

"Well, don't ever touch the dog," he said. "I'm the super here. Are you here to pay them?"

"Pay who?" I asked.

"Them," he said, gesturing to the door to my left. "For what the boy did to their daughter – to Francine."

"I know nothing about this," I said.

"That boy should be locked up," the man said, and so saying, he turned around and, the dog following, went back through the door at the end of the hallway and down the stairs.

I hesitated only for a minute or two – my heartbeat, due to the dog's attack, had accelerated – and then walked up three flights of stairs and knocked on the door to Mister Rofman's apartment. Nobody responded. I knocked again, and then again, after which I tried the door. It opened, as I expected it would.

I entered the apartment and called out – *Mister Rofman? Daniel?* – several times. Just as I had not been surprised to see the man in the window, so I was not surprised to find that the apartment was deserted. Everything was as it had been on the day when, concerned about Miss Rofman, I had first come here, except that the table upon which Miss Rofman had, in the bedroom, been making her drawings, was now in the kitchen. In readiness for the Sabbath, there were two candlesticks, with candles, on the table, a flask of wine and silver goblet beside them.

In the bedroom, both beds were neatly made.

I pushed aside the curtain and looked out the window. Nobody was on the street below looking up at me, but I suspected that Detective Kelly or one of his associates might be nearby. I was not worried about Daniel's ability to avoid Detective Kelly or Mister Tompkins, of whom he was properly wary. Rather, I was concerned about his innocence regarding his father, for despite Daniel's overt expressions of hostility towards Doctor Landau, I was acutely aware of how nearly impossible it would be for him, as for any child, to believe that his father would willfully do him harm.

This thought came to me, and not for the first time, while I lingered in the bedroom, and when, out of habit, I found myself smoothing down the blankets and pillows on each of the two beds – an unnecessary task, since they were already as smooth as they might have been had a hotel housekeeper attended to them – and, in my mind's eye, recalling times I had, at night, sat on the side of my daughter Gertrude's bed in our house in Linz, and talked with her. Sometimes, when she fell asleep, she would do so while holding fast to one of my hands.

What I soon found myself imagining was that Miss Rofman was lying in the bed across from Gertrude, and that after I had said good night to each of them and left the room, they had talked in happy whispers from one bed to the other in the way sisters might have done. The feelings that welled up in me of a sudden at this thought were so strong that it made me wonder if one who had not been a parent could ever know what it was I had felt once upon a time, and what I was, embellishing upon that memory, feeling now. How, not raising and loving a child over the course of time, could one ever achieve that *Herzenbildung* – that cultivation of the heart in which lies our true value as human beings?

This thought was allied, concurrently, to a sense that my desire to spare Daniel the harm his father or others might do to him was somehow bound up with my rather foolish desire to spare the German and Austrian peoples the harm that was befalling them (consider, in this vein, the arrogance of my belief that a letter from me to Adolf Hitler could actually have been a force for change!). And this feeling, coming fast upon my imagining Gertrude and Miss Rofman as young girls – each of whom had grown up without siblings – befriending each other, made me conscious of the degree to which my confused mingling of desires and fancies was itself a source of my flawed ability to be an effective agent for good.

It also occurred to me when I imagined sharing my thoughts with Miss Rofman, that she would have chastised me for my view, doubtless presenting for proof the person of Doctor Helen Taussig, a woman who is herself unwed and childless, yet who, from Miss Rofman's accounts, is second to no parent in her love and understanding of children.

When, such thoughts preoccupying me, I passed back along the narrow corridor between bedroom and kitchen, and when I pulled open a closet door on the chance that I might come upon some of Daniel's possessions, I was more startled than I might otherwise have been to have a large figure suddenly come at me screaming wildly and forcing me to recoil so swiftly that I struck the rear of my head hard against the wall behind me.

"Daniel!" I exclaimed even while I experienced a sudden, blinding wave of nausea. "Then you *are* here!"

"I saw your face!" Daniel cried out. *"I saw your face! I saw your face!"*

"Yes," I said, and I reached out to embrace him. "I am so happy to have found you, my child."

It was Daniel's head that now snapped back, as if I had struck him – in my excitement, and momentary light-headedness, I had forgotten how upset he became whenever one tried to touch him – and it was only then that I seemed to *see* him for the first time, and to notice that he had combed his hair across his forehead at a diagonal and drawn a dark, square moustache under his nose.

His right arm shot up into the air. *"Heil Hitler!"* he cried, after which he fell to laughing and, delighted with himself for having startled me, repeating over and over again that he had seen my face.

"Well," I offered, "and I have seen yours."

"Do I look like him?" he asked. "*Do* I? *Do* I?"

"No," I answered. "Not at all."

"You're *bleeding*!" he said then. *"Look – !"*

I reached a hand to the side of my head, behind my left ear, and felt the moist seepage of blood, after which I moved into the bathroom while explaining that the scalp was highly vascular and rich in sensory endings, and that there was no cause for alarm since the quantity of blood produced by even a minor cut could often be misleadingly dramatic. What I did not say was that a large and swift loss of blood could sometimes lead to sudden and life-threatening shock.

"But I scared you, didn't I – *didn't* I?" he said, and when he did I had the distinct impression, from what I can only describe as a ravenous look in his eyes, that he was pleased to see me bleeding.

"You did," I admitted, even while I looked around in search of a towel, to stem the bleeding. "But it is a superficial wound."

The towels on the bathroom rack were white, but I recalled that in the bedroom there were towels hanging at the foot of each bed that were a dark green, and so, my hand clamped over the cut, I returned to the bedroom, the impulse to reassure Daniel mixed – like blood and hair? – with the desire to ask him what exactly had happened between him and the young woman the superintendent of the building had mentioned.

Daniel followed me, telling me about how he had gone to a movie theater where he had seen newsreels of Adolf Hitler. When I had been a soldier, he asked, had I ever killed anyone? Had I ever goose-stepped the way the soldiers did when they paraded in front of Hitler? Was I still intending to send him a letter? Had I ever ridden inside a tank or flown in an airplane?

I pressed a towel against the back of my head, and stated that yes, I had, when a soldier, killed men, but before I could reply to his other questions, he interrupted me.

"I read your journal, you know," he said.

"I know," I said. "It is why I am here."

At this point, without acknowledging what I had said, he began stumbling towards the kitchen, laughing and repeating again that he had seen my face.

FOURTEEN

From the Journal of Doctor Eduard Bloch
December 27, 1940

Daniel will live.

As of this writing, he is being attended to by Doctor Landau's colleagues at Columbia-Presbyterian Hospital where, in a short while, Miss Rofman and I will visit him. He is conscious, and the bleeding that resulted from the injuries he inflicted upon himself, having been stemmed by the quick and expert intervention of his father, who applied direct pressure to the wounds and the surrounding areas (following upon Daniel's arrival at the hospital, Doctor Landau's colleagues did what was necessary to seal the wounds and prevent infection), no longer presents a life-threatening danger.

How I wish I could state that I had had a premonition that Daniel would attempt upon himself the surgical procedure that he and his mother feared his father and the administrators at the Salisbury Home were planning. Alas, I cannot, and so I find myself obsessing about the interventions I did *not* make, and the consequences that will not, for the rest of Daniel's life, follow from them.

Daniel's letter to me, promising that others would never succeed in doing to him what they intended, should have alerted me to his intention. That he took with him my copy of *Gray's Anatomy* should also have been a sign to me of his resolve, yet I chose to believe instead what has, sadly, also proven true – that he had taken the book not because of an interest in *male* anatomy but because of an interest in *female* anatomy. I am also guilty of a grievous lack of foresight in not seeing to the contents of my physician's satchel, from which, we now know, Daniel took one of my small scalpels, along with several curved needles to which were already attached, for suturing, braided China silk thread.

I fault myself, of course, for these failures both of perception and vigilance, yet I must admit, given what Daniel has now proven himself capable of – and given that he is alive! – that I am not unhappy about what has occurred. Perhaps, as Doctor Landau and those responsible for Daniel's care at the Salisbury Home, believe, it really *is* for the best if Daniel not be endowed with capabilities his appetite is unable to control. Perhaps, too, it is for the best if his innate and destructive impulses are not transmitted to future generations.

I suspect also, given the excruciating pain Daniel must have endured, that he was unable to consummate his intended act and that his father, or the doctors into whose care his father placed him, completed the surgical procedure Daniel had begun. Whether or not it was medically necessary to save Daniel's life we will never know.

Contemplating not merely the act itself, but the mind, dispossessed of reason, that led Daniel to it, I hear again a saying from my wartime experience, one we doctors would use with one another (the visceral force of the German – *Ich kann ja nich so ville fressen, wie ick kotzen möchte* – seems nearly untranslatable) to cover a multitude of situations: It makes me want to throw up, we would say, more than I can possibly eat.

Doctor Landau has given assurances that all of Daniel's functions, other than those associated with his reproductive capacity, are intact, and for this, one is grateful. Perhaps, when he learns of the outcome, Daniel will be able to believe what he desires to believe: that in his act he was both successful *and* heroic, and perhaps believing this will help to guard him from future acts of self-destruction.

Perhaps, too, I think in my self-exonerating logic, if, suspecting Daniel's intent, I *had* intervened, he would have panicked and done himself even greater harm. As to his other impulsive and violent tendencies, particularly those directed towards women, his new and altered condition, biologically as well as emotionally, may, one hopes, lessen his inner perturbations and their worldly issue.

Although it gives no pleasure to write, even in summary fashion, of these events, yet do I find that it provides consolation to be able to put into words just how horrible they were. But my primary concern, now that Daniel's survival is not at issue, is for Miss Rofman. I must consider the ways in which I may be of service to her so as to maximize the chances that she will not blame herself inordinately for what has happened, and that she will be able, with time, to find peace of mind not unlike that which I experience when I contemplate my efforts to make such peace of mind possible.

I cease here from consideration of what these efforts might entail, for although one may discern the unseen from the seen (as, for example, when one infers the inner workings of the body from its outer appearance), I do not think it useful, as I once did, to believe one can anticipate the future by one's understanding of the past, or by giving undue credence to one's hopes.

Therefore, to the events themselves: I was, less than twenty-four hours ago, about to write of the conversation Daniel and I had after I had discovered him in Mister Rofman's apartment. At this moment, however, Miss Rofman awoke, and so I put aside this journal and told her what had happened, after which we prepared to go together to the apartment.

Since I wanted as soon as possible to return home and give Miss Rofman the news that Daniel was alive and well, and that I had seen a man I recognized from her drawings as her father, and that he was – my inference – apparently caring for Daniel, I intended to keep my conversation with Daniel brief.

Daniel was eager for my company, however, and intent upon telling me of a young woman named Francine, and so I sat with him in the kitchen for a while, where he took from the top compartment of the ice box a container of chocolate ice cream from which he ate. He seemed to have put out of mind any thoughts of my journal and its contents, or of the letter he had written to me.

This was his story.

Shortly after he had taken sanctuary in his grandfather's apartment, having, in his words, "borrowed" the key from his mother's purse, Francine knocked on the door and asked if he would like to play with her. She told him that she knew who he was because she remembered seeing him in the building, and he told her that she was correct – that he had visited the apartment several times when he was younger, that Mister Rofman was his grandfather, and that Miss Rofman was his mother. He invited her in and offered her a bowl of ice cream.

While they ate, he showed her drawings from *Gray's Anatomy*, and informed her both that his father was a surgeon and that his mother made anatomical illustrations like those in the book. It was at this point, he claimed, that Francine asked if he wanted to play doctor-and-nurse with her, which game, according to Daniel, she said she had often played with her brothers. I will not repeat here his account of what ensued, except to confess to being so captivated by the zeal with which he described what they did with each other that I did not do what I should have done: I did not tell him I thought he was, at the least, exaggerating grossly, and that whether he was or was not, the actions he described were reprehensible.

I shied away from doing so for several reasons: first, the fear that doubting his word or chastising him would cause an upset in him that might prove violent – his nervous mannerisms, especially the way he picked at the sores on his thumbs, being markedly in evidence – and second, my desire not to compromise the trust, evidenced by his very willingness to tell me such tales, we had established.

In taking this course of action, as subsequent events have shown, I erred terribly.

After telling me about the games he and Francine played, he began to talk of his intention to marry her. He did not think that when he was, say, twenty-seven, and she eighteen, the difference in their ages would matter. Moreover, he believed that the universe was so constructed that each man and woman on earth was destined from birth to fall in love with one and only one other person, but that oftentimes what happened was that, seduced by lust, we erred when we chose our *first* love-object and were punished for this error by being disabled forever after from knowing our one *true* love. One did not, in Daniel's philosophy, if I understood it correctly, receive a second chance.

It was, therefore, their great good fortune, he said, that he and Francine, despite their tender ages, knew instantaneously – love entering through their eyes, and journeying directly down to their hearts – that their match had been foretold in whatever heavens existed. They had, he said, and in a chilling echo of words I recalled from National Socialist propaganda, experienced the true "ecstasy of destiny."

I was somewhat dumbfounded to hear him present, in effusive detail, a confused, confusing, and banal mix of views on romance – he talked, for example, of how "the voice of the blood" had spoken to them – and would have inquired about his reading habits, or if he had, at the Salisbury Home, occasion to attend the cinema, so as to ascertain where such views had come from – but, in truth, I did not have the heart to dampen his enthusiasm, for there was about his views an innocence that was endearing. That they were also deadly was not, in the moment, apparent.

I made a decision, moreover, not to inquire about his grandfather, since it seemed more judicious to allow the two of them that secrecy and collusion that were enabling Daniel to evade those who were pursuing him.

For his part, Daniel never mentioned either his grandfather or his mother, and the longer he talked, the more agitated he became. When, in the midst of telling me of the many children he and Francine were going to have and, room by room, of the elegant home by the ocean in which they would raise their children, he paused to eat a large spoonful of ice cream, I took the opportunity to announce that I was leaving. I pleaded the need to attend to my wound, and told him I would return as soon as possible and that when I did, if he thought it proper, I would hope to meet the young woman of whom he was so fond.

He reacted as if I had dealt him a physical blow, turning his back upon me, and striding into the bedroom. This behavior was yet another reminder that he was, despite his physical size and strength, very much a child, and that his fantasies, as I believed them to be, were largely compensation for severe self-doubts, these engendered in good part by the intense shame that derived from his being put away from others in an Institution for those who, in my native land, would be and are being subjected to laws of racial hygiene.

When I informed Miss Rofman about Daniel and her father, she became resolute. It is time, she declared. She would dress and we would make our way to her father's apartment. Her cheeks were ripe again with that unique flush of beauty that make it difficult for me to refuse any request she makes. And the cause of both her decision and her exhilaration was, I soon discovered, the following: When she was a child, she explained, she had lived in fear that the courts would take her away from her father. This fear had been particularly acute during a time when her father's hand had been infected in a way that threatened to disable him for employment – a poisoning of the blood that might, she later came to understand, have proved fatal. But this fear – that the courts would intervene to separate them – was never realized.

When, therefore, she reflected on the parallels between her childhood situation and that of her situation with Daniel, she concluded that it would be wrong – and cowardly – to allow fear to possess her and, thereby, to dictate a course of action. What she had come to believe, given especially Daniel's proof of his own resourcefulness, was that the courts, seeing her and Daniel in front of them and hearing their story, could not possibly deny them the right to live together. She was certain that, at the least, she could get a judge to stay, for a brief period of time – time enough for Daniel to attain his majority – any attempt on the part of Doctor Landau or the Home to separate them.

To this end, she would inquire of Doctor Taussig and Doctor Blalock of their acquaintances in New York City, and receive from them a referral to an attorney to represent her and Daniel. A threat she had made to the Director of the Salisbury Home, she said, could now become a reality. She also concluded that I had been correct in my judgment that we could not keep up indefinitely the kind of hide-and-seek maneuvers in which we had been engaged, which was why we were now going to her father's apartment in an open and public manner.

I protested that I had never claimed she should behave in any way other than the way she had been behaving, and had surely never judged her choices or actions. At this remark she laughed, called me a liar, and, pushing me against the brick wall of an apartment building, grabbed the lapels of my coat and kissed me hard on the mouth.

And I was a desperate woman, she said.

But such spirited playfulness was soon brought low, for when we turned onto her father's street a few moments later, there waiting for us in front of her father's building were Detective Kelly, Mister Tompkins, and Doctor Landau. And when we endeavored to enter the building, Detective Kelly and Mister Tompkins barred our way, Doctor Landau informing us that the three of them had arrived only a minute before, and with the express purpose of forestalling our entry.

With a warrant, I am certain, Miss Rofman said, after which she demanded that we be allowed to pass. When Detective Kelly said this would not be possible, and when Miss Rofman tried to enter the building, Mister Tompkins pushed her back roughly.

I did not hesitate, but grabbed this large man and pushed him against the building so that Miss Rofman was able to move past him, to open the door, and to take several steps into the building's interior. Detective Kelly, however, moving quickly, grabbed her by the wrist to pull her back onto the street, and when he did, I seized his arm.

He let go of Miss Rofman and stared at me quizzically, as if astonished I would even attempt to stop him, and it was in that moment that we heard the first scream. Then there was another, and another. Miss Rofman started up the stairs, but Detective Kelly and Mister Tompkins were upon her at once, and, a fury rising in me even while, in the vestibule, the screaming from above grew louder and was joined by a dog's shrill barking, I was upon them with all the strength I could summon. The superintendent's dog slouched towards us, howling miserably, and suddenly I stopped and saw what we all saw: that the dog was accompanied not by the superintendent, but by another man I knew at once to be Miss Rofman's father. In his right hand he carried a thick, jagged piece of wood that might have once been part of a railroad tie.

The white material around his neck, I realized, was a bandage, and when he spoke my name, his voice was raspy, thin, and virtually inaudible. From above, screams continued to descend upon us even as, our eyes fixed upon Mister Rofman and the dog, none of us moved. Other doors opened, however, and tenants appeared behind us and crowded on the staircase and on the landing above.

Miss Rofman came back towards us and asked her father if

he was all right. What had happened to his throat?

Instead of answering, Mister Rofman stepped towards Detective Kelly and Mister Tompkins.

We should go to Daniel, Miss Rofman said, indicating to her father, and to me, that she wanted us to accompany her.

Detective Kelly shoved Miss Rofman aside and withdrew from his pocket a dark implement which I later saw to be the kind of small, heavy cudgel Americans call a Black Jack, or sap. He ordered Mister Rofman to put down the piece of wood he was carrying. Mister Rofman, who seemed, in his weakened condition, barely capable of standing, made as if to place the piece of wood on the floor, then suddenly rose up tall and in a ferocious whipping motion struck Detective Kelly hard across the face, opening a gaping wound there and felling the Detective.

In the commotion that ensued – from behind and above, tenants were shouting and screaming – I had lost sight of Doctor Landau, who was, I saw, climbing the stairs two at a time. Mister Tompkins, with no seeming thought to Detective Kelly, followed Doctor Landau, first hitting Miss Rofman a blow upon the side of the head that knocked her against the stairway's banister, after which, but too late, he realized that Miss Rofman's father, approaching him, still held the piece of wood. Mister Rofman now struck Mister Tompkins across the front of his face so that he fell upon the floor beside Detective Kelly.

Miss Rofman, dazed, seemed not to notice what her father had done and, putting her hand on his arm, asked him again about his condition. Why are you so thin? she asked. And: What happened to your throat? Talk to me, please. Tell me. Are you all right? Are you all right?

I have been better, he whispered.

At this response, and at what she must have intuited about the source of her father's condition, she went quite pale. I put my arm around her and drew her with me back out and onto the street, sitting her down on a front step and forcing her to lower her head below the level of her heart. She talked, somewhat confusedly, of a paraffin lamp under whose light she had removed gauze from the wound in her father's palm. Did I know where it was?

Behind me, I saw through the doorway, Mister Rofman was bent over Detective Kelly and Mister Tompkins.

They are alive, he said when he joined us a moment later. Then, seeing that Miss Rofman's eyes were closed, he spoke to me: I did not want my daughter to see me in my weakened condition.

Miss Rofman raised her head and spoke: Is that why . . . ?

If I had told you not to visit me, you would have suspected the worst.

So fast, Miss Rofman said. So fast.

Mister Rofman reached down to touch his daughter's face, but before his hand reached her, her head fell against my shoulder and she lost consciousness.

Mister Rofman touched the back of my hand with one of his fingers. You will take care of her, yes? he said, and without waiting for an answer, he walked away.

A police car, passing Mister Rofman in the opposite direction, now came down the street, its siren preceding it. There were also, I realized for the first time, several dozen people, including many children, gathered around us. Gently, I lay Miss Rofman down upon the sidewalk, my wool scarf under her head, and asked a young woman to fetch water. Looking up at the young woman, I saw, above her, that two young men were climbing down the fire escape of the building. Between his teeth, one of the young men carried what appeared to be a long-handled screwdriver. An ambulance now appeared, and then a second police car. Although Miss Rofman's skin was cool and her breathing shallow, her heartbeat was strong. Someone handed me a glass of water, and I raised the back of Miss Rofman's head and put the glass to her lips. She drank.

My father? she asked.

I gestured to the policemen who were approaching us.

Yes, Miss Rofman said.

She did not ask about Daniel. I thought of her father, and of how he had tried to protect her, and thinking, as I did, that this was ever Nature's way – to want to protect and succor those we love – I thought also of what, if anything, might yet be done for him. My thoughts, that is, were the thoughts of a physician.

As ever, I mused, our great search was for that mechanism that would seek out a target of its own accord and, by virtue of its chemical properties, directly attach itself to, and thus be able to kill or weaken the infecting organism, yet leave the tissues of the infected patient intact. I thought also in this moment of how foolish it was of the German authorities to divest themselves of those exceptional physicians and scientists of our race who, along with educated and skilled men like myself, might have been a force for the well-being and redemption of our homeland.

All around us, the world had become quiet and still. People stared at us without moving, and the police, doctors, nurses, and various medical assistants went about their tasks noiselessly. When I said that it was imperative we return to my apartment as soon as possible, Miss Rofman did not resist. Would I, later on, she asked, retrieve her drawing supplies? Not yet knowing of Daniel's fate, I wondered if she was in that moment thinking of drawing a picture of her father as he had just appeared to her, and I considered, in advance, discouraging her from such an undertaking. Why not, I thought of saying to her, picture the world as it might yet be instead of the way it was.

Miss Rofman reached up to me then – had she discerned my thoughts? – and caressed my face with great tenderness, feature by feature – eyes, nose, mouth, cheeks, chin – as if, I sensed, to set them forever in her heart and memory. I want to draw the world, yes, she said then, but I also want to draw the world to me. Is that all right, do you think? Or is it best to just sleep for a while?

I kissed her eyes, and she fell at once into a deep sleep, while – curious thought – I found myself believing that when we arrived home, Doctor Landau's wife, Sonya (in my imagination, she was wearing a nurse's uniform), along with her three children, would be there waiting to welcome us and to tend to our needs.

I informed a policeman that I was a physician and asked if he would be able to provide transportation for Miss Rofman and myself. He looked towards the building's entrance, where more than a dozen policemen were gathered. A second and much larger ambulance had arrived by this time, and I saw that the bodies of Detective Kelly and Mister Tompkins, on gurneys, were being lifted into this ambulance. Several nurses were attending to the wounded men, the nurse's starched white caps fixed on their heads like tiaras.

The policeman, receiving permission from a superior officer, ushered us into the back seat of a police car. Miss Rofman opened her eyes but did not inquire of Daniel, nor did we wait to see Doctor Landau and others carry him down the stairs.

I do not know where Mister Rofman is, or, given the speed with which the malignancy has apparently taken hold in his body, how much longer he will survive.

I do not know whether Detective Kelly or Mister Tompkins are dead or alive.

I see, in this afternoon's newspaper, that tens of thousands of children are being evacuated from Berlin, Hamburg, and other large German cities. In these cities, shortages and rationing continue. Hot water is limited to one or two days weekly, church meetings are forbidden, the Berlin Technical College, Berlin University, and the Berlin Public Library have closed. Rumors abound concerning Germany's impending alliance with Francisco Franco, dictator of Spain, and of Germany's intention to abrogate its treaty with Russia and to invade that nation.

Earlier in the day I turned on the radio in the hopes of receiving additional international news, and curious also to discover whether or not the fates of Detective Kelly and Mister Tompkins would be made public. Instead, I could find only orchestral music, and Miss Rofman, somewhat angrily, asked me to turn off the radio. Music, she said, offended her.

It did not offend me, though I certainly understood why, given the events of the past few days, music might in this hour darken her mood. For my part, I am aware of my growing preference for words over music, and in this newfound infatuation with words I am also reminded of what I sometimes forget, and have, until recently, given little thought to: that I too am a Jew. Also: that the joy I feel when I can record events I witness, along with thoughts engendered by the events, and by the process of writing itself, which provides a personal liberation of an intensely pleasurable nature, is unlike any experience I have previously known.

That this is so, given the culture in which I was raised, is curious, for the preference in my world has ever been to elevate music at the expense of language. Music is itself, I was taught, the universal language, the very essence – *das Ding an sich* – of things: it is the return to nature, and the purification of nature, and nature transformed into love. Music is magical – and language, by contrast, as Nietsche famously wrote, a terrible sickness – because it elicits and inspires those feelings that pass beyond ordinary reason and that join us more directly than words ever can to the ineffable.

Many, of course, with regard to the belief that music, by its direct appeal to the emotions, is superior to language as a mode of expression – reason, thus, becoming the enemy – have deemed this view a flaw, perhaps fatal, in the German and Austrian character.

I did not and will not discuss such matters with Miss Rofman. The better course, I have decided, is to be conscious of them while refusing to understand them.

Will Miss Rofman, within weeks or months, return to Baltimore, and will I go there with her, I wonder, or will she remain here with Daniel? And how is it possible that we have known each other for only three weeks? At the hospital this morning, Doctor Landau confided in me that, shortly after the New Year, he is going to leave Columbia-Presbyterian Hospital in order to accept a research position at The Rockefeller Institute, and that when he does, he is certain he will be able to find employment there for Miss Rofman as a medical illustrator.

Before Miss Rofman makes any decision, I intend to make inquiries concerning Professor Brödel, and of why it is a man who grew up in Germany (and in Leipzig, a shamelessly beautiful city – city of Wagner, Bach, and Mendelssohn – in which I would hope to one day have the pleasure of walking with Miss Rofman: of showing her the splendid Elizabeth Gardens – Professor Brödel's daughter, Elizabeth, it seems, was named for them – and the magnificent new Shocken department store) has chosen to abandon his homeland forever in order to live on these shores.

Miss Rofman, who has begun working at her illustrations for Doctor Taussig here in my apartment, and who becomes immediately enraged if I in any way interrupt or distract her, has promised that we will celebrate the Sabbath together this evening, and she has asked me to remind her, during our return from visiting Daniel in the hospital, to buy candles, *challah*, and a bottle of wine. The Sabbath begins in a few hours, at sundown, and I am hopeful that when it does, its peace will descend upon us.

The End